FOR ELAINE

WHO PUT UP WITH ALL THE SHENANIGANS THROUGHOUT THIS PROCESS OF MY TORTURING HER TO LISTEN TO MY STORIES.

TREAD 'N WATER

BY: FRANK C. BRINDLEY

CHAPTER 1   Tread lightly

   Through discarded time and tortured moments wind caught
leaves and trash sending them spinning in tiny tornadoes wildly
toward unknown destinies until they spun themselves into
nothingness reaching a dead end.

   Drive carefully and slowly, he thought. Jack had to turn the car
around. He missed seeing the sign that read dead end. Don't
get caught. Don't make any sudden moves you might regret
later, he told himself.

A light rain fell earlier and slicked the road surface. Dark clouds
hung low in the sky ominously, as if to burst any moment like a
giant, overfilled balloon. A light sheen of oil could be seen in
the reflections of the oncoming headlights on the road surface.
The smell of ozone lay heavy in the air. Reflections blurred and
melded into tiny globes caught in droplets of rain gliding slowly
across the car's windshield. It was early afternoon although the
diminished light and grayness of the falling rain made it seem
like quickly approaching twilight.

Jack Kahill turned the car around. He was driving a borrowed car very slowly along Elizabeth Avenue northbound into an approaching storm. The sky increasing in darkness and foreboding. He kept his focus straight ahead and didn't move his head. He didn't want to arouse suspicion from the patrolman in the police car he just passed parked along a side street. He trembled when he took his eyes off the road just long enough to check the rearview mirror. He had to be sure and he cocked his head just enough. The rearview mirror was empty except for a glow of hazy reflections off the road surface from the red tail lights of the beat up 1973 Buick he was driving. He could feel the beating of his heart in his chest. He heard the haunting rhythmic thumping in his ears and it made him feel dizzy. Jack checked the gap between his teeth with his tongue and took in a gasping breath. The car's engine made sounds like it was gasping and coughing for life. He could see the instrument panel of the Buick lit up like a Christmas tree blinking S.O.S for help there in the subdued light. He hit the panel with a closed fist trying to make it stop. The car rattled with the slightest bump in the road. It ran more like an army tank than a car. It hit pot hole after pot hole with almost a certain glee, like a child running purposely through mud holes just for fun. This was anything but fun thought Jack. He felt pain welt up in his neck and leg with every bump.

Jack wiped a light glistening bead of sweat that formed at his temples and caught his reflection in the rearview mirror. His eyes were bloodshot, like the glow of the stop lights on the wet pavement. Got to get more sleep, he thought. His face was gaunt, too thin, and the beard he let grow was now coming in more gray, than the red of his youth. He was thirty years old and his hairline now receded, and, like his beard, it too was graying at the temples. Behind the red, his eyes reflected ghostly gray like the moors of Ireland, then the shamrock green they used to be. His weight was down, and he knew it. He almost walked hunched over with constant sciatica pain. He felt sick at times, but he just didn't have an appetite. It was the constant nightmare of the accident three years ago that robbed him of his health. He wanted to stop the car and throw up.

He remembered when, at night the constrictions got too tight to bear, he would scream into his pillow until the guards became pissed off. The guards, when his banshee wailing became unbearable, would rattle his cage with night sticks across the bars in a cacophony of thunderous rage until he cried himself to sleep. They would torture all new inmates regardless just for the fun of it.

The sudden screeching of brake drums on thin pads startled Jack back to reality. He had to slam on his own car brakes. The car slid on the wet oil slick pavement like a slithering snake. It came to rest just slightly with the car's nose past the red light

4

and into the intersection almost hitting the car approaching from the other direction.

"Hey, wake up, you asshole!" A man shouted with a burly face through the open window of a car stopped just inches in front of the Buick.

The window wiper stuttered just enough to wipe away a few years of unwanted abuse. Through the light mist on the windshield Jack could see the outline of a huge mass spilling over the steering wheel. Jack again flicked the switch that controlled the wipers but this time only the passenger side worked freely. The wiper on the driver side moved in stutters as it mopped a mix of old mud smashed bugs and fresh rain across the windshield. Finally, the driver side wiper blade moved to clear his view. He jumped back away from his own steering wheel. What filled up most of the other car's driver's seat Jack hoped suddenly would stay put. He didn't need an ass kicking as the huge mass in the other car Jack felt was certainly twice his own size.

As Jack sat there with his hands frozen to the steering wheel a panic feeling welled up in his chest and he soon began to feel faint. He bit down, sucking in the inner side of his cheek between his teeth. He felt the small hole in his cheek forming from the constant abuse. A full-blown panic attack was fighting him for birth. He had to get the hell out of there, but this time the face of hate and rage kept him frozen in his seat.

"What the hell are you looking at, asshole?" The man shouted out the driver side window of his car. "Move it! What shade of green are you looking for?"

At that moment Jack snapped at the opportunity to hit the accelerator and get the car and himself out of danger. As the car responded in a choking gasp from the pressure on the accelerator, Jack took one eye off the road and focused on a split image in his mind as he sped off around the other car. One eye he kept focused on the fading image of the other car in the mirror and the other on the road ahead of him as his car fishtailed down the road. This was something he had learned to do as a child when playing hide and seek at the orphanage.

Two images registered in his mind's eye at once. Jack found it a bit confusing at first, but as he began to focus and practice playing the game he found he could make out two images at one time. And with time, he taught himself to move one eye slightly left or right for an even better image. If anyone had been looking at him when he did this he imagined that he must have looked like a human chameleon.

Through the years of growing up in and out of different orphanages he never lost a game of hide and seeks. Old Mr.

Sampson, the caretaker of the Sunny Side orphanage, would see Jack playing and always say, "That boy got second sight."

So, he employed two images a once. He focused each eye independently.

A second light ahead now turned green and Jack wasted no time. He cleared the image of the burly man in the other car out of his head and focused his attention on getting the hell out of there. Again, he stepped down on the accelerator, but the wheels slipped on the oil slicked road before they found their grip. It was a good block past that intersection that Jack mustered up the courage to slow the car and look back to see if he was being followed. Looking back, all he saw was the man's head and arm sticking out the driver's side window, flipping him the bird and mouthing some obscenities.

Passing the next light Jack slowed easily into the curb and came to a resting stop in an effort to catch his breath. He shivered as his body was now covered in sweat. He could see that a small black Toyota was now backing into the parking space he had hoped for. "Shit!" He whispered aloud to himself. That was a perfect spot a few hundred feet away from the Lord Building, where he was to see his parole officer. He could have parked there and not been afraid of Mike Shannon seeing him from the window of his sixth-floor office.

Mike was his parole officer and Jack considered him a hard ass that took no shit from any of his clients. Mike wouldn't think twice at flipping a coin and sending a parolee back to what he like to refer to a jail as, "The iron bar hotel." Breaking his parole agreement would have been enough to get him a few more months in the county jail. If Mike had known that Jack borrowed a car and was driving around with a revoked license he was sure Mike wouldn't think twice about turning him over to the authorities. He would bust him a new asshole.

As a parole officer and ex-Marine, you didn't keep Mike waiting. Mike served two tours in Vietnam and, as the men on the line referred to it, they took heavy shit. Mike's job as a side gunner on a recon helicopter would be to lean out the side of a flying chopper and fire on any unfriendlies or gooks, as the men in his outfit called the enemy. Mike was tall and broad shouldered, and he sported a square flat top hair cut that looked like gray icicle clippings short to the scalp. Jack always thought that if he touched Mike's hair he'd walk away with bloody fingers from how sharp it looked.

Driving around the block, Jack came upon a spot where a car was leaving just in front of the parole office. Damn, he thought, nope. It was on his third time around the block when, just after turning right on the side street of the building, a space opened next to a sycamore tree. Jack thought it a perfect spot to hide his activities.

8

With the car backed in, Jack shut down the engine. The engine rumbled and sputtered its displeasure at being cut off from its life supply. It sputtered and caught itself in an endless loop of post ignition as it died and then coughed up life again time after time.

"God fucken dam it!" He screamed. "I'm going to kill myself."

Jack slumped back in the seat and let out along sigh as the car finally died. He sat there for a long moment staring at small droplets of water running into small streams that formed on the car's windshield. The wet windshield gave the images of people walking by a kaleidoscopic effect.

Jack just sat there intrigued with the light bending images and the soft sounds of the raindrops tapping on the car's roof. The images reminded him of a mescaline trip he had as a teen living on the streets of L.A. Suddenly an image pressed up against the driver's side window came into focus. Jack recognized first the badge on the officer's rain slicker. It was even clearer seeing the engraving on the metal read: OFFICER COLLINS, ELIZABETH, N.J. Now this is a bad trip, he thought. Jack froze in his seat.

"Hey buddy, you going to sit there all day?" A voice asked through the window.

Jack could see the officer reach for something under his coat. He thought to duck for cover but quickly came to the realization that an odd move, would only serve to arouse the suspicion of the man in the rain slicker. He decided to just sit still and hope that the officer would go away. Jack forced a split image in his mind's eye. One eye trained on the rearview mirror and the other on the image in the side window. Because of the way the mirror was turned from its previous alignment with the burly man, Jack could see a full view of the driver's side of the car and a full view of the police officer. Out of the corner of his right eye, Jack could see that what the officer had in his hand was a night stick. After a few taps on the driver's side window by the police officer, Jack finally mustered up the courage to roll down the window. A gust of windswept rain preceded the very large mustache of the officer through the window opening.

"Hey mister, you okay?"The officer questioned.

Think fast; think fast, Jack told himself.

"Huh? Oh, yeah." He answered, "Just day dreaming, I guess."

Shit, is that the best you can do? A voice spoke to Jack in the back of his mind. Shut up he answered.

"Well I just didn't want you to leave your car before you shut its headlights off." The officer tucked the night stick back into its holder on his belt.

"Oh yes, thank you, officer." Jack nodded his head and pushed in the light knob on the dash board.

"I've seen it a hundred times. Folks get caught in the rain with a dead battery, ya know?" The officer leaned into the small window opening and Jack followed the officer's eyes with his own. It seemed to Jack that the officer was now doing a little snooping.

"Well thank you, thank you very much, officer." Jack pulled the door handle and the door immediately popped open with a low thud sound as it hit the officer's night stick. Jack could feel his heart pounding in his chest and he was certain it would explode. The little voice inside his head crept up again urging him to run. Again, he urged it to shut up. Better not he answered. Please don't ask me for my ID he thought.

Suddenly a flash of light streamed across the dash. The police officer held out his flashlight and began to search the car like a lighthouse beacon searching through the fog for a lost ship.

"Oh shit, I'm late." Slipped from Jack. He started to roll up the window with the mustache face still in it. The officer jumped back as Jack started to open the door but not before being hit in the knees buy the wind-swept door. Jack eased himself out of the car.

"Oh sorry" Jack said turning to shut the car door.

"Well you better get a move on if you're late and all." The officer tucked the flashlight into a pocket of his slicker.

Jack slammed the door shut and took off in a mad dash for his appointment. He could hear the officer yell out that he should be using an umbrella because it was now raining heavier. Jack paid him no mind and just made a beeline for the entrance.

Mike Shannon would be waiting with a verbal tongue lashing for being late. He knew he couldn't tell Mike the real reason he was late, that he was sharing recipes in a car with a nosey police officer. Jack could feel the rain hit him in the face and as he slowed to turn the corner of the building he knew he was late but just how much was uncertain.

A watch was something he always told himself he would one day purchase again, and he wondered if the Tag Heuer his father had given him was still at the pawn shop. It was just after getting out of prison that he settled for far less than what the watch was worth. He knew he was being taken for a ride when the pawn shop owner assured him that the three hundred dollars he offered was a great deal. As a child he was happy to have inherited it and never questioned as to how his father gained possession of such a fine time peace.

He could now see the front of the building and started to run. Wet leaves caught him in his next step and he hydroplaned about ten feet, arms flailing wildly like a turkey in mating season. He went head first sliding into a bush at the bottom of the building's stairs. Instantly rain soaked through his trousers. He could feel the front of his pants soak up water like a sponge through to his underwear.

"Mother fucker." He shouted.

As he entered the foyer the sounds of his boots sloshing, and squeaking echoed in a swirling motion from wall to floor and seemed to surround him at times. Jack stopped to see if he could follow the sound as it bounced around the marble floored halls. Slowly he caught the sound as it skipped along the walls and followed it past glass doors and faded paintings until it stopped and again swirled around him. Looking down he realized quickly that it was time to keep moving when he noticed a small pool of indigo stained water now forming around his boots.

When the elevator door opened a wave of perfume hit him like a ton of bricks and Jack just stood there momentarily frozen in time. "Well what's it going to be sunny?" An old woman said tapping at her wrist. But Jack saw no watch there. "On or off?" She added impatiently.

The ride up in the elevator to the sixth floor drew quite a bit of head rocking, glares and stares. When the doors opened on the fourth floor, a little old lady tisked and made a face at him as she walked on the elevator. Jack tried to avoid eye contact by employing the split image eye trick he learned as a child just to keep an eye on the others in the elevator. People moved off toward the right side of the elevator, crowding around each other as if a plague was set loose around the wet body that was now Jack Kahill.

In the split image of Jack's mind, he could make out on one side the image of the little old lady repeatedly pushing the stop request for the next floor. Nothing seemed more important to her than to get as far away from the dripping man in the rear of the elevator car as she could. Eagerly she kept at the task of trying to get the machine to overlook its regular set of motions and skip the sixth-floor destination in favor of her choice of the first floor.

Jack heard the buzzer of the elevator announce its arrival at his stop and he brought his focus on the little light above the elevator door confirming the stop. As he stepped off the elevator he could feel the heat of unwelcomed jeers staring him down from behind. He could see in a glass reflection of an office door in front of him the smirk of the little old lady just before the elevator door closed behind him. "Fuck you too."He mumbled. He thought of raising the bird above his shoulder but didn't. He had enough problems in front of him and quickly realized that he needn't bring on any more. As the elevator

14

began its descent, Jack wondered how many times, would the old lady push the first-floor button before the elevator reached its destination.

A quick look left and right and Jack realized he was alone. The bell of the elevator rang out again on its descent and echoed in the hollow halls. The only presence that came was a shadow through a smoked glass door directly in front of him. Jack recognized the outline of large breasts belonging to the figure of Billie Mathison, Mike's secretary.

She's a lovely young lady, Jack thought. She had curly blonde hair and was tall and slender with legs that seemed to run all the way up her back. She had large, beautiful green eyes that, when Jack considered them, reminded him of the beautiful island photographs of Ireland he saw in the prison library. He thought she was a bit out of his league. She seemed clumsy around the office, always bumping into things, dropping papers and breaking pencils when she was taking notes. Jack remembered that once a letter he received from Mike's office had a great deal of misspellings. She was beautiful though, and once Jack thought of asking her out, but the idea quickly faded. What would she want with an ex-con, he asked himself. Besides she must be Mike's main squeeze. The way she grew flustered when Mike came into the room was the dead giveaway. She looked like a school girl on a prom date, batting her eyes at Mike every chance she got.

Jack opened the office door as quietly as he could, trying not to make a sound so he could soak up her beauty a few seconds more before she noticed his presence. The squeak of the door busted him cold.

"Hi Mr. Kahill, Mike will be with you in just a sec." She had the accent of New York. Probably Brooklyn, he thought. He watched as Billie pulled out a small blue specimen cup from a drawer in her desk and placed it on top of the desk before him. It was part of his probation to be tested for substance abuse. He felt degraded but more embarrassed being handed a cup to piss in by a beautiful woman.

Billie pointed to the small rest room across the hall, but he already knew the routine. As Jack went about the task the word "Mister" rang strangely in his mind. Mister Kahill. Not since before going to prison for the last three years of his life had anybody referred to him as mister. The prison guards always referred to a new inmate as shithead and once you got labeled, it became hard to get rid of.

Jack wondered if Billie might just be a bit dippy too. She hadn't noticed that when he came back into her office he was drenched to the bone and dripping all over the floor. He placed the full specimen cup in the tray on her desk and took a seat opposite her desk and proceeded to thumb through the magazines spread out on the table. Jack let his mind drift for a moment aboard a tall sailing ship making way to port in Belize. His eyes fell shut and he could feel the gentle breeze catch the sails and smell the cooking coming from the island. People sun drenched tan glistened in the sunshine dancing there to the music of steel drums along the beach.

Billie got up from behind her desk and went over and tapped on the door of Mike's office before she opened the door a crack and stuck her head in and announced Jack's presence.

A whiff of cigar smoke took the opportunity to snake through the opening, taking a chokehold on the fresh air and breaking Jack's spell. He followed it with a split screen eye, one on the pear-shaped ass of Billie and the other on the slithering snake of cigar smoke leading back to Mike's office.

"You can go in now, Mr. Kahill." Billie pointed to the door.

Jack moved toward the door and was stopped dead in his tracks by the sight of Mike seated behind his desk pounding a fist on top of it. A deafening rhythm billowed out of a tape player on a file cabinet from across the room. Jack recognized the music as that of a Marine marching overture. Mike held out a finger like a stop sign in Jack's face and raised his other fist in time to the marching beat, right to the last crashing crescendo.

"Shut that off, will ya, darling?" Mike yelled out to Billie as the song faded.

17

Jack spun on his axis. He didn't realize that Billie was standing right beside him through the concert. Both men followed the curves as Billie performed the task.

"You're late." Mike pounded a fist on the desk, this time at his displeasure of Jack being late and not the music. "What the hell happened to you?" Jack just stood there at attention afraid to move for welcoming a coming storm.

Jack was still in the trance caused by Billie gliding past him a moment ago and he didn't answer the question.

"Billie, get this fool a towel, will ya, hon?" Mike pointed to a closet across the other side of the room. Jack followed the action intently.

"Yo...Jack!" Mike snapped a finger in Jack's face.

"Huh...what?" Jack answered.

Billie handed him a towel and walked over to Mike's desk and sat on an edge. A light sent of her perfume lingered there in the air behind her.

"Got to love them Marine boys. They don't take no shit." Mike pointed to a poster on his wall that had the United States and Marine flags with the words "Simper Fi" highlighted across it.

"Honor and duty." Mike shouted as he pounded a fist on the desk. This time Jack jumped back a little. He wondered when Mike was going to let him have it. He braced himself for the barrage. Honor and duty, he thought. It was something he now believed he knew nothing about.

"I slipped and fell; it's raining like hell outside." Jack finally answered Mike's question.

"Bullshit!" Mike shouted. "You don't know what the hell rain is until you spent eight fucking months in 'Nam. There it rained for three months night and day in jungle sweat and heat and the fucking gook bastards kept coming at you. You don't know what it's like until you've seen rain fall up."

Jack took the offered towel from Billy and went about drying himself watching her all the time as she walked slowly past him. Jack took a seat and just listened. It was always the same routine whenever he had to check in with Mike. Jack thought that Mike was probably born to be a parole officer. He was a hard ass and didn't like to take any shit from anyone and a half an hour each month Jack would have to sit there and take the lecture. It was all part of what Mike called becoming rehabilitated. Jack remembered that once in their conversation Mike told him that he found out from his C.O. while on a recon flight just what the Pentagon boys valued his life at as a side gunner. "Eight days...can you believe that?" He had told Jack on many occasions. "Well fuck them, I did. I lived. I got out of that hell hole, eight months with a second tour of duty back in the States."

Mike leaned back in his chair and re-lit the cigar he'd been chewing on. Gray smoke danced in the air around his head like a cobra.

"Ok, Sport," He waved a finger at Jack in the air. "Listen, you get your ass in here early next time." He snapped. "If I was ever late just once for my duty, death would have snuck up on me and slit my throat. No sir, it ain't going to happen when I'm on watch!"

Jack watched Mike with a trained eye as Mike produced a letter from his top desk drawer and slid it across the desk at Jack. Jack stood there doing nothing. "Well pick it up sport." Jack leaned forward and picked up the letter. For the first time since Jack sat down in Mike's office, silence took hold of the passing moment. Jack held the letter between two wrinkled index fingers like a piece of corn on the cob, his fingers still showing the signs of being wet. He recognized the return name on the letter, but the address was unknown. The name was that of his grandmother, Margaret Kahill. A cold chill ran up his spine as if old man winter took hold of his bones and sucked out the marrow till the bones were crisp like dried leaves on a hibernating tree. How was she able to find me, he thought? He had refused contact with her when he went to prison for vehicular manslaughter.

The time he spent in prison was more than three years and he had never responded to any of her letters in all the time he was confined there. Now the ghosts of the past trembled in his wrinkled fingers.

"Read the damn thing, man!" Mike demanded, puffing new glowing life into his cigar.

Jack turned the letter in his hands and took notice of it already being opened. It was annoying to have someone pry into his life. He tried to pay it no mind. It was a practice of the parole office to screen the parolee's mail. Mike wanted to make sure the parolees in his charge weren't into something bad with people on the inside or out. Most letters Jack received through Mike's office came from the state prison in Warren, Maine. They were always from a cellmate he shared a six by eight-foot prison cell with.

His cellmate for most of the three years he had spent in the Maine state prison system was a beefy little bald man with one eye. Most of the other inmates called the little man Popeye instead of Fred. Jack, on the other hand, thought that the stubbiness of the man's face and his pot belly led more to the Wimpy character than Popeye. It didn't take long for Jack to befriend the man. It seemed Popeye had a good outlook on life, even while in prison, that Jack liked. Through many long nights of wordy conversations, Jack discovered the real reason the other inmates called this little world traveler Popeye. It was because no matter how Jack tried to steer their conversation in any different direction, Popeye would always come back to talking about the sea and fishing. Jack didn't mind it much. It passed the time and at times it was fascinating to hear about strange exotic ports Popeye had claimed to visit even if at times it seemed hard to believe. The real ports of call Jack surmised were more than likely from the books and magazines in the prison library. Popeye could be seen there at any given time scouring the shelves for his next self-proclaimed adventures.

He and Jack would talk for hours about how, when both got out of prison, they would go into business together. It was going to be, a bait and tackle shop in Florida that Fred's father had left him in a will. Jack was out of the lock up for almost four months now and the last he had heard about Fred was that Fred had two more years to go on his charge of embezzlement from the Bank of Portland.

Jack sat staring at the letter, a light sent of lavender floated in the air. He didn't have to open it. The light smell of lavender gave it away. There was no mistaking that it was from her. She always had a light sent of lavender about her he remembered. Yet, he wished he didn't have to open it. He knew that was not going to happen if he had Mike staring at him from across the desk and tapping a finger impatiently. The return address read: St. Elizabeth Hospital, Elizabeth, NJ. Jack slid a finger into the opened end of the envelope, took a deep breath and continued to open the letter. A drop of water fell from his hair and bled the ink across the letter. Jack's eyes followed the drop as it stained its way across the page. He didn't get past the part of "Dear Jack," before Mike burst his concentration.

"Your grandmother is dying, Jack. You better honor her wish and go see her." Mike stopped tapping the desk and stared directly at Jack pointing the red dragon of death cigar in his face.

 Just what Mike had dictated Jack was now reading for himself. The letter began: "SEEK THE PRESENCE OF HIS LORD ONE – JACK KAHILL." She might be gravely ill, but she still had her wry sense of humor. She is the only person that ever called him "Lord Jack." When Jack had finished the letter, he sat for a long moment staring blankly out the window. It seemed to him that the rain was now one sheet of water thick as far as his eyes could see.

"You alright?" Mike asked.

"Yeah, just dandy." Jack folded the letter and stuffed it into his wet jacket pocket.

"Listen, Jack, if your grandmother is as ill as that letter suggests I'm going to cut our time here together. You do the right thing and go see her." Mike pressed a button on his intercom and again appeared a vision as lovely as a sunburst peeking through a developing rain on a Sunday morning.

"Billie, honey, would you please get Mr. Kahill's file and signature sheet? He will be leaving us presently." Mike leaned back in his chair resting his legs atop the desk and went about puffing new life into his cigar. Again, it sparked to life like a dragon.

Billie nodded to Mike and both men followed her with their eyes as she turned and walked back to her front office. Jack signed the papers pressed in front of him and breathed in a long breath of Billie's perfume. For all that he was concerned Billie could have held the notepad in front of him forever. Jack would often pretend to need a piece of paper and pen from her. He would wait if he could in the presence of Billie, eyeing all her godliness all evening. For some reason she seemed not to catch on to Jack's routine each time he came to see Mike. She seemed to enjoy the attention and Jack wondered if she deep down understood his little perverted but innocent act?

As Jack closed the door of Mike's office and headed toward the elevator, again he heard the wailing banshee cries of marching feet screaming from Mike's tape player.

Jack pressed the down request button for the elevator. He was glad that his clothing was a bit dryer. When the elevator door finally opened Jack was met again by some of the unwilling passengers from his first trip. All he need do now was to push a button and upset their day. Jack wanted to step back away from the opened door. He stood there contemplating whether to get in or just find the staircase when his eyes met the little old ladies. Jack could see the blood boiling in her eyes and she gave him the same warm 'tisk' welcome.

"Well, come on!" She demanded in a raspy voice, sounding like two pieces of rusted steel scraping together. Her voice hurt Jack's ears and he jumped on the elevator as the doors scraped his back side. Jack didn't push the button for the ground floor. It was already illuminated, and he was certain the little old lady would push it a few hundred times before the elevator would come to a stop. If he had pushed the wrong button he was sure she'd explode.

He then scampered into the rear of the elevator car like a cockroach running from a pointed shoe, hoping not to get squished. He needed to get as far back as the car would allow so that he was positioned behind the little old lady. This way, he wouldn't have to be stared at by the rusting old hag.

Jack pressed his back to the wall and found the crumpled letter in his pocket. The letter was devastating news. He felt his eyes blur with tears and his breathing becoming heavy and labored. It was so long ago that Grandma Kahill loved and toiled for Jack's wellbeing. She even tried to care for him the long time he spent alone in a foster home.

Jack had managed to stay in contact with her no matter where he was by letter, an occasional phone call and even a rare special occasion in person appearance. "Is that you, Lord Jack?" He remembered her calling him when he finally paid her a visit. But now it seemed so long ago. He felt ashamed now. He ignored any letters that piled up in his forwarded mail box and chose not to contact her while in prison. How could he? He couldn't bear to face her with his shame of being a common criminal. He remembered their time together was always festive. Grandma Kahill would always whip up a batch of her famous clam chowder that Jack loved so much.

Jack would pry her to talk about the family history. The characters that she would bring to life and the yarns she spun would always leave Jack wondering if any of it was truly real. She spoke of a funny story about his mother and her alcoholic friend. They were leaving a bar after drinking there for some time and while walking home along a river bed spotted a barrel floating along the river. "Your mother." She continued. "Said that she could catch the barrel and she fell into the river trying. She came up on top of the barrel about a quarter mile away and now floating out with the tide. When she finally swam back and up out of the river, what do you think they did next? They went right back to the bar. She looked and smelled like a river rat. And ya know Jack, the funny thing no one said a dam thing." She and Jack shared a laugh together. She would always finish the story by saying, "Remember, an Irishman would rather tell you a story than to tell you the truth straight out." But now there would be no more Sunday afternoon brunches, no more studies of ancestral history, no more commenting on daily events and no more social commentary that became so prevalent in many of their special times together. All of this was now rapidly coming to an end. Grandma Kahill was dying.

There was only one thing Jack could do...see her. Would she forgive him? The thought briefly entered his mind. He was certain of one thing that she loved him no matter how great the distance between them and how much time had passed.

Jack held his breath for a moment and crumpled the letter back into his pocket. He closed one eye and with the other traced the ceiling tiles until he found the elevator mirror on the left wall. It allowed him to see the faces of whoever got on or off the elevator without having to face anyone himself. This was a trick he learned while in lockup, from Popeye the sailor. This was a way to keep a watchful eye on his surroundings without making himself vulnerable to those around him.

The elevator stopped on the fifth floor and two more people crammed in. Watching the mirror Jack could see that one was a man, well dressed, suit and tie, probably a lawyer thought Jack. The other was a woman also well dressed. An overstuffed satchel hung from her right shoulder making her list to that side. Jack wondered why the man didn't carry the bag for her. But as they got on the elevator it became clear when they stood at opposites sides of the car that they were traveling alone. She was pretty but not like the goddess he left back in Mike's office.

Suddenly the walls were closing in on him. Jack felt dizzy and faint. The pounding in his chest grew heavier and he heard the pumping of the blood through his veins in his ears. He felt his chest tighten as if his heart was about to burst. He had to get the hell out of there. He couldn't take the pressure. Everything seemed to be crashing in on him. The prison doctors called it a panic attack but to him it felt as if he was about to lose control and die. His hands shook as he tucked them into his coat pockets. The tiny cramped elevator room began to spin. At any moment he felt he was going to lose it and wind up leaving his body, go insane and never recover. He closed his eyes and with his tongue found the hole in his inside cheek that he started by biting on his cheek long ago. This time he bit down hard. He tasted blood immediately when his teeth cut through the ragged flesh of his mouth. Jack thought that the panic attacks were all behind him. He hadn't experienced them since being released from prison over three months ago. Think, think, he told himself, I've got to get a newspaper.

"Bing!" Jack opened his eyes, hoping that the sound meant the elevator had reached its final stop. He was horrified to see that that elevator had only reached the second floor. He felt he couldn't breathe and was sure he was going to pass out at any moment. Newspaper, newspaper, he kept saying in his mind. A newspaper was the one thing he felt sure would calm him down.

While in prison, when the lockup became too much, and panic began to surface its ugly head like the darkness of mortal sin, Jack would immerse himself in reading a newspaper. With pen in hand he would begin to make social commentary on everything he read, going so far as to even rewrite a news article or heading. He would rewrite it in a socially funny or ironic commentary. He thought it a scream when he read that a newlywed couple on their honeymoon was attacked by a shark while sailing a personal watercraft. The bride got eaten by a shark while the groom watched. Jack found this to be so ironically funny that he fell off the commode while reading it. Through laughing at the news, he could calm himself and put off a panic attack.

So now when the elevator door finally opened on the ground floor Jack rushed past the other occupants, bumping the little old lady. Pushing people out of his way, he ran desperately through the lobby searching for the newsstand. He paid little attention to the little old lady as she cursed him from behind.

CHAPTER 2

THE WALLS HAVE EARS.

 Junior Leeds had just finished pouring a cup of coffee for a patron when he heard change hitting the ceramic bowl he had placed atop the register counter. Two dimes and a nickel registered in his mind. Being blind had its disadvantages but sounds registered with the utmost clarity in Junior's ears. It was the sound of someone leaving change for the purchase of a newspaper. He placed two cups of coffee on the countertop, sealed the lids and went about fishing a paper bag out of the cubby under the counter when his radar picked up the sound of an elevator door closing. Junior registered the sound of a man's heavy footsteps rushing ever closer toward his coffee shop. He recognized the tapping of heels on the marble floor. Wait...one more, he told himself.   He shifted his sensitive receptors slightly left. Yes...that's it. It was no mistake now. There was only one boot that made that kind of tapping sound and he recognized it every time as belonging to Jack Kahill. Junior made it a point to get to know the customers that frequented his café. But this time the sound of heels heavy against the floor had a rap of urgency and he could tell that Jack must be in trouble.

"Quick, Junior, just a Daily News." Jack mumbled, swallowing hard.

Jack placed a damp dollar bill into the ceramic bowl and didn't wait for Junior to make change before he turned to find a secluded table to sit at. The voice, above the screeching stop of a boot heel on the waxed floor, confirmed the identity of the person now standing before Junior.

"Whoa, Jack, hold on a minute. What's the rush?" But it was too late. Jack already had his back to him and was now making a beeline to an empty table he spotted under a staircase next to a potted miniature Bloodgood tree.

Junior Leeds had been blind since birth, but he never let his disability bother him. He ran the Elizabeth Town Hall coffee shop for ten years along with his wife. He always had a kind word and loved to chew the fat with anyone that stopped long enough at his shop.

Jack would stop by after he had finished with his parole officer and the two men would share comments on any event Jack found interesting in the news. Junior's kindness reminded Jack of old Mister Sampson, the caretaker at the Sunny Side Orphanage, and he felt comfortable enough around Junior and his wife to talk about anything. Most of the time, Junior sat with many of the people who passed through, often discussing politics of the day. He quickly became a good listener when someone needed to pour out their troubles. The lawyers on the second floor nicknamed him "The Wall" because at one time or another, Junior became a sounding board to talk out any problem. It was often Junior's way to disappear into the back of his café and then reappear with a fresh pot of coffee. He'd then go about sitting himself down to listen to your troubles long into the night, well after the building had closed. He would never chase anyone away if they had some interesting gossip or just something to say.

So, it was no different this time when he recognized Jack's erratic behavior.

"Mary." He said, handing her his apron. "Watch the café. I've got to go talk to a man a moment."

Mary nodded even though Junior couldn't see, and she waved him off. She knew he was about to butt into someone's business. Junior grabbed a fresh carafe of coffee and tucked two ceramic cups into the fold on his arm. Following the sound of a man's labored breathing, he slowly made his way over towards where Jack had taken up residence. As Junior came closer it became apparent to him just what that ruffling noise he heard was. It was Jack flipping through page after page of a newspaper.

Jack sat studying the newspaper and didn't notice, Junior setting down the coffee or taking a seat beside him. Jack felt his heart racing. He had to calm himself down. He knew that flipping through a newspaper always did the trick. He especially liked to write his own satirical comments on any story that seemed funny to him.

He was beginning to lose himself in the pleasure of writing his commentary as Junior sat. It was an article about a single engine plane that crashed into a Kentucky Fried Chicken restaurant in a poor section of an urban city. Jack was fiddling with a photo of a man commenting about how he had seen the crash. Jack wrote a caption above the man that read: THE PLANE DONE HIT ME UPSIDE MY HEAD...WHERE MY LAWYER AT? The second story he came across was of a funeral and how the priest had crashed his car into the limo of the grieving family as they were departing for the graveyard. The story continued how at the repast the two sides of the family who hated one another started a fight, turning over tables leaving some people with broken bones. The whole melee ended with three cop cars showing up. Jack laughed leaving this story alone, it didn't need a commentary. Oh, how his grandmother would have found it a real hoot, he thought. Jack chuckled to himself and sat staring at the newspaper until the aroma of the coffee caught his attention.

Wiping tears from his face, he looked up and found Junior pouring the two men a cup of hot coffee. Jack watched in amazement at how Junior could pour just the exact amount of Joe without spilling a drop or even worse burning himself on the hot liquid. Jack quickly surmised that Junior's other senses must be of heightened awareness to compensate for his blindness. How else could he have found him in a room full of people surrounded with all kinds of distracting noises?

"What's the hurry, Jack? You okay?" Junior finished pouring the coffee like a surgeon performing a delicate operation. "So, what's the problem, Jack? Did you see your parole officer today?"

Junior held out an open hand and Jack shook it. Junior noticed that Jack had a tremor in his grip, but he made no mention of it to Jack. He also noticed that Jack's grip was something like that of a wet raisin and made a mental note that Jack should be carrying an umbrella.

"Yeah, Mike was his usual self." Jack sipped at the coffee. "Geese, you make the best cup of coffee."

"Did he have that dang blasted symphony going again? I swear, sometimes you can hear it all the way down here in my café."

Jack didn't answer. He sat there a moment staring at a photo of an old woman celebrating her 98th birthday. The photo showed her holding in her arms her great, great grandson. Immediately, Jack thought of the crumpled, wet letter hidden in the inside pocket of his jacket. Jack took a long, slow sip of his coffee and reached into his pocket, hesitating a moment before his fingers locked hold of the crumpled mess.

Finally, the question that Junior asked broke through the fog that was now Jack's mind. He didn't believe that Mike would play the Marine marching band music so loud that the people sitting in the café would be able to hear it. It was probably just the ultra-sensitive hearing Junior developed.

"Yeah." Jack answered sipping at the cup. "Mike was playing the same god damn shit he always plays. I swear he's stuck living in the past." Jack thought about that for a moment. .... At least he was living.

Jack placed the crumpled wet letter on top of the newspaper, covering the photo of the old woman. He watched Junior's face and a little twitch gave away the knowledge that Junior heard the two pieces of paper meet.

"What's in the letter that's got you so upset, Jack?" Junior reached a hand across the table and extended a long finger, tapping it on the crumpled wet letter.

"Bad news." Jack answered and he let it die there saying no more about what was in the letter.

Jack wondered if there wasn't anything that Junior could not sense. There were many times Jack would visit Junior's café, sit and shoot the bull with Junior since getting out of jail almost four months ago. Although the time he knew Junior was short, Jack felt there was something genuine in the caring that came through in the talks they shared. At this point, Jack felt he could probably refer to Junior as a friend and on more than one occasion he told Junior how much he reminded him of old Mr. Sampson the caretaker. Mr. Sampson would play checkers with Jack when he lived at the orphanage. He, too, would listen to Jack's problems with a caring ear.

Jack was six years old when he went to live at the orphanage. He wanted to live with the one person who truly loved him, his grandmother. But her second husband put a stop to it. He despised children and wanted little to do with Jack. He made it a point that Jack could not live with them. Even on those rare occasions that Jack came to visit he let his displeasure grow into a fight with the grandmother, often abusing her.

A few months after his arrival at the orphanage, Jack came into the temporary custody of a family named the Henderson's from Long Island, New York. It was with the not too soon arrival of Jack, that the pregnancy of Mrs. Henderson, her first biological child, Jack had to go. Mr. Henderson always believed that his wife was infertile. But the constant moaning and bed squeaking Jack heard through the adjacent wall of his bedroom led him to believe that Mr. Henderson was a determined man. So, it was that when Mrs. Henderson became pregnant, Mr. Henderson was determined to get rid of Jack. Often was the occasion that Jack was bounced from foster home to foster family and then back again.

One day, shortly after Jack was dumped off by the Henderson family, Mr. Sampson invited him to engage in a friendly game of checkers.

"Checkers is like life, boy." Mr. Sampson would go on... "You got to think on your feet and make all the right moves at the correct time. When all else fails you got to trust your gut." Jack wasn't sure he knew what the old man had meant and how he could learn anything by playing checkers.

It wasn't long after that when Jack was engaged in another game of checkers with Mr. Sampson, he let on to another fact of life. He said, "Just remember, Jack you need a license to have a dog, but any scum bag can have a child. Where's the justice, my boy, where's the fucken' justice? And remember this most important fact my boy." He pointed a finger in Jacks face. "Life is absurd and humor the antidote."

Jack remembered how he laughed at the thought of Mr. Henderson now with a newborn baby, having to change messy diapers and all.

Jack thought it funny, but this was the first time in a long time that he thought of his time spent in the orphanage. He sighed openly this time and didn't try to hide his feelings from Junior.

Jack pushed his empty cup across the table. The rising tide of caffeine was about to overflow its banks. He needed to calm down, not race into the unknown.

"You know, Junior, we've been sharing a cup of Joe each time I come here. We always sit and discuss the bullshit of the day, but what I can't figure out is why you bother to talk to a guy like me at all?"

Junior sat there for a moment and then faced Jack. It seemed to Jack that Junior was purposely blinking a blind gray stare at him. Everything around him seemed to darken out of focus. Sounds became mute. Everything seemed to slow to a crawl. Jack could see his own reflection in the cold, gray marble frosted dead eyes of Junior. The reflection of himself suddenly turned into a small boy running to sit on the knee of a woman seated on a porch step. Jack recognized the woman as the same person who authored the letter he was now fumbling with at the table. Another blink from the dead eyes and as quickly as she appeared she vanished. Jack sat there with his mouth agape, staring blindly into Junior's face. Suddenly the face moved, and Jack jumped back in his chair. Junior didn't see Jack's reaction but like a Doberman he heard it.

"What does it hurt taking advice from a blind man? I can't see you, but I can hear in your voice your soul and I know your trouble. In my life I'm constantly surrounded by what people might refer to as a constant evil of darkness, but just because I can't see...in the torment of darkness... he paused for a moment.... don't mean I can't see."

Jack looked back at the soggy letter on the table. His hands trembled as he went to reopen it. There were many questions he needed to answer for himself. How bad was his grandmother? How long had she been in the hospital? It had been a little more than three years since he last went to see her at her summer cabin in Maine. There he told her something he thought he would never have to do. It was a lie that he had taken a job with an oil rigging company in the Gulf of Mexico. He felt guilty for having to lie to her, but he couldn't tell her the truth that he was going to prison. He couldn't tell her the truth that he had killed two people while drunk driving. Three years in prison was a long time to be away and out of contact with the outside world. Before his sentencing, his court appointed lawyer assured him that he would only serve fourteen months. She was a young lawyer who was over pressed to service too many charity cases to really spend time with any one case. The judge handed him three years plus. Before Jack could respond to the sentencing and make a grab for his lawyer's neck, he felt the hard pressure of the two sheriff's officers clamping down on his arms and dragging him away.

There were so many questions circling around his head. Jack slipped a finger into the corner of the envelope and pressed it against his now throbbing forehead. He peeled back an edge slowly and even though the envelope was damp with raindrop moisture, the agonizing torture seemed to echo, ripping fibers separating from itself across the marbled hall. Jack watched Junior's head perk up, his ears working the subtle fluttering of the wind like a Doberman. Jack couldn't tell if it was really the echo of the envelope opening or Junior's keen sense of hearing that perked Junior's attention.

Jack turned to face Junior and in a purposely slow, low tone of voice asked, "How do you measure a life? One minute you're here and the next you're not."

He felt his stomach do a flop and sink into a burning, bottomless pit. He felt empty except for the heavy weight of guilt, pounding and cutting a valley through his heart.

"I didn't know the two people I killed. I never even saw their faces. I was drunk. The fire department had to use the Jaws of Life, to cut the two people out of their car, but it was too late. My car was totaled, and I hardly got a scratch. Everything was a blur, but I'll never forget seeing all the blood gathering and spilling down a drain." Jack sighed and crumpled the letter into a ball, flinging it into a nearby trash can.

"Life flowing down a drain." He whispered sitting staring at his hands as tears rolled down his face.

"I believe things always happen for a reason and the force of natural occurrences... call it karma... yes that's it karma." Junior answered holding out a hand. "Take it from me Jack there is only one thing you can believe in and that is the force of KARMA. Life happens to you no matter how well you try to prepare. Often faced with unimaginable odds, the one thing you can be sure of no matter what you do, remember this Jack it's always karma that will be the great equalizer in the great mystery of everything."

Jack took a firm grip of Junior's hand. "Thank you, I don't know." After a long pause finished... "You're probably right."

Chapter 3

Dying is a messy business

Margaret Kahill held the small controller in her frail hands, desperately trying to push in the button so she could get the attention of the nurses' desk but the arthritis in her fingers made it impossible for her to get a good grip on the key pad. It was early in the afternoon, just after lunch, but not quite dinner time. She never paid much attention to a formal timing of those rituals. A person should eat when they're hungry, drink when they're thirsty and sleep when they're tired, she would always say. She was left thirsty from all the tests of the early morning.

"Why doesn't this damn thing work?" She asked of the air. Everything bothered her. The room was one moment too cold and then the next too hot. She felt humiliated at the thought of having to be taken to a rest room by a stranger or having someone who didn't speak English force a bed pan under her ass. She thought why was it that in all her ninety plus years that someone still had to wear a hospital gown with their ass sticking out the back. She refused to wear one from the very first day she was admitted. "No sir." She would say and put on a house coat instead. The head nurse tried to put up a fuss and insist at first, but her doctor put the head nurse at ease.

The window curtain was opened too much, letting in too much light and the damn television had a fuzzy picture of an old rerun of the Honeymooners she had seen a dozen or so times. Her thumb now ached from pushing the button on the controller in her hand. Enough is enough, she thought, and flung the controller across the room at a trash can. The controller flew until the cord became taut and recoiled like a rattle snake snapping back and crashing into an IV bottle suspended on a pole near her bed. The force of the controller broke the bottle and sent glass shattering. A small piece lodged itself into her skin just above the IV tube that protruded from her forearm. Suddenly two nurses came rushing into her room followed by an orderly larger than any black bear she'd seen while at her summer home in Maine.

Had it not been for the fact that she could no longer walk, she would have gotten up out of that hospital bed, skipped down the hall and gotten her a Nephi pop out of the vending machine.

As she became an adult walking became more of a task with each passing year. Growing up as a young child surrounded by

43

poverty in the depression era ghetto port of Elizabeth, she had to make due sharing other siblings and neighbors shoes. Over the years of abuse from having improper fitting shoes and having to force her foot into ones that did not fit, she developed a deformity where her toes overlapped each other, increasingly making it more difficult for her to stand and walk.

She was now ninety-eight years old. Her body was breaking down, but her mind was clear as a bell. She had lived through four wars and the Depression. She could sing any tune from JOLESON, SINATRA, and even enjoyed the BEATLES. She was never much of a drinker, so the time of prohibition didn't bother her in the least. She referred to alcohol as the creature because the more someone would drink the more it released the creature. Her favorite movie was THE WIZARD OF OZ and if it was an inside joke or not, she was said to root for the wicked witch saying she got a bum steer.

She remembered the sinking of the Titanic having been twelve years old at the time of the ship's sinking.

She still had a full head of hair, although now snow white rather than the blondish red it had once been.

She joked about her height. "I'm sinking. I think the gravity on this hell hole of a planet has gotten heavier. I think I was six feet three." The truth of the matter was that the arthritis in her back had her hunched over at five feet two, but she was five feet four. She never smoked and insisted on eating a banana every day even if the banana was black as coal.

"What, I got to kill myself before I can get some attention around here?" She yelled.

The male orderly immediately went about the task of cleaning up the broken glass from the floor.

"Hey, what do I have to do to get some attention around here?" Margaret flinched when the head nurse picked the small shard of glass from her arm and wiped it with a cleaning swab and went about bandaging her cut.

"Now Miss Kahill, you know we've got more patients than nurses. Honey, we didn't forget you. You can't fly into a huff any time we don't answer you presently." She spoke with a French Creole accent that Margaret found hard to understand at times.

Margaret was about to pull out the IV needle but was restrained this time by both nurses.

"Now, Miss Margaret you don't want to be doing a thing like dat." The head nurse motioned for the orderly and the burly man held Margaret's arm as the two nurses went about the task of securing the IV tube with sterile adhesive pads.

"Listen, mumbo-jumbo, when the hell am I going to get out of here, so I can go home and die in peace?" Margaret was now waving her other hand in the woman's face trying to get the nurse to stop what she was doing. Her body was giving out, but her mind was as sharp as a razor. It had been three weeks since the first day she arrived at the hospital and it had been a constant barrage of poking, prying and tests.

When the doctor arrived the following morning, she knew. No matter how much Doctor Jain tried to hide his emotions behind a poker face, she could tell that it pained him to have to tell her she was going to die.

"Miss Kahill, I am sorry, but there no-ting I can do." Doctor Jain spoke with a Hindi accent that made Margaret strain to understand what he said, and she asked him to speak a little slower. "The liver tumor is grown too large. The cancer is too far spread. The best we can hope for is to make you as comfortable as possible." He held her hand and squeezed it. Then he took a stethoscope from his lab coat. "Let me take a listen to your heart."

He listened for a moment and then asked her to lean forward, so he could listen to her breathing. She grabbed the stethoscope and spoke into the tiny listening device.

"Hello…anybody home? Listen, Doc, I don't want to live forever, not in a wrecked-up suit like this." She made a twirling motion with her finger over her body. "Just tell me when I can go home and die in peace."

Doctor Jain smiled at the joke she made. "Now please let me listen." He gently patted her hand and took back the stethoscope. "Good, good, all of your vital functions are as good as they can be for your condition." He tucked the stethoscope back into his pocket.

She thought to herself and replayed that word over in her mind…condition. "What condition…slow boat to China?" It wasn't the fear of dying that got to her. It was going to the end of the road alone that bothered her more.

"I thought you had a grandson. Has he come to see you?" Jain asked.

"No…I mean yeah, I have a grandson, but no he hasn't come to see me." She fumbled to rebutton her blouse but the arthritis in her fingers made the task difficult.

"Oh, I am sorry Miss Kahill. Please let me get that for you."

As the doctor helped her button her blouse, she sighed, thinking to herself that the letter must have gotten to Jack. But why didn't he come? She thought. Where could he be? Most importantly, how would he take the news that she probably had less than six months to live?

As she sat there contemplating the devastating news, she wondered, as she did every day, if he would come. It had been over a month since she had sent out the letter saying she was going in the hospital. The news Doctor Jain had given her was something that she felt coming. For a few months now, she hadn't felt like herself. Although she had great difficulty walking and her body was failing her, she felt she had the mind of a young girl.

"You know, Doc, how about transferring my head on to one of those young, good looking nurses out there in the hall? I'll be sure Medicare throws in a couple of extra bucks."

"You are funny one lady." Jain said in a mixed-up sentence. But she knew what he had meant. Lately she felt herself tire more easily and the abdominal pain grew slightly more intense each day.

"Now Miss Kahill, the nurses tell me that you call them often. What is it that I can get for you presently?"

I wish Jack would come, she thought. "I'm thirsty and hungry." She said.

"Good, good. You have no dietary restrictions. You can eat anything you wish."

"Why don't you hop your ass down the street and get us a bucket of Kentucky fried chicken?" She pointed to the door.

"Before I go I will tell the nurse on duty to let you have anything you wish. I need to do a blood sample in the morning and then I will release you, so you can go home."

Doctor Jain sat on the side of her bed and gave Margaret a hug. He then walked out of her room and headed towards the nurses station.

Margaret felt tired and decided that instead of food, she would try to get some sleep. Today, she kept thinking. Maybe today Jack would come.

CHAPTER 4

PANIC ATTACK

It was late in the afternoon when Jack left the company of Junior and made his way back to the car. The rain had finally given up all but a light mist that now swirled around his face. A thick fog was now forming in the mist and the darkness of the late afternoon was giving way to the setting sun. On the walk back to the car he thought to himself of the promise he made to Junior, that he would see a doctor about his panic attacks. But he had only been at his new job a short time and it would be months before he would make the carpenters union and get his med card. It would have to wait, money was a luxury. He would have to suffer through it as he often did. He only hoped that he wouldn't chew threw his face when biting the in-side of his cheek when the devil came calling with the sudden rage of a fearful gruesome slaughter. They were always awful, starting the same way with a sudden pressure in his head and then a feeling of dizziness. His heart would race followed by the feeling of impending death. It always gave him the feeling that he needed to run away, and it didn't matter to where, just as long he was moving. It always left him with a shortness of breath and a shakiness he couldn't control.

The car grumbled to attention with a huge puff of gray smoke from its exhaust pipe. It fought Jack as he turned it into the flow of traffic along Elizabeth Avenue. The hospital was on the other side of town and the car seemed to know the way before Jack had the opportunity to navigate the street. The faded green light on the dashboard of the car flashed the time as 4:15 p.m. It was a little late starting a trip to the hospital. Would he be allowed in or better yet, would she still be there? There was one certain thing he had to do. He had to make the trip, there was no turning back. She deserved that, he told himself, and if she asked where he had been all this time, he would try to change the subject. But deep down inside, a gut feeling told him that she already knew the truth about his being in prison. That would explain how she managed to get a letter to him at Mike's office. He wondered how many of the letters he refused to pick up from his mailbox while in prison were from her. He'd remind himself later to ask her how she was able to track him down. The rain grew heavy again, looking like waves whipping across the street in front of him as he drove. Again, it saddened him to realize that he had lied to her.

CHAPTER 5

THE COLD DARK

Montgomery Barry sat at his desk performing his favorite task when he looked out the window and noticed that the sun was peeking out from behind a swift moving front. A ray of sunshine gleamed in through the window and reflected in a blinding sheen across his desk. It pissed him off that the weather was changing. Why couldn't it rain more? He wished. Now the noises of the living would come out of their hiding places and start their haunting. He loved the rain because of how it calmed the world and silenced everything. He pulled himself from his desk and went over to pull the shade, again encrusting himself in the wonderful subtleties of the dark. In the now darkened room he again seated himself at his desk and went about playing. At least he had this to himself. At least he had this to escape into.

The wallet lay on the table just where he positioned it the night before. No living soul would dare disturb his game and once he had laid his wallet there, the one part time helper who worked at the funeral home knew never to come into this room. He took a deep breath and just sat there for a moment staring at the wallet and making a mental calculation as to its precise position on the table. He had to be sure that no-one had come into the room and touched the wallet. He sighed, and a smile came upon his face. It was perfect. He admired its fine Italian construction, the intricate detail of its stitching and the perfect fold no matter how much he stuffed it with trophies.

Wait, wait...let the suspense build, he told himself. He closed his eyes and let the feeling wash over him. It was the feeling of total bliss. It was almost the same kind of feeling he got when an October storm was brewing hard rain and he was shut in tight, alone in his den in a darkened room listening to the rain smack against the porch window. But now it was time to get down to business, time to play the game. He opened his eyes and scooped up the wallet in one hand. The hand stopped with the wallet in his open palm just a sixteenth of an inch below his nostrils. Slowly he breathed in its bouquet. All the smells registered at once, the scent of leather, the smell of plastic photo holders holding in its secrets of past years and lives, and his favorite smell of all...dead Presidents. This time, though, a new smell arose from among the folded faces. It was unmistakably the smell he recognized the most...the smell of new money. He didn't need to smell it again as he lowered the wallet to the table. It was the way new money always had the wonderful bouquet of a woman laced upon it that he liked the most. New money in his wallet always had the smell of a woman's perfume on it and he loved this smell more than anything in the world. He shut his eyes for a moment letting the full sense take hold of him.

 Rain again pelted at the covered window and the wind whistled through the rotted window panes, blowing back the drawn curtain. He smiled when the cold chill feathered the hairs on the back of his neck. It reminded him of a recent burial.

It had rained the entire day of the funeral. It had been a funeral for a prominent lawyer in town who died suddenly of a heart attack. Everyone was miserable with the rain and all, but he remembered how overjoyed he was that day. He was glad it had rained that day and he was glad too that the old bastard was dead. He was prouder of himself, though; of the fact that he had overcharged the family a few thousand dollars. He wanted to screw them hard because the old bastard was one of the lawyers who had handled his father's will.

All of that was behind him now. Somewhere on the wall was a photo of the dead lawyer nailed to a dead president's face staring, back at him. If he looked hard enough he could find the trophies of that funeral. He knew he could find it fast if he wanted to because the funerals he hated most got a nail hammered through the trophies while others got a simple stapling.

He placed the wallet in the center of the desk and brushed his hair back between his fingers like a comb. He shut his eyes before laying his hands open on top of the wallet. He hoped that it had stopped. The doctors assured him that it was all because of his nerves that his hair was falling out and that the medication he was prescribed would help. He hated medication. He believed that it was an evil force that was trying to control his thoughts.

He didn't need to open his eyes. Just by rolling his fingers he could feel the hairs between them. He was fifty-eight and he despised the idea of looking like his father, bald with just a touch of gray at the temples. The hairs he saw in his hand were still darker than coal. He meticulously counted each one before he placed them in a jar of formaldehyde on his desk. It was twenty-three this time, less than the day be fore's, thirty-one. He still had a full head of hair. From the top drawer of his desk he produced a mirror. The room held just enough light for him to see his reflection. He wanted to be sure. He disliked the haunted reflection he saw. His hair was well groomed, dark as a moonless night. He had deep, dark eyes, beady like two small oyster pearls. His eyebrows were dark, gray showing through more than black. His nose was sharp, and he always thought it a bit long for his thin face. His shoulders were broad, and he wore the white collar of his starched pressed shirt high on his neck covering his large Adam's apple. He wore an Armani suit, always double breasted. He stood a bit hunched over, not because of any deformity or disease but because of his height. He stood six feet eight inches tall and always had to bend forward to talk to customers who came to the funeral home. It was a bad habit he developed. Most times he seated himself to put the customer at ease. He despised an ex-girlfriend who once referred to him as Lurch during a fight. But the image that haunted him the most was that as he grew older he was becoming the image of the one person he hated most, his father. His emotions peaked, and he flung the mirror across the room where it shattered on a casket.

Montgomery Barry felt disgraced that when his father died three months ago the decree of his will declared that another funeral home in Bangor would take care of the arrangements and that Montgomery was not to do the burial. But when his father's lawyer went public with the reading of the will, Montgomery was put out of the greater part of his father's wealth. The New York Times ran an article shortly after his father's death. The article related the three hundred-million-dollar fortune amassed by his father as a self-made man was all going to charity except for the inheritance of the funeral home bequeathed to Montgomery.

The smell of money called to him and again he turned his attention to the wallet. He spread the folded bills on top of the table. In different piles he placed all the dead Presidents. He crisped all the bills, folding them slightly vertically so they stood up slightly from the table. He handled each bill carefully and with the attention of a craftsman straightening a folded corner of a hundred-dollar bill gliding it ever so carefully between the nails of his thumb and index fingers. He rubbed them over and over again until they were silky smooth. He counted aloud with each pass the number of times he passed the bill between his fingers before all the creases were gone and the bill appeared like new. Again, a light whiff of perfume rose from the bill. He let out a sigh of delight.

Another pile held various forms of identification. Slowly and methodically he pinched the trophies and placed them in a vertical row on the table. Each trophy a photograph of a recent burial he performed. The first photo was showing a small child hit by a car. The boy ran out on a busy street chasing a ball. It was a closed casket, but Montgomery's trophy showed the left half of the child's body crushed by the car's tires. Not even the parents had seen the child's mangled left half. Montgomery flipped the photo over to see the notes he had written on the back side. The date of the child's death was printed on the top. It was a date that he remembered well as it was just a bit over three years ago, about the time of his father's first stroke and the time he had to take over running the funeral home alone. It also held, printed on the back, the total cost of the funeral arrangements, $8,000. Still stapled to the back was the crisp twenty-dollar bill that the child's grandmother had given to Montgomery to place in the casket for the child's sixth birthday a day after the accident. Montgomery held the twenty dollar bill up to his nose. He found it remarkable that the bill still held the scent of perfume.

Six new photographs now lay on the table, all with the exact information of the person's cause of death and the circumstances pertaining to the event. The photos also held stapled to them the costs and any money found in the casket that Montgomery took out before it was sealed for its final journey.

Montgomery found the stapler in his desk and made his way over to his trophy wall. Yes, that's it, he thought, that will do just fine. The boy will look perfect between the photos of a small girl drowning victim and another small girl who had been sexually assaulted and then strangled. He held up the photograph of the small boy and stapled it to the wall. He let his eyes scan the walls around him; hundreds of trophy photographs were stapled there, some fading with time. He paused for a moment on a photograph of a young woman who had died because of a drug overdose. It was a shame, he thought, for someone so young and beautiful to hate life so much as to extinguish one self. He thought back to the day he was called to come and pick up the body at the girl's home. The gruesome discovery was made by her mother when the girl had failed to show up for dinner. She was found naked on her bed. The police had discovered a suicide note and a mixture of pills spewed across the bed and determined that the girl had been dead for hours before the mother's arrival. The mother had to be taken to a psychiatric hospital and to the best of Montgomery's memory, she was still there.

It had been late in November and Montgomery was in the middle of stapling another photograph to the wall one early afternoon when he received a phone call to come and pick up the body of the young girl. The drive was a long one out town into an affluent neighborhood of Bangor. Out of the darkened window of the hearse he could see stately mansions behind ornamental iron works with well-groomed lawns. The drive through the front gate and up to the front of the house he estimated at a quarter of a mile winding under a canopy of large oak trees that darkened the road. He loved how it blocked out the sky making it seem like driving through a cave.

Three patrol cars took up the parking places in front of the house. A detective in a long trench coat came up and greeted him just as he was getting out of the car.

"Mr. Barry, thank you for coming out. I'm Detective Pool." The officer held out a hand and Montgomery wrapped his long fingers around it like a spider's tentacles and shook it firmly, just enough to greet the man. Montgomery wondered why the formal greeting when he and everyone in town knew Detective Pool as just Dave. Montgomery's hand was almost twice the size of Pool's and he could have easily crushed the man's small hand if he had wished to.

"Good evening, Detective." Montgomery went to the back of the hearse and opened the door and started to pull out a gurney and a body bag.

"If it wouldn't be too much trouble, Mr. Barry, would you give us a moment here? The mother is still upstairs and she's quite frantic…you know, before you bring in your equipment and all." The detective was now standing in front of Montgomery and with his hat on, he only came up to Montgomery's chest.

Montgomery towered over detective Pool like a gargoyle perched on the gutter of a tomb vault.

Montgomery looked past the detective towards the house. The front door was open, and a police officer was attending the entrance. Just past the opened doorway he could see the figure of an elderly woman pacing back and forth in front of the interior steps. She was flailing her hands in the air as she paced around.

"I can get a couple of the boys to help with your equipment if you'd like. Excuse me a moment." Pool stepped to the side away from Montgomery.

The detective opened his jacket and pulled out a walkie-talkie and in a static laden voice held a brief conversation with the officer on the front porch.

"It's okay now; Vern says we can go up." The detective motioned for him to follow. "Do you need a hand with your equipment?"

Montgomery waved him off. "No, I'll be just fine."

Detective Pool watched as the giant man picked up the gurney and cradled it under one arm and held the body bag with the other hand.

"I could use a hand on my way out," Montgomery said as he followed the detective into the house. The steps were easy for Montgomery to navigate. His shoes scraped the kickboard of each step as he walked up. If it wasn't for the fact that he was being escorted by Detective Pool, he would have taken two steps at once. At the top of the steps he had to duck his head going through the entrance. It was a magnificent house.

"This way," Detective Pool pointed up the stairs. "Follow me."

Montgomery ducked just in time, almost hitting his head on a crystal chandelier that hung above the first step. He felt a tingle run its way up his back. Magnificent paintings hung from every wall. This house had the smell of money, he thought. He was just about to turn a corner on the staircase when a great yell came from an adjacent room at the bottom of the stairs.

"No! Not like that!" The woman screamed up at the two men.

Montgomery could now see that the woman was forcefully being restrained by two police officers, the officer from the outside porch and new woman officer who just arrived.

"She's not decent, for Christ's sake!" The woman tried to shake loose from the grip of the officers.

"Wait a moment." Detective Pool held a finger in front of Montgomery like a stop sign and called the woman officer to come up the stairs. The officer made her way up the steps and stopped at the turn of the stairs next to Detective Pool.

"Wanda, this is Montgomery Barry. He's from the Barry Funeral Home." Wanda nodded a hello at Montgomery. "Listen." Detective Pool shook his head. "Wanda, go up ahead and get a blanket from another bedroom and just cover the body. When you're ready come back and escort Mr. Barry. I'll go down and try to comfort Mrs. Kate."

The officer turned and proceeded up the stairs without saying anything and Montgomery stood there like a vulture perched on a ledge waiting to pick a carcass clean. He tried to hide himself in his surroundings, but his six-foot eight figure stuck out like a giant bird perched at the turn in the stair. He tried to find something to look at while he waited for the officer to come back. His eyes wandered the walls around him and stopped, admiring the vast paintings hung along the walls. He could feel the heat of something staring back at him. As he turned his eyes caught the heat in the bloodshot eyes of Mrs. Kate staring back at him. The bright green of her eyes spotted in a sea of red bled through and shot a grip on his soul. He felt as if he was staring into what the good Reverend Kelly referred to as the fires of Hell. He could see her face beginning to change and contort with the expression of pain only the Devil could deliver. The gripping stare of the woman held him frozen.

"Excuse me, Mr. Barry," Officer Wanda tapped him on the back. "If you please." She pointed at a room down the hallway. "Follow me. We can go in now."

Montgomery blinked away the staring hold of the woman. As he followed behind the officer he could feel the racing beat of his heart. The feeling he had was that of a powerful evil presence at work here. It was a presence that just stared its way deep into his soul. He felt the presence inside him, looking and searching his mind and thoughts. The feeling of that kind of power excited him and he wished that the officer had not broken the locking stare. As he turned to follow the officer he stopped in mid stride and glanced over his shoulder, hoping to catch one last glare, but all he could see was the woman being led into another room by another police officer.

At the top of the stairs Montgomery could see a room at the end of a small hallway, its door ajar. The room was dark, just the way he liked a room to be. He thought to himself that all he needed now was the sound of rain hitting against a window. He suddenly felt a rush of excitement wash over him. It was the excitement of the opportunity to collect another trophy. It didn't matter that a young girl had taken her life so tragically with an array of sleeping pills and was now lying in a state of early rigor mortis just a few feet in front of him. It was the chance to see what he could really make of this wonderful event.

Montgomery placed the body bag and folded gurney down at the top of the stairs and walked slowly towards the opened door. He crossed the threshold and paused momentarily. A faint breeze of perfume floated across the room just in front of him. He closed his eyes and filled his lungs deeply with the heavenly smell. He thought of taking out his wallet and comparing the fragrance to that of the money it held. With the police officer standing just a few feet behind him, he thought best to just enjoy the fragrance with only one of his senses.

"Mr. Barry, would you like me to adjust the lighting?" Officer Wanda stood by an open window moving a curtain and about to pull the shade open.

"Please, no, the lighting is just fine the way it is." Montgomery was accustomed to working in the dark.

In the darkened room Montgomery could make out the image of the body under the light cover as if he stood by it with a spotlight. The body was still in the position that the police had first found it. The young girl had fallen forward on the bed facing the headboard face down. Her feet stuck out with the right leg folded under the left. From under the sheet a hand stuck out, the fingers constricted as if still holding the bottle of pills that took her life.

"It's a shame, don't you think?" Officer Wanda adjusted the sheet to cover the body totally.

"Yes, I suppose so." Montgomery answered as he walked back to the hall to pick up his tools. In the hall he was met again by Detective Pool.

"Here, let me give you a hand with that." Pool took up the other end of the gurney. "I supposed you've seen the body. That's just the way we found her. This is a clear case of suicide. What a shame. Damn shame it is."

Montgomery just nodded his head yes at Detective Pool as he followed in tow with the officer.

"Geese, it's like a morgue in here. Oh sorry, Mr. Barry. Officer Wanda is that you over there? Wait, I'll put some lights on."

Montgomery wanted to stop him, but it was too late. The room flashed to life with a blinding light that made both Montgomery and Officer Wanda squint like a cat. The bright lights hurt Montgomery's eyes and he was momentarily stunned blind. He had to stand there a moment to what he thought was the nastiness of the day light.

He placed the body bag next to the deceased girl and instructed the female officer to help him flip her body. Officer Wanda pulled off the sheet covering the girl as Montgomery unzipped the bag. He then walked over to the doorway where he had placed the gurney and went about setting it up to carry the body. Behind him he could hear the two police officers struggling to get the body rolled over. When he turned around he could see the nakedness of the body fully exposed.

He stopped in his tracks, awed by the beauty of the dead girl. She had strawberry blond hair flowing long and straight that stopped at her breasts. Montgomery took extra notice at how her hair seemed to caress her breasts. Her eyes were closed, and Montgomery found himself wishing that he were alone there for a moment, so he could open her eyes to see what color they were. He told himself there would be time to investigate that later. Her face was thin with thick eyebrows and a small nose. The skin of her face still had a soft complexion to it.

She looked peacefully asleep. He thought all he need do was to reach out and touch the girl and wake her from some happy, deep, distant dream. But from the rigidness of her body with the beginning of rigor mortis starting to set in, he realized from the contortion of her fingers that she once held the key to another threshold. The police had removed the bottle of pills for evidence. Her skin was tight and there was not an ounce of fat on her body anywhere to be found. The only imperfection that he could see was the scar tissue just above her pubic hair where her appendix had once been.

She was as lovely as any woman he had seen in the private rooms of Ms. Mary's bar in Bangor. Ms. Mary also ran a not advertised illegal brothel upstairs of the bar. Some of the local flesh he had the pleasure to associate with.

He felt the blood begin to boil in his veins as if he was suddenly hit by a lightning bolt. The swelling of the blood to his penis set an arousal throughout his entire body. He had never felt so thrilled and alive as he was there at that moment, staring at death and the nakedness of a dead girl.

With the help of the officers it was an easy task of carrying the dead body of the girl toward the winding steps. At the threshold of the door way leading to the outside he felt a tight grip take hold of his jacket pulling him back. If it wasn't for the help of the other officer, he could have easy lost hold of the body bag and drop the body.

He turned to see a screaming woman pointing a gnarled finger at him.

"*DEATH...DARKNESS...EVIL*" She shouted.

Montgomery turned to see a woman who now looked as if she had grown older before his eyes. Her hair seemed grayer and the smoothness of her face was now replaced with wrinkles. He wasn't sure if the woman standing before him was the same lady he met on the way in or now someone else. Her clothing was the same and he told himself that it was nothing more than the change in the rooms lighting.

The officers stopped cold. Wanda grabbed her arm as another officer took hold of her other arm dragging her kicking and screaming into a side room the entire time screaming...

"DEATH... DARKNESS... EVIL."

With a tap on his shoulder he turned toward detective Pool again grabbing hold the body bag and walked toward the waiting hearse.

Montgomery smiled into the rearview mirror as the officer closed the door. It was now dark, and he was sure that the detective had not seen his act of impropriety. It was wrong to smile at the pain of someone's misfortune. He didn't care though. He felt light on his feet and almost skipped his heels as he walked down the stairs with the police in tow carrying the sealed body bag to his awaiting car. He could hardly wait to get home, so he could place the body bag on the operating table and start the process of making another trophy. But this time it was somehow different. He had never felt the lustful feeling he had for the victim lying in the bed of his hearse in all the body pick-ups he'd ever done before. He had shortness in his breath and a tingling feeling in his hands as he gripped the steering wheel, turning into the funeral home drive. Again, he felt the surging blood of lust throbbing against his thigh.

The door of the hearse was hard to open at times and he had to use some force to open it. He grabbed at the rollers of the gurney and proceeded to pull the body out some so that the automatic wheels would fold out, making it easier for him to wheel the body into the house.

Suddenly a flash and instantaneous roar of thunder surrounded him. The sound of the cracking lightning flash left a ringing in his ears.

As he grabbed hold of the end of the body bag a light whiff of perfume floated up from the gurney and he noticed that it wasn't the same smell of the contents of his wallet. It was purer and sweeter, like the smell of dew on honeysuckle. It wasn't like that at all in his wallet. That smell was old trophies. It was now time to get busy. Another flash of light, this time illuminating his way, and the heavens opened. Much to his delight it began to rain. Out with the old and in with the new he told himself.

CHAPTER 6

ROUGH GOING

Rain battered the Buick as Jack pulled up in front of St.
Elizabeth Hospital. Standing in a doorway trying to duck out of
the rain a police officer, stood stiff like a graveyard statue. His
eyes glowed there in the darkness like two red coals with the
focus of his attention clearly on Jack. Jack froze stiff in his seat
when he locked eyes. Instantly he could see a bony hand
protrude from under the man's rain slicker like a snake popping
up out of a hole waving Jack to keep moving on. The
intermittent movement of the windshield wipers sloshing a film
of oil and rain across the glass made it hard for Jack to see the
man's head shake from side to side. It was now early evening
and he wished he could have parked where he was. He drove
on, not wishing a confrontation with a police officer who was
wet and probably miserable from the downpour.

Sliding the car into an open parking space on the top level of a
parking garage, Jack reached around and under the car seats,
desperately searching for an umbrella. He would still have to
walk in the open rain. A smile came to his face when his fingers
wrapped around a cylindrical object. He forced it from its hiding

space. "Shit!" he shouted when he realized the handle of the umbrella was a dried up old Coke bottle. He could feel the irritation well up and tighten in the back of his neck. He flung the bottle into the back of the car and flinched just in time to avoid being hit by ricocheting shards of glass. The back dashboard was now covered with glass and a crack ran diagonally along the window where he smashed it with the Coke bottle. Looking through the window he could see that it was now raining heavily again.

He wiped the perspiration that was forming on his brow and as he brought his hand down over his face he felt a sudden sharp pain sear into his skin just above his left eye. He pulled his hand quickly away from his face as his eye closed from a stinging liquid running into it. With his other hand he wiped away the warm trickle above his closed eye. Squinting with one opened eye he brought his hand into focus to see that fresh blood trickled down his finger and began slipping into the ravine of his lifeline across the palm of his hand. A shard of glass reflected back a devilish jagged smile as it imbedded in his finger.

His teeth got a grinding workout as he pulled the demon from his skin. He found a few old Dunkin Donut napkins in the glove compartment and adjusted the rearview mirror, cleaning away the glass dust above his left eye. Jack sat there a moment applying pressure to the cut in the hope that he could get it to stop. He saw that it was one straight cut across his left

71

eyebrow, deep and about an inch long. It could use a few stitches, he thought, but he didn't have time to address it now. He didn't want to arouse any questioning from emergency room nurses and especially the trench coated police officer he passed a few moments ago near the parking area.

Now he had to get into the hospital. He searched around again in the glove compartment and found a small band-aid, its wrapper faded brown from old age. It didn't stick well to his skin and its size was too small for his wound, but at least it slowed the bleeding down. Inside he would look to steal a gauze pad and maybe a few larger bandages from a nurse's cart if the opportunity arose.

As he exited the door of the Buick a swift gust of wind caught hold of the door and whipped it from his grip. He moved out into the rain and kicked the door shut behind him with the back of his foot. He made a mad dash toward the side of the building adjacent to the hospital entrance. He slipped along the side of the building pressing his back against the wall desperately trying to become part of the mortar. It seemed to help a little as the wind circled the building front like a cyclone. No matter which way he faced the rain seemed happy to be a constant companion and play tag with him all the way.

"Quite an evening" The police officer said, as he held the door open for Jack.

Jack stood there for a moment trying to shake the rain from his body like a wet dog.

"Hope I'm not too late." He said with a shiver, keeping his hand over the wound and his head turned out of a direct sight.

"No sir, your fine you have an hour before we close up for the evening." The officer answered.

Jack waved back over his shoulder as he passed the officer and could see a little old lady seated behind a long counter dressed in a candy striper's uniform. A large sign hung over her head that read reception. The lady looked almost childlike sitting at the giant table. She paid no attention to Jack as he approached the desk. Jack stood there for what seemed like forever as the lady went about shuffling papers. Jack decided to clear his throat in a false attempt to be inconspicuous and try to get the lady's attention at the same time. A memory flashed into his mind. It was the face of old mister Sampson. His eyes now yellow from a failing kidney, he said. "If you lose your sense of humor, Jack your dead."

Startled by his presence the lady notice Jack and jumped back in her chair.

"Whoa, make some noise there when you come up son. You'll give an old lady a heart attack." She laughed a toothy grin at

Jack. She smiled from behind thick glasses that looked like two soda bottles suspended on a chain.

Jack kept his head turned slightly towards one side but wasn't too concerned as he was sure the little old lady was as blind as a bat.

"Raining out there eah? You should have an umbrella." She slapped a knee.

Fuck you thought Jack, but what came out was. "I'd like a pass to see my grandmother. Her name is Kahill.

"Devil?" She answered. "No —no devil here. You sure you're in the right place son?" Again, she slapped a knee.

Jack found the hole in his cheek with his tongue and bit down slightly sucking in his cheeks.

"No ma'am. The name, he spelled out slowly, K.a.h.i.l.l."

"Well now let me see." She answered.

Jack looked up at the clock behind the old lady. Ten minutes had passed since the time that he walked in. He watched the clock as two more minutes passed when finally, the old woman came up for air.

"No —no Stay mill. I've got a Kahill. Who did you want to see again?" She asked.

"That's it." Jack almost shouted. He could feel a knot tighten in the muscles of his neck.

"Well why didn't you say so?" She said, handing him the pass.

Jack stood in front of the elevator. He watched the metal arrow move backward indicating the descent of the elevator. The door opened, and a young woman got off pushing a wheelchair in front of her. Jack turned his head away and watched the movement of his feet as he got on the elevator. He turned and looked up at the girl only when she had her back to him. He watched as she turned a corner and disappeared. He gave a sigh of relief to find that the elevator was empty. He held the room card and focused the room number to memory. He bent the card in half and with a slight bit of force folding the plastic laminated room pass and tucked it into his back pocket. He hesitated for a moment and then hit the button for the seventh floor with a tight fist. Jack stepped back in the elevator and pressed his back against a support bar and watched as the doors began to close.

"Wait, wait! Hold the door!" A voice echoed in a swirl around the elevator car.

Jack could hear the desperate footsteps running toward him and the rattling of a cart being pushed along a hallway. His eyes widened, and a sudden surge of fear ran a cold streak through his veins. He jumped and desperately tried to push the buttons on the control panel to close the door, but in his panicked attempt his fingers fumbled and slipped, landing on the door open delay button. Shit, he thought. He covered his face with his hand and tried to walk off the elevator but was forced back by a nurse's station cart hitting him in the abdomen and knocking the wind out of him. Jack watched as the contents of the cart spilled to the floor.

"Oh, I'm sorry mister. Thank you for holding the elevator." A young girl said in a soft voice.

She didn't look up and quickly skirted around the floor of the elevator, scooping up the spill.

Jack could see she was dressed in a candy-striped uniform just like the terror that he left behind in the reception area. He tried to step around her, but the car's door was now closed, and Jack felt the sudden engagement of wheel and pulleys as the elevator responded to its task.

I'll get off at the next stop, he thought, and he watched as the floor stop indicator illuminated the next floor. He breathed a sigh of relief, but the elevator didn't stop. He pressed his back against the wall and shut his eyes tight. He felt the room starting to spin and bit down on the inside of his cheek. He could hear the clinking of bottles and the rustling sound of papers. He opened his eyes. The young girl was still kneeling on the floor and with one hand placing the spilled contents spewed on the floor back onto the cart in a haphazard way. His eyes widened. There in front of him on the cart various bandages poked out from among the growing heap of items the young girl was restoring to the cart. Don't dare blink, he told himself as he reached a hand out in a magician's snap and grabbed what he could of the bandages. He watched in slow motion, split screened one eye on the girl and the other on the object of his theft. Time for the moment seemed to slow to a crawl but he knew his magic act happened in only a flash. He crumpled the bandages into a ball and quickly stuffed them into a coat pocket.

He focused all his attention on the girl and she slowly came into focus. He took notice that the forced split image in his mind seemed to take longer to readjust than the last time he used this trick back in the car.

"Can I help you?" He said as he knelt to pick up some of the mess.

"Oh, thank you, no, I have it all." Said the girl as she stood, still adjusting some papers she held in a folder tucked under one arm.

Jack tucked his chin down into his chest and put his hand up over his eyes to hide his face. He could see through his finger that the girl was paying no attention to him and still engaged in tidying up the cart. He wiped at his face and felt the warmth of the blood still oozing out of the cut above his eye. Suddenly he felt a shift in the elevator as the door opened on the seventh floor. He watched as the young girl backed out of the car, pulling the cart as she turned and went about her way. Jack stepped out of the car just as it was about to close on him. He found himself slithering along the corridor like a snake, moving along the wall ready to tuck into a crevice if need be to avoid contact. He felt sweaty and cold at the same time.

The hallway was long and straight, and he could see a set of doors he guessed to be fifty feet ahead. Through the small glass windows of the doors he could see a nurses' station with people coming and going. Jack slithered along the wall and came across a side corridor that was hidden from his view. It seemed to be new construction and there was no way of knowing it was there. Jack looked up to see if an exit sign hung from its ceiling, but he found none. Down the corridor a mop and bucket rested just at the bend. Jack spun on his heels at the sound of approaching footsteps. Looking over his shoulder he could see a ghostly figure approaching, a young man completely dressed in a white jumpsuit dictating into a small voice recorder. As the man approached Jack bit on his tongue and covered his face. He paced the man for a few seconds, slowing his stride and allowing the man to pass. Jack stopped at the mop pail and watched the man pass through a set of doors all the while dictating into the recorder. Jack wondered if the man had even noticed his presence. Jack took a deep breath and tried to clear his mind, but the smell of soaps and wax was the same cleaning fluid smell that turned his stomach when the prison janitors disinfected the showers at the Main State Prison.

The janitor closet door was left ajar and Jack slipped inside. The closet was small with just enough room for one person to stand over the oversized sink. The room was overstuffed with toiletries and a few new mops lay on a makeshift shelf. Jack had to squeeze himself in and up against the sink basin to close the door behind him.

From his pocket he took out the crumpled bandages, pushed the mops over on the shelf and laid the bandages alongside them. The water from the sink was warm on his face yet it felt refreshing against his skin. Jack washed his face and winced when the water found its way into the cut above his eye. Jack looked up and caught his reflection in a small mirror that had been taped to the wall just above the sink. He stopped and stared at the blank reflection in the mirror.

A small trickle of fresh blood stung his eye. His face was thin, with a pale color reflected in the soft light of the room. A three-day growth of gray stubble formed a raccoon mask around his face. His stomach turned and grumbled. He wondered if she would recognize him. He watched in a frozen stare as a drop of blood dripped from his cheek and became captive to gravity, exploding into tiny droplets as it hit the bottom of the sink.

At that moment he felt life drain out of him. All that had happened in the three years since the last time he had seen his grandmother rushed into his consciousness like a whirlwind. Images came entangled into one another, blending into a kaleidoscope of thoughts. He shook himself and bit down hard on the inside of his left cheek. Blood instantly began flowing in his mouth. He spit out the salty mess and watched as its life surrendered itself to the emptiness of the drain.

Jack tore open the box of toiletries and wrapped his hand a few times with toilet paper. Again, the cut above his eye sent a note of displeasure at being fumbled with. He pressed hard against the wadded paper, holding it against the wound with one hand. With the other hand he fought to open one of the gauze bandages, finding he had to use his teeth to tear it open.

He pressed hard against his forehead and held the bandage there for a few moments. The bleeding had stopped. He opened a bandage that was too large for the wound he had. He bit the corner of it and tore it in half. He placed it on the cut and immediately his forehead stung from the contact made by the bandage. A small strip of adhesive tape held it in place. He checked it again in the mirror, a small red stain formed in the middle of the pad. He crumpled the remaining half in his hand and then gathered up the other bandages stuffing them into his coat pocket. With one last look he was satisfied with his appearance; no-one would take a second look at him. After all, he was in a hospital and he would look normal for anyone who just received medical attention.

He held the pass in his hand and gently closed the closet door behind him. The hollow hall picked up the clasp of the lock slipping into place and it reverberated around the marble walls until it faded into an empty adjacent hall. He walked gently away from the new construction area and again found the main hallway. A red sign suspended from the ceiling, its arrow pointing the direction to the elevators, flickered faintly like a heartbeat. Each step he took echoed back from some hidden area. As he walked he could see his reflection as a shrunken figure in the tiny marble fragments of the floor. Each step took on a kaleidoscope entanglement of disfigured forms that began to swirl around his head. He had to shake himself to stave off the mesmerizing effect.

The afternoon faded quickly and as he passed a window he could now see that it was now dark outside. The hospital must be closing soon he thought. He walked softly almost on tip toe cat like trying to sneak past the nurses station hoping not to be noticed. The corresponding card room number was dead center of the station. He faced the wall and shielded his face with his hand as he walked by. No one seemed to notice him. The nurses were more involved in their paper work and paid him no attention.

He slowly approached the room and the first thing to hit him was the smell. The smell of disinfectant wafted around the room like a swarm of bees waiting to stick to anything that moved. He could feel his stomach turn with each breath and he forced himself to breathe through his mouth. The bed was half hidden from view from a security curtain. White shoes could be seen making small steps, side to side. Oh, shit he thought someone is here. He wanted to turn and head back out the door when the curtain was pushed back. A nurse turned toward Jack she had a finger pursed to her lips. "Shush." She whispered and with the same finger motioned for Jack to come near.

"We had to give her a sedative she was having a hard time sleeping." She said in a soft voice.

"Are you okay?" She pointed at Jacks forehead.

Without moving his head Jack kept one eye on the nurse and with his other eye he caught his reflection in the mirror above the room sink. The bandage above his eye was full of blood but it was dry and not bleeding. He moved closer to the bed.

"I'm fine he whispered back." And let that conversation die there offering no further explanation.

"Can I speak to her? He asked over his shoulder as he approached the bed taking hold of his grandmother's hand.

The nurse answered but he didn't hear what she had said. He could see that as he held his grandmothers hand she pulled back making a wincing face as if in pain. He quickly let go her hand. The nurse now stood next to him. "Best let her rest" She said. Jack stepped back as the nurse slid past him and went about adjusting the bed covers.

The nurse now turned to Jack who was standing looking out the rain covered window into the dark void.

"She's going to be out for the night. It's probably best that you come back in the morning. She will be rested and fresh then. You're Jack?" She asked.

Nodding, Jack answered." How did you know?"

"She speaks of you all the time. I'm sure if I had to, I could pick you out of a line up." She laughed.

Jack caught his reflection in the glass. Brushing at the whiskers coming in on his face, a lineup he thought, he was clean shaven then. It had been a long time since he stood in a lineup. It was an experience he soon rather forget.

"You're welcome to sit awhile and visit if you wish but I'm sure with the heavy sedative we gave her, she won't awake, and she will sleep through the night."

The nurse turned and walked toward the door. Jack followed her with his eyes. She suddenly stopped at the entrance. "Oh wait." She pointed a finger to the table next to the bed. "I almost forgot." She said as she walked back into the room going to the table opening the draw and fishing out a large envelope handing it to jack. "Your grandmother said to give this to you the moment you arrive no matter what happened, and it was of great importance that you have it."

Jack didn't watch her leave but instead fixed his gaze on the heavy envelope he held in his hands.

CHAPTER 7

COLLECTING TROPHY'S

A flash of lightning lit the garage door as Montgomery backed in the hearse. Rain hit him in the face as he made his way to the rear to retrieve the body. How delightful he thought. It was late evening, but he was alive with excitement for the task before him. He couldn't wait to prepare the body and add her photo among the others of his trophy wall. He unlocked the automatic door stepping on the floor control pad. The double wide doors swung open and he rolled the gurney inside stopping next to a long table. He didn't care that he was wet from the rain and allowed his jacket to slip from the back of his chair in his office, falling to the floor. He was too anxious, and his hand shook in excitement as he placed a new digital card into his camera and set it on the table next to the body bag. Slowly he unzipped the bag. The smell, like that of delicate flowers burst forth taking life in a desperate attempt to escape the dark hollow grip of death. Stiff, the body took a little effort for him to remove from the bag. Usually an assistant would be present to help with the dead weight of a body being removed and placed on top the table. But, on this special occasion he wanted to enjoy it alone. He called no one and left the light dim. He wanted this moment to suck up all the pleasures for himself.

This was a moment for all the senses to come out and play. This was a time for all his heightened awareness to enjoy the beautiful bouquet the gods bestowed upon him.

Montgomery stepped back and stood frozen letting the wave envelop him. There were no fresh meadows of flowers; no young life prancing along a cool stream in the glowing warmth of an afternoon sun light. There was no young girl skipping along catching butterflies resting on newly birthing angel trumpet. No, it was the scent of money. He closed his eyes and took in all the wonderful fragrance, holding his breath as long as he could. He stood there remembering the reading of his father's will and the scent of the perfume worn by the old lawyer as she read aloud his being written out of his father's will. He stood there thinking of the horrors he could inflict upon her cold dead decaying body given the chance.

The will had stated that the fortune amassed by his father was estimated at three hundred million dollars. It consisted of many properties and large sums of cash that would go to various charities to be named at the will of the executor lawyer now reading the will.

"Montgomery." She pointed a finger at him from directly below her nose. "He will inherit the sole property that being the funeral home here in Monson Maine."

Jenny Harrows lifeless eyes now stared blindly from some distant plain up at Montgomery. Her eyes, round like marble glass, gray and lifeless. There was nothing he could see in them only the reflection of himself distorted and bending like the way a reflection did in a Christmas ball. They no longer held the moments of her life. No longer were the images of the girl running through mountain fields picking wild strawberries along the banks of rolling hills. There were no images of stepping stones across the small summers winding brook. It was just too late for him to capture the fading of the measurable life once wondering for direction from within her. She was completely different then the many others he had the pleasure of observing. Her body lay too long before he could get to it. It was truly a shame he thought, it would have been wonderful to watch all of her memories move on to new paths.

On many occasions if the bodies were brought to him in time he would be able to force open the deceased eyes. He would then hold the eyes open with his finger and position his face just inches away and stare into the dead person's eyes. Many times, if only for the briefest moment he would catch a glimpse of the soul of the person leaving the body. On rare occasions the magic lasted for a few moments before the eyes only stared back like a blank canvas.

Once he saw in the deceased eyes the actual murder of the person taken place. He saw the rage of the murderer slashing the victim repeatedly with a long bowie knife.

He stepped back away from the body of Jenny Harrows wiping the salted beads of sweat from his face with a handkerchief from his pocket. Montgomery imagined her eyes what they used to be, jade green, he guessed and how wonderful they must have looked surrounded by her strawberry blond hair. He caressed the side of her cheek with the back of his hand. It was velvety soft. She needed no makeup. Her skin glowed with a veil of softness like milky cream. He was glad that her suicide was from an overdose of sleeping pill and not the bloody mess of a gunshot wound. He held the camera steady rapidly firing off shot after shot. She's going to make a beautiful trophy he thought.

CHAPTER 8

NO ANSWERS

Jack sat in the chair just staring at the envelope he now held in his hands. He felt ashamed that he refused to answer any letters that his grandmother or anyone had sent to him while he was in prison. He knew that she was the one person that was always there for him. Even when she couldn't take him into living with her in her cabin in Maine, he knew she loved him. His mother had died, while in child birth. It was because of the hatred for children by his step grandfather, that Jack was not taken in. She sent along money and letters of well-wishing to all the different foster homes he stayed at even if they were only temp arrangements. She always somehow found a way to send him a letter.

His attention was broken when he heard a long sigh come from his grandmother as she wrestled there in her sleep. The constant humming of machines monitoring life signs and blinking lights acted like a constant annoying alarm clock. He slowly stood trying to stretch out the glue of old decaying bones and placed the envelope at the foot of the bed. Standing at the side of her bed he wondered how without being sedated, anyone could sleep with the many distractions surrounding them. What a horrible situation to be in, when at the time in one's life, when you have accomplished so much to be abandoned by one's own failing body.

A noise came from over his shoulder and he turned to see the young nurse approaching.

"I am sorry Mr. Kahill but visiting time was over a half hour ago. If you like you can come back tomorrow at 11 am when we release her to the nursing home that is going to take care of her. I wrote the info on this piece of paper." She handed Jack the note.

Jack folded the paper and tucked it into his shirt pocket. "Would you just give me one more moment alone?" He asked.

"Sure" She answered, over her shoulder as she walked away. "But don't be too long."

He turned back facing his grandmother and he could see the look of pain on her face. So many questions swirled in his mind. How did she get back to her home town? What happened to her home in Maine? Was his step grandfather still alive? Who else knew she was here? The last question he knew he could answer quickly just by asking the young nurse and he made a mental note to do just that on his way out.

Jack wished that she was awake to answer the many questions that now need answering. But, most of all he wished she was awake so that he could again share a special moment with her again like the times visiting her as a small child, even if for only a moment. How would she know he was there? Surely the nurses would tell her, but it wasn't enough.

At that moment he remembered the necklace she had given him as a child. It was a saint Christopher's medal. She told him a long time ago that the gap between his front teeth meant that he was a traveler and how he would go places some day and that he would be on great adventures. The medal she told him was to protect him along his journeys. He removed it from around his neck and held it in his hand. Looking at it he laughed to himself. For all the time he had it, he didn't really feel it help too much and went about placing it in her hand. As he placed the medal in her hand, he watched her recoil her hand and wince in pain. The medal fell from her hand, but he let it lye there as the necklace part entangled between her fingers.

Jack scooped up the envelope and folded it in half and stuffed it into his jacket pocket. He quickly made a plan of coming back tomorrow when his grandmother would be well rested. He would open the letter discussing life with her then. Tomorrow was Saturday and he didn't need to worry about going to work and if he was lucky he might be able to borrow the car again to get back to the hospital. It didn't matter; he was determined to come back even if he had to walk. It was too important now. He had to see her. She deserved that, and he needed her to answer so many questions that were swirling in his mind.

Jack walked away swiftly only to look back once as he started to close the room door. He could see his grandmothers face. She looked at peace now. Maybe it was the drugs or maybe she was just at peace with the world there in dream land. Whatever it was he hoped she was at peace. He hoped that she was not consumed in thinking about his problems and nightmares. He paused at the nurses station to ask if anyone had come to see her. But when he approached the station he found it abandoned.

Nurses must be on rounds he thought. It's another question for tomorrow and he thought no more of it. From the looks of the room it seemed that no one had come to see or look after her. He could see no cards or flowers in her room and the way the chairs set in the room it seemed she had no visitors.

The elevator was empty when it came to his floor. He stepped inside and breathed a sigh of relief glad not having to share the ride with strangers poking at him from behind interrogating eyes. The elevator came to a stop its door opening at the entrance level. He found himself alone again except for a maintenance worker at the end of the hall mopping the floor. When he came to the reception desk, he realized he forgotten the pass card leaving it behind on the room chair. "Fuck it." He mumbled when he found that the little old lady he had done battle with earlier was no longer there.

Outside it was no longer raining, yet everything was still wet. Jack found he was now limping as the sciatica pain now resurfaced in his leg. He dreaded the idea that he would have to squeeze back behind the steering wheel of the Buick. No matter how he tried to adjust the seat it would not budge. If the sciatica pain hadn't been so much, Jack thought of leaving the car and just walking.

CHAPTER 9

IF WALL COULD TALK

Montgomery Barry was careful not to place the staples to close to the photo of Jenny Harrows and applied just enough pressure to the corners of the photo to hold it in place on the wall. He rubbed his hands together with anticipation. What wonderful treasures would he find in the casket? He stepped back for a moment and almost wanted to turn the lights up so to breathe in the mass collection around him at once. But, he chose to only adjust the light knob, so a shallow light glowingly hung on to the victims with just the slightest amount of life. He knew he still had some work to do in finishing the prep of Jenney Harrows body but, the walls whispered … it's time to play. And, just for fun this time he thought of doing it all backwards.

He would start with Jenny Harrow the latest victim of a self-inflicted suicide and end with the photo of the little baby, Francis who died during child birth along with the mother Mary Kahill. The photo of the baby still had a key he found in the casket pinned to it. He cracked his knuckles and placed his wallet on the desk, not before holding it up to his nose taking in a long breath of the little dead men inside. He was smiling at the same time as the wonderful aromas of woman's perfume delicately waft up like a flower from deep within. He shuttered there for a moment when he finally realized that the tapping on the window was from the rain hitting it. He felt the moment could have not gotten any better when he pulled back the curtain and saw the darken sky with a storm approaching. He turned back to the wall that was now holding the photo of the recent deceased Jenny. But, he stopped when he caught a reflection of himself in a small mirror hanging there next to a gruesome detailed photo of a gunshot victim.

He reached out with his left hand touching the mirror and studied it for what seem a long time. He didn't recognize the person looking back at him. His face had become thin and shallow. His eyes reflected dark like two pin points on a faraway road. He could see now his hair was graying and dead, lifeless like a gravestone. His beard hung there the way Spanish moss hung from a Savannah tree. What happened to the once young man who hoped to travel the world on his father's fortune? He flung the mirror against the opposite wall. It imbedded itself there, like a ninja star, in the chest of a man who had died some 15 years ago.

Pinned to the photo was the pull tab of the man's favorite beer. Montgomery had taken it out of the coffin along with a small solid gold cross that the grieving wife had placed there at the funeral. The caption, although fading, he recognized as his hand writing read: price $4000 dollars and the date of death when the man fell through thin ice on Monson pond. It also had how much money Montgomery had found while searching the coffin. He remembered it being a wonderful night, moon less and the atmosphere stiff dead cold, grave quiet. He remembered being a bit disappointed when he searched it after the second late night showing. He found nothing more there after the grieving family had gone home for the night. The crumpled dollar bills were still pinned to the photo.

He sold the body of Mr. Kingford to a cadaver school for eight hundred dollars claiming he was unidentified. No one was the wiser and he estimated his weight at two hundred fifty pounds. It was the first time he had gone to Home Depot and purchased bags of sand, placing them into the coffin to resemble the weight of a corpse.

There in the faint light, hundreds of faces some in hellish agony, some grossly disfigured, wildly stared blindly at nothing from a ghostly realm. They were the trophies of all the many years of accepting the departed and prepping them for their next journey whether heaven or hell, Montgomery didn't care witch.

Montgomery walked over to the wall and slowly pulled the small mirror out of the chest of Walter Kingford. He then placed the crumpled dried out dollar bills and beer pull tab back on the tack holding the photo to the wall.

The dollar bills crumpled into a fine dust and fell like ashes slowly to the floor. This made him angry in the fact that he had wasted money buy his careless actions and knowing that there was no way he could put it back together again. He bent down and scooped up as much of the ashes as he could into the palm of his left hand and went about placing them into a pile on the desk. The pile was not enough to fill a whisky glass, but he wasn't going to throw away money no matter how dead it had become. Just then a flash of lightning illuminated the entire room and a spark ignited in his mind. All is not lost he thought. He had the brilliant idea that he would add it to the next cremation that came his way and charge that customer for his misfortune.

From the corner of is eye, he caught a fragmented smile reflecting through the shattered mirror at him. He walked back to the window and pulled back its curtain. Touching the glass with his nose, his breath fogging the window, he made a dollar sign in the vapor. He laughed out loud as he dropped the mirror into a waste basket.

CHAPTER 10

DRIVE THROUGH HELL

The Buick bucked and rattled never missing a single pothole. Every nerve in Jacks body flared with pain with each jolt as if they were super heightened. He felt sick and tried to roll down the window to get some fresh air in case he had to throw up, but the window was frozen in place and would not budge. Fuck it he thought if he needed to throw up he would just open the door and besides it was now pouring rain again. The windshield wiper slopped a mixture of dirt, dead bugs and muddy rain making his view of the roadway a kaleidoscope of broken images.

He felt miserable not being able to speak to his grandmother and have the chance to explain his absents. What could I possibly tell her? Just how miserable prison was, the sooner he could forget that the better. But he knew he had to thank her for being there for him as a child even though, because of her husband, she couldn't take him in. Yet deep down inside he felt that she knew all. He shook his head. "She always knew all." He spoke aloud. He felt himself tearing up and pounded a fist on the dashboard splitting the plastic and exposing the foam from underneath. What could she possibly tell me he thought?

He reached into his jacket pocket. He still hadn't looked at the letter that was left for him lying in the dresser table in his grandmother's hospital room. He placed it on the passenger seat eying it occasionally in a split vision of one eye on the road the other on the letter.

The envelope being addressed to him in the hand writing he recognized as that of his grandmother it read in capital letters:

LORD JACK.

He drew in a deep breath and exhaled in a long drawn out sigh. Biting down on the inside of his cheek, he attempted to ward off the feeling of a panic attack fighting him now for life.

Fighting the feeling of panic, he eased the Buick into a curb parking space in the shadows of an old abandoned building far from the reaches of the street light across the road. He recognized the building as Joe Tiger's.' It had once been a night club and eatery and he could barely make out the building's letters faded by neglect. The area was dark and for the moment also seemed to be abandoned.

He closed his eyes tightly fighting the panic sensation and began a long slow breathing technique he was taught by Junior the blind newsstand attendant. He felt his hands trembling and, yet they had the odd sensation of being touched. It was the feeling as if someone was holding his hands. It was the same way his grandmother would hold his hand and speak comfortably to him. He remembered crying each time as the authorities forcefully would remove him from her loving arms and take him away to some ungodly orphanage.

Rain pounded the car in a defining roar. Lightning cracked and bounced ghostly shadows off the abandoned doorways and windows of the bar. He opened his eyes and found that what he was feeling was the letter held tightly in his trembling hands. It wasn't a newspaper, but it would have to do.

He told himself that it was something to read and he hoped that reading it would take his mind off the panic attack. The parking space proved to be too dark. He reached for the overhead light pushing the sensor knob, but it didn't illuminate. He forced the knob off and when he hit the button for the window, this time it opened just enough for him to toss it out in disgust and frustration. Jack dreaded the idea of having to start the Buick again, but it was the only possibility of reading the letter.

The Buick fought to life and he slowly nudged it forward in the parking space just enough to let the smallest amount of street light fall on his hands. He sat there for a moment wondering how the saloon had come to its demise. It had been a long time since he had a drink.

Three years sobriety was a long time he thought but now with his hands trembling onto the steering wheel he wished the bar was still open. He could feel the demons deep inside locked away fighting faded memories for life. He licked his lips, but they were dry. He swallowed hard, but it was just a dry lump that he almost choked on. He thought about licking the window to relieve his thirst. What would dead bugs and mud taste like he thought? He remembered what Mr. Sampson had taught him a long time ago as a child.

"Little man," he would say. "Find you a round pebble, not too big and not too small. For, you don't want to be swallowing it. It's got to be just right. And you put it into your mouth and let it rest just under you tongue. Before long, Mother Nature will take hold and you will have a mouth full of liquid. It will curb your thirst."

Fuck that he thought. I'm not getting out of this car and start looking around for no dam dirty rock to suck on. He searched around the car and found a small used Styrofoam cup lying under the seat. He opened the window and placed it on top the windshield wiper against the glass in hopes it would collect rain water. But, the moment he let go wind blew it away. He looked around again but the only thing he found was the folded letter resting on the passenger seat.

Jack held the envelope in his trembling hands for the longest time trying to summon up the courage to open it. "Fuck it I got to know." He whispered. He slowly unfolded it, letting the creases glide between his fingers smoothing them out. He ripped the corner open with his teeth and caught the edge of the envelope with the corner of his mouth leaving a long paper cut. Instantly he felt a salty brine of warm liquid flow into his mouth. He opened the letter unfolding its multiple pages and tried to wipe off the blood from the top edge. But it was too late it was already stained through. He shut his eyes for a moment and there before him stood his grandmother.

The letter began... *Lord Jack as you begin to read this please know that I love you and know that there is nothing that you can do for me now as I am surely gone. Shed no tears for me Jack be happy that I have lived a somewhat comfortable life but a troubled one in the fact that I couldn't have done more for my grandchildren. (Grandchildren?...Jack thought...what the hell is she talking about? What grandchildren. I thought I was the only one.) He shook his head in disbelief. The truth be told ... the letter continued. Your family was rotten. Jack laughed aloud. He really didn't know his family, other than the watch given to him, but he felt it to be true if she was saying it.*

I'm sorry that I couldn't take you in when your mother died, but your second step grandfather hated children. He was a monster Jack and ultimately treated me like shit. You must know that he was extremely wealthy. But, before I get to that, there is something you must know now.

Jack felt his heart pounding in his chest and he wished he could just run away from all this.

Jack ... you were born a twin. But, your brother died in child birth as your mother was having a very difficult time. You too almost didn't make it. But by the grace of God you did.

Yea lucky me thought Jack.

And so too the stress was too much for your mother, she died just shortly after your birth. Though you never knew your father, know this, he was a bum and a drunk. He abandoned your mother when she became pregnant. He died shortly after your birth when the cops found him holding up a bank. They shot and killed him in a hail of bullets when he opened fire on them trying to escape while holding a hostage. You were better off not knowing him or having him involved in your life. Trust me Jack he was scum.

Jacks body was now trembling, and the letter fell to the floor of the car. Tears welted up in his eyes and he wiped his face in his shirt. He reached for the letter and tried to continue but his hands were trembling so much it made it hard for him to continue to read. Often, he found himself reading the same line twice and he cursed it. "Holy shit" he said aloud. His grandmother he knew was one to never hold back the punches.

And now you must be made aware of the fact that you also have a step sister her name is Sara from your mother's first marriage. She's a lovely young lady that I hope you meet some day.

Jack felt the dryness in his throat but as he tried to swallow he realized it was for nothing. He felt like he was trying to swallow sand paper.

Now to the point Jack. There is a key to a box. I placed the key in the coffin of your twin brother, and yes, I knew it was foolish. But you need to understand how much I grew to hate your step grandfather. Without him knowing I stole from him every chance I could get, money, gold coins, diamonds, jewelry, whatever I could get my hands on. Over the years I stowed it away in a box. Go to the cabin and search there you'll find directions tucked away as to where to find the box. It's yours now Jack but promise me one thing that you'll spend it. Go Jack, go to the cabin and find it.

LOVE YOU JACK

Mother Kahill

Jack sat there physically shaking. It was unbelievable what he was reading. He felt panic welting up in his body. He quickly opened the door and threw up. He had a hard time catching his breath. The dryness of his throat left him heaved over with acid burning in his throat. He tilted his head back sticking his tongue out trying to catch some rain, but the little amount of moisture gathered there wasn't enough. Jack crumpled the letter into a ball and stuffed it into his pant pocket. Panic was now fighting him for control of his body and all he wanted to do was get the hell out of there.

This time when he turned the ignition key the Buick jumped to life. He quickly shifted into drive and hit the accelerator hard, the wheels spun in place on the wet pavement. When the wheels finally dried, they caught hold of the ground hard and sent the car fishtailing out of the parking space. The car took off hitting a parking sign bending it in half with the rear side panel. He gripped the steering wheel hard and caught the reflection of the sign in the rearview mirror as it fell over of its own weight. The car jumped the opposite curb nearly missing the building as its wheels slid from side to side on the wet grass. He bit his tongue as the car jumped off the walkway and finally met the road. Rocks flew up behind the wheels and he could hear them bouncing around the wheel wells. His hands gripped the steering wheel tightly as the car became a raging bull of heated adrenaline. Like a bat out of hell he took off down the street heading nowhere in particular. He just drove as fast as he could to get away. Time quickly became a blur and the street, lamp posts, buildings faded into a blend of mixed melting colors. The Buick rumbled as if it was coming apart at its seams. Jack shook in his seat as if he was a test pilot in an experimental jet.

It was at that moment in time when time itself seemed to flicker in slow motion. Jack could see that he clearly had the green light, but his reaction was too late. In a split vision he could see the other car as it ran through the red light and straight into his passenger side. The impact sent his head into the driver's side window smashing it and opening a gash in his face. In a slow-motion dance between time and reality Jack could see the passenger side of the Buick flicker. Sparks of twisted metal and glass flew in all directions. The Buick slid sideways coming to a stop with its front end imbedded in an abandoned store front.

Jack shook his head trying to shake loose the cob webs but immediately stopped when a searing pain shot its way up his spine. He quickly took stock of himself buy feeling his body with his hands. Nothing seemed to be broken but when he tried to look out the window half his vision was a blur. He could feel a stinging in his eye. He quickly reached for the rear-view mirror to check his face. With the back of his hand he rubbed at his eye and slowly it came to focus on a long gash above his left eye bleeding heavily and running into his eye. He quickly searched the car and found nothing he could use to help stop the bleeding. In the cramped space of the driver seat he managed to get off his jacket and ripped off his sleeve of his shirt and pressed it against his forehead and for the first time he felt dizzy. Concussion he thought.

Wiping the blood from his eye, it was difficult to see in the darkness the other vehicle. Across the intersection, he could make out that it lye upside down against a telephone pole. One body was lying on the ground a few feet from the rear of the car and another could be seen half way sticking out of the front windshield.

I've got to get out of here he thought. And again, he took stock of the situation around him. The door to his left, the driver's side was blocked in buy the building. With great difficulty he moved himself over to the passenger's side of the car, but as he pulled the handle realized that the door would not budge. It was too crumpled from the impact. Jack leaned back and with all the might he could muster kicked at the door, but it would not give, suddenly the second kick took hold, and the door flung open. He stumbled to his knees as he exited the car.

Jack could see that there was no movement of the body that lye next to the car. In the darkness he heard moans and a call for help. What he saw made his stomach turn. The calls for help came from a man whose body was caught in the windshield. Jack couldn't make out the man's face there was too much blood. Jack limped over to the first body and tried to feel for a pulse, there was none, too late he thought. The second person, a man bleeding from the side of his head was awake and conscious. Jack stood there next to the body and immediately grabbed hold of the man trying to pull him out of the wreckage and through the windshield.

"Don't." The old man spoke in a garbled fragment sentence. Jack eased in closer placing his ear next to the man's mouth. "Too late he said it's not your fault. I ran the light ....I'm sorry."

Images swirled in Jack's mind .... How could this happen to me? Where are the police, where is the help? Why is no one showing up?

Again, Jack tried to lift the old man out of the wreckage, but the old man stopped him in his course. "Don't it's too late I'm stuck...the lady?" Jack shook his head.

"A... letter in my jacket pocket, get it to my granddaughter."

Jack reached into the man's jacket and pulled out the envelope.

"Please promise me that you will deliver this letter. No matter this, please promise me that you will do it."

Jack held the blood stain letter in his hands. He looked the man straight in the eyes, holding his hand and swore on his oath that he would deliver it no matter how hard the task might be. Softly, his voice fading, the old man continued... "It's addressed follow that."

Jack could feel the man's grip loosening and the life leaving the man; again he thought how do you measure a life. The idea that one moment you're here and then the next you're not bothered him. There must be more.

This time two people lye before him. Could he explain that it was not his fault and that liquor was not in play? He hadn't had a drink in three years since going to jail. But the fact that he was driving while on the revoked list was certainly enough to send him back to jail for a very long time. I'm not going to take the heat for this he thought.

He felt the life slowly leak out of the man as the death grip slowly eased. Crystal clear eyes now stared blindly at him ... just like junior's they were dead, but a different kind of death was at pay here. It was the kind of death that once there, they didn't let you come back or walk in between realities.

Suddenly the realm of reality forced it presence upon him. He could hear sirens in the distance getting louder by the moment. Whether it was panic or something else he tried to run but fell to his knees. "I got to get the hell out of here." He said aloud. He ran slipping and fell in the street but quickly got to his feet. This time he was soaked to the bone.

He turned the corner and slipped into an alley. He stopped just long enough to peak back seeing that the authorities were not yet on the scene. Surely once they were on the scene it would take them some time to put out a police bulletin alerting others to be on the lookout for him. He figured he probably at best had a half hour to get to his house gather up his belongings and get the hell out of there before they could put all the pieces together and pin him. He had no choice he had to get to his house to get his things.

If he stuck to the alleyways he could make the mile or so trek in about fifteen minutes and he had two things in his favor. It was dark outside, and it was raining again. But what was not in his favor worried him more. One, he was bleeding and two, if he walks out onto the street he would currently stick out like a sore thumb. Because it was raining, no one was out. He knew the area and was accustomed to using the back alleys along the buildings. He would only have to navigate the main street for one block when he got close to his house and only when he had to cross the street in front. He wanted to go slowly but he knew that was not going to happen he would have to run as fast as he could to keep ahead of the authorities figuring out who was driving the abandoned car.

Jack quickly realized that the alleyway had changed since he was a child running around the neighborhood. The long alley way he was running along abruptly came to a dead end and his way was now blocked by a six-foot fence. He could turn back the way he came in and hope that no one was searching the area and maybe get lucky. Maybe he could find a new way around. The mix of rain water and blood stung his eyes and made it difficult to see. He looked back to where he had come from and in the distance, he could see for what seemed like a moment a red flashing light illuminating the end of the alley far in the distance. There was only one way and up was it. At the top of the fence he could see that the red light was now moving closer along the alleyway. When he got his second leg over the fence his jacket pocket caught the top of the fence and pinned him to the top. With all his weight he forced himself over ripping the sleeve off the jacket as he slipped and lost his grip falling on top of trash cans. The sound of him crashing echoed around the brick row homes but no one came out to investigate. But, he knew that the sound was like sending up a signal flare there in the darkness. Quickly he followed the path as it turned right and then stopped between two building staircases. He paused for a moment and looked back along the alley way. No one was fallowing that he could see. Ahead of him he could see the open field of the park and entrance hallway of the flop house he was staying at.

Run or walk he thought. Running would clearly bring attention to him if someone just happens to look his way. Walking slowly and staying in the shadows he decided was the safer bet. Just as he stepped from the shadows of the two buildings a red flashing light appeared turning the corner at the intersection. He breathed a sigh of relief and smiled to himself realizing that the patrol car was racing away from him. He stepped out tucking his head into his chest and pulled his jacket up around his neck. Slowly he made his way to his house.

Chapter 11

SHE'S A LIVE ONE

"Gather around closely, close your eyes and grab hold of the persons hand next to you. You must listen very carefully." A light whiff of lavender filled the air from the candle she lit. "Sometimes it's just a whisper."She added.

Sara Gardner kept her dark brown eyes open surveying the room around her. She pushed back her thick brown hair from her eyes. She wished she had it pulled back in a pony tail like she often did, but tonight she just felt to let it flow freely. She got up from the table and walked over to a shelf and picked up a book of spells and walked it back placing it in the center of the table. She wore a long dress that touched the floor as she walked along. She had been seated at the table for almost an hour when she checked her watch. She gave the customers an extra fifteen minutes time at no charge.

It was her nature to give it all and sometimes a fault to give too much. She went about lighting a second candle the glow casting disfigured shadows around the room. Five ghostly figures danced in unison on the wall copying that of its living hosts now seated around the table.

This was the seventy fifth séance she was hosting in her shop since opening her Mystic Book and gift shop a little more than three years ago. Books of the occult were selling well, and she enjoyed bringing the community together to see if she could again contact what she liked to call...angel protectors. Not all her hosted gatherings were successful sometimes no one showed up and her paying customers left without a single contact. Most often was the case. Everyone especially loved it when they received a response. She always tried to stay positive and would quickly end a session abruptly if anything negative would try to come through and made it a point to never tell the customers of the negativity or evil entities trying to come through.

This was a gift at times, and when she didn't want to be bothered, a curse. The ability to feel or see spirits she struggled with since a small child. Spirits would come to her all the time. There was most times no warning of foresight. Unwanted, uninvited, they showed themselves. She was frightened at first but later as a young adult she gained the confidence to control just how much contact she would allow in.

Tonight, didn't seem to be the night, yet everyone seemed to be having a good time. Two younger female adults sat at a side table and entertained themselves with a Ouija board, moving the planchette themselves trying to spook each other.

"I'm sorry." She said to the people gathered around the table. They seemed to know all at the same time. "It's ok." Said an elderly woman seated across the table. She had come to the gathering trying to contact her recently deceased husband.

"I'm sorry." Sara closed the books. "Sometimes they just don't want to come through."

She got up and made her way next to Millie at the front store counter to help check out a customer wanting to purchase books. She and Millie had been friends since their college days and had pooled their savings together to open the shop.

"I can offer you all a discount on a future visit." She offered. Everyone shook their head no, but the one woman accepted the coupon offered.

It was late when everyone finished their good nights and the last of the customers were finishing up their purchases. She waved goodbye to everyone and she and Millie went about closing the shop. She was just about to turn out the lights when she noticed two figures standing across the street.

An elderly man and woman stood holding hands staring back at her. She quickly took stock of what she was observing making a mental note of all the details of the encounter she could remember.

The first thing she noticed they looked ragged as if they were in a horrific accident. She swallowed hard when the images of the two people turned bloody. She blinked, and they were gone. She was certain of one thing. They were new, and she was certain they would try to visit again. That was the one thing she really had no control of. She could only control how much she would allow coming through. She pulled down the door shade and walked off to the small back kitchenette.

In the frig she found the rest of a half-eaten bowl of salad grabbed the newspaper sat herself at the séance table and went about finishing her lunch even though it was well past dinner time. Millie went about the task of straighten up the shop.

The day seemed gray to her with no one coming through except for the new comers outside across the street. They, like everyone else would have to wait their turn. She wanted to forget them all now and finish reading a story she started early that morning. "Dam rotten article." She murmured.

"What's that?" Millie asked taking the seat next to her.

Before opening her own store, she had worked briefly for a small independent local newspaper covering small stories, anniversary notices, birthday celebrations, and birth announcements. The death announcements she almost always knew about before contact was made to the newspaper. She had studied investigative journalism in college and always dreamed of working for the New York Times as an investigative reporter.

"Something keeps gnawing at me and I can't seem to get it out of my mind. I'm sure something is odd about the Barry funeral home. I'm called to it." She laughed. "Like a moth to a flame."

Millie patted her on the back. "You know what happen to the moth when it got too close? It got burnt. Don't wind up a moth." She laughed.

115

Sara continued reading a follow up story of a multi-millionaire leaving nothing to his son except the funeral home and how the IRS had a pending investigation on going. "Wow." She said. "Now the feds might be getting involved with a possible investigation into improprieties at the funeral home. It seems like this guy might have forged a name on a dead person's life insurance paper work to get access to funds."

The article continued: Funeral director accused of stuffing organs from one corpse into the body of another after cremating the first body without all its parts. Another line that stood out to her read: funeral director embalmed the body of an organ donor before her bone and tissue could be harvested. It went on to describe a family who opened an urn and found strange bits of metal among the ashes. The story continued with a strange explosion of a crypt where methane gas had built up in the casket blowing the lid and doors off the crypt. The body was found hanging in a tree. Sara flipped the paper over without finishing the article. It was too much for even a hardened investigative reporter. She wiped away tears from her eyes. How many lost souls wondered in the eternal empty darkness created by the evil of Montgomery Barry? "Wow, this creep should be hung out to dry by his balls."

Sara walked over to a small book rack with a sign above the rack that read travel, vacations and maps. She was just about to reach for a map of Maine when Millie out of the corner of her eye caught what she was about to do. She dashed over and snatched it up before Sara could get hold of it.

"Oh no you don't, I know what's going on in that investigative mind of yours."

Sara held her hand out expecting Millie to fork over the map.

"What would it hurt just to see where this Monson Maine is at?"

Millie rolled her eyes and threw her hands in the air. "Do you know how far Maine is from New York City?" Millie's question went unanswered as Sara snatched the map out of Millie's hand and went about unfolding it atop the table.

Millie was trying to talk her out of it but soon realized that her words were falling on deaf ears. Sara had her nose pressed against the map and was already a hundred miles away.

Sara's eyes were wide with excitement. Her fingers busy tracing roads over stream and valleys. All of it she hoped to be exploring soon by a kid who couldn't control her excitement. She felt like a child with a nose pressed up against a candy store window.

"Promise me you're not going to do anything crazy. I don't want to come here in the morning and find the place empty. Don't get up I'll use my key and lock the door behind me." Mille went to wave goodbye but the only response she got was Sara nodding her head.

CHAPTER 12

EMPTY GRAVES

Darkness swirled around the brightness of the stinging windswept rain, but it was a lovely night for a walk. There was hardly a moon only a sickle sliver seen deep behind the clouds. Statues danced in stillness projecting horrid glances as they seemed to briefly come to life in the momentary glow of lightning flashes.

There were no smells; the only sound was that of the thunder echoing among the tombs. Everyone lay still just where they had been put. Even the recent arrival of the young sweet corpse now tucked away like a morphing moth tight in a cocoon six-foot-deep below his heels was laying there motionless.

Montgomery Barry paused for a moment and sat down on a large granite slab opposite the grave and monument of Jenny Harrow. Hers was a special one. She was there. She was too beautiful, and he left her body alone. He prepared her body with the finest of care. She lay there dressed like an angel. He only stole the mementos the family had placed in the casket before making its final journey. He sat there studying the figures of a woman and child holding a basket of fresh flowers. A female feathered winged angel stood in front, her arms reaching out ready to except a humble gift. It was meant to represent the holy trinity the monument cost the family one hundred and twenty-five thousand dollars. Montgomery smiled knowing that because of his having made the arrangements he over charged the mother five thousand dollars. He walked over to an adjacent grave and pulled out the plants from the ground in front of a head stone and placed it into the empty basket held by the trio.

"There." He laughed. "A little thank you gift." Yet deep down inside he felt empty. He let the nothingness of the evening take hold of him by pressing his face toward the sky and allowing the rain to soak his face. He breathed out a long sigh, wonderful, wonderful he thought. He was surrounded by darkness and he didn't mind it that when he sat down he sat in a pool of water gathered there on the granite slab. He laughed knowing that the tomb he was perched on was indeed empty. He had overcharged the family, stole the mementos they left behind in the casket, removed the body and sold it to a science cadaver school. He, claiming it was an unknown person that they were going to use for science experiments.

There six feet below him was nothing more than an empty coffin filled with just the right amount of dirt to mimic the weight of a dead body. Suddenly Montgomery felt something strange come over him. It was the empty feeling of loneliness. He really had no friends and the children in town along with many adults would point at him behind his back as he went to the local cafe for coffee. They all thought that they had gotten away with it, making fun of his large stature. But he felt it and he knew they were there. And now it was his turn to laugh, pointing from grave to grave and speaking aloud to the darkness. "Empty." He said repeatedly laughing, looking down a bony finger pointing from grave to grave. "Empty." He repeated. The family would never be the wiser and the photo hung on his trophy wall in perfect company of all the others. It was pinned there holding tight its many treasures never to see the light of day again.

The passing storm was now right on top of him and each flash of lightening was immediately pushed out of the way by instant thunder. The whole graveyard flickered like a neon sign with each lightning strike. In the distance he could see his objective illuminated then fade back into the abyss. But, he didn't need the momentary flashing to find his way he could do it blind folded. This was a weekly ritual he enjoyed but it was a delight in a storm.

Ahead, he could see the massive sepulcher with its angels of death standing guard at the entrance. Another flash of light momentarily brought the two Cathates aura back to life as their wings seemed to reach out of the shadows. But, there was no purifying breeze, only death, rock solid slowly decaying in everlasting torment. This massive ossuary was not his doing and he had no input into its construction. It had been constructed when his father was alive. Montgomery James Barry had it commissioned as a final resting place for himself and his wife.

Montgomery was aghast when he found a receipt in his father's papers at the exorbitant amount paid for the monument.

Montgomery stood at the bottom step of the entrance and there in the darkness he could easily make out the plaque.

ABANDON HOPE OF HEALING FOR THE DARKNESS HAS STOLEN THE LIGHT OF DAY ALL THE HEAVENS AND RAINBOWS HAVE TURNED GRAY.

Montgomery rolled his eyes. He always hated his father's poetry. He walked up the steps closer unzipped his pants and went about urinating on the plaque.

"Shove that rainbow up your ass you mother fucker." He yelled finishing with a spit.

CHAPTER13

KEEPING PROMMISSES

When Jack opened the outer hallway door a breeze of garlic hit him in the face. His stomach growled, and he felt hungry but there was no time to stop to eat. Dam he thought. It would be nice to stop and call on old Mrs. Colandra. She often made spaghetti and meat sauce and would often bring Jack a plate. But, it was better that she didn't even know that he was there. His hand shook as he fumbled in his pocket for the key to his apartment. Jack opened the door, it squeaked loudly with enough noise to wake the dead. He went to reach for the light switch but thought it better to leave them off in case someone was watching. Fumbling around in the dark he threw off his wet clothing as he made his way around his small apartment. His head ached, and he swallowed two aspirin dry from the bottle he found in the bathroom.

Looking in the mirror he wondered just how much more abuse his face could take before he wouldn't recognize himself anymore. The cut on his face took two gauze pads and a large BAND-Aid to cover.

He quickly toweled off and put on a fresh shirt and pants.

On the floor next to the bed he found a small knapsack and grabbed whatever medical supplies he could from the bathroom cabinet stuffing them into the sack. He then went about stuffing it with another set of clean clothing, two water bottles from the refrigerator and the bottle of aspirin.

He opened a small box on the dresser and looked at the money crumpled in his hand. He quickly thumbed through it realizing that Four hundred and eighty dollars was not a good start to get to Maine. Jack shook his head; at least it was enough to fulfill a promise. Reaching into his pocket he found the letter he promised to deliver. He could have easily crumpled it up and thrown it into the trash, but he remembered something old Mr. Sampson had said to him a long time ago.

"Jack." He said. "Happiness and moral duty are inseparably connected."

Mr. Sampson was always quick to quote some learned fact on life to Jack. As Jack remembered he was often seen reading anything he could get his hands on. He was sure that he wasn't anywhere close to being happy or knew what moral duty meant. The only thing he was sure of was that he had to do the right thing and maybe for once in his life keep a promise made.

Jack took note of the name on the letter folding it; he placed it in the sack and carefully zipped it closed.

His jacket was still wet and missing one sleeve, but he wore it anyway. It was the only one he owned. Jack thrusted the knapsack over his shoulder and tossed the keys to his apartment on the kitchen table. He didn't look back as he walked out the apartment. Stepping over the threshold and out into the hallway he left the door open. He mumbled, "Fuck it, I'll never see that again." He opened the outer door and quickly stepped back into the shadow of the doorway noticing a police car slowly making its way up the street towards him. In a running dash he ran back to the apartment and shut the door and locked it behind him. He tried the back bed- room window but found it stuck shut. With a small pocket knife he quickly cut along the windows edge breaking the paint seal. He wrapped a wash cloth he found in the bathroom around a closed fist and hit hard around the base of the window and finally on the third strike was able to force it open. Swiftly he kicked out the screen with the back of his boot and gently let the knapsack fall to the ground below. Luck was on his side and the climb out the window he felt would be easy. The fall, he calculated was less than eight feet to the ground. He winced in pain as he forced his leg up over the windowsill. He hung on the ledge by his fingertips until the pain became overwhelming and he had to let go. Hitting the ground his right ankle slid under him sending him off balance. Desperately trying to right himself, he went stumbling and crashed into garbage cans. The uproar quickly brought unwanted attention. He could see lights coming on in many apartments. Jack didn't stop to look back as he scooped up the knapsack and swung it over his shoulder and heard a familiar voice of Mrs. Colandra yell out.

"Hey who's out there?"

Limping, Jack turned the corner of the building and slowly peeked around it edge. "Shit." He said. A police car was now parked in front of his apartment, but he noticed it was empty. He felt his heart thump in his chest and his eyes widened. That meant one thing; the police officer was now inside the building. If he was lucky, Mrs. Colandra would have the officer occupied for some time.

Jack limped as quickly as he could around the corner and down the street trying to keep to the shadows. Noticing a street light out across the street, he made his way there stopping for a moment to look back. He could see no one following. He kept his head tucked to his chest and quickly crossed an empty ball field. A hundred yards ahead he came to a tunnel under the central railroad crossing.

The tunnel under the tracks leading to the trains smelled like piss and a few of the lights were smashed out the results of vandals he thought. On the wall he noticed a sign that read: No loitering, that made sense, but he couldn't figure out why it was also printed in Braille. Were there a lot of blind people loitering about?

The walk was dark, and his footsteps echoed in swirls around him, loudly sending signals to anyone ahead of his approach. Jack curled his fingers into fists and tensed his body for a fight. If someone was to jump out at him he would have to fight with all his strength. He couldn't afford to be robbed of the money he was carrying.

This time of the evening the ticket booth was closed and the train schedule on the bill board read that the next train to Newark would be arriving at 7 pm. He looked at the clock that hung there above, 6:50 pm. "God dam it." He shouted startling the three other people standing there on the platform. He would have to run back down the stairs and purchase a ticket from the automated machine.

He fumbled there with the machine. He could hear the ticking in his ears as if a stop watch was being held against his head. He quickly realized it was his blood pressure thumping in his eardrums.

Before him the ticket machine sucked in dollar bill after dollar bill only to regurgitate them back up like an overstuffed bird trying to feed its young. He was getting nowhere when on his third attempt to feed the beast, it spit out its offerings. The wind caught hold of the bills scattering them on the ground in a desperate attempt to flee. A long whistle from an approaching train broke his concentration as he tried to scoop up the bills. He wasn't sure if he had them all as he slung the knapsack back over his shoulders. He clenched his teeth in pain trying to make a fast dash up the platform. The pain in his ankle thumped with every steep.

A conductor was waving at him yelling out. "All aboard."

He took the first seat he came to quickly and planted himself against the window. His eyes teared as pain mounted in his legs. He placed the knapsack on the seat next to him hoping to discourage anyone from sitting there. He shook his head realizing that he would have to pay extra for not buying a ticket beforehand.

Ahead he could see through the window of the closed door between the cars. A conductor was now approaching, collecting fares. It was well past rush hour and the train was quite empty for the evening ride. The car he was in, he shared with only four other passengers. In front of him sat a woman traveling with a baby stroller with a small child. Behind him sat a man in a suit with a dark briefcase. Across the aisle, sat a young man wearing head phones that Jack could hear were much too loud. Every

127

beat of the noise coming out of the speaker's Jack saw the man's head go up and down with every beat of the music. Something was odd, and Jack could feel the hairs on the back of his neck stand up. He split the image in his mind. He focused one eye on the door in front and the other on the odd feeling of the young man seated to his right. He watched the woman with the baby rush out of their seat making a beeline to another car forward.

He thought of closing his heavy eyes and get some rest but worked against it for the fear of falling deep asleep. Jacks attention was now again focused on the door of his train car as the conductor made his approach.

Suddenly his eyes widened in fear as he caught a glimpse of a police officer tagging along behind the conductor. Jack wanted to get up and run to the back cars, but he quickly realized it was too late. The conductor had just finished collecting the fare from the woman and child and was only a few feet away. Jack sat frozen in his seat when the officer made direct eye contact with him. Shit I've had it he thought. What could this police officer be thinking looking at the tattered spectacle seated in front of him. Jack must have looked like a mess. His clothing was tattered, his face all banged up and he's wearing a jacket with half a sleeve missing. He thought he now resembled a hobo. The gig is up. He felt his hand tremble as the two men approached.

Suddenly to his right he saw head phones hit the police officer in the face. The conductor ducked just in time. Now the image of the man seated to his right became a huge mass moving swiftly at the two men. Jack could now see blood pouring from the officer's nose and reaching for his weapon. But, the huge man body slammed the conductor and he fell backwards hitting the police officers hand and knocking the gun loose falling under the seat.

Three men now wrestled each other for possession. There on the floor in the entanglement of arms and bodies a shot rang out. Jack felt it rip pass him and through the seat. He spun on his heels only to catch the sight of the man in the business suit gagging and holding his throat as blood pored through his finger. He saw blood spattering everywhere with every beat of the man's heart. Jack caught the horror in the man's eyes as he fell dead on the seat. He wanted out of there, but his escape was blocked by three men still in a wrestling match. He tried to step to his left side hoping to climb over the seat. But, his foot hit something. Looking down his foot rested on top the gun. He bent down quickly coming up with the gun firm in grip and placed it to the back of the head of the young man.

"Get up motherfucker or I swear I'll shoot you!" He shouted.

With the gun firmly pressed against the man's head Jack backed up some allowing the officer and conductor to stand. He was tired and scared but mostly pissed off at the situation unfolding before him. He felt the rage boiling in his veins and with all the force he could muster he hit the man in the back of his head with the metal handle of the gun knocking him out cold. The man fell onto the seat and Jack kicked his feet into the booth as he stepped around him handing the gun back to the police officer. The conductor stood there in shock, covered in blood and had to be helped to a seat. The police officer holstered his weapon and moved to check for a pulse on the man in the business suit. He looked back at Jack and just shook his head. "He's gone."He said.

The train now arrived at the station, police and medical personal poured in from every direction. Jack could here sirens wailing in the distance. Looking out the window, there had to be a hundred police officers gathered around the station with more arriving from stairwells and escalators. A group of EMT'S boarded the train and went about placing the body of the dead man on a gurney while three other officers placed hand cuffs on the young man and were dragging him away, still unconscious. Jack could see that this was his chance to slip away. He grabbed his knapsack and quickly turned away from the commotion hoping to slip out the rear of the car. He made his way sliding the car door open when he suddenly felt a firm grip on his wrist. Jack spun on his heels and came face to face with the bloody nosed officer.

"Waite." The officer said handing Jack a crisp one-hundred-dollar bill. "I want you to have this. You look like a guy a little down on his luck."

"I can't take this." Jack waved him off.

The officer rubbed at his face with his hand, blood still trickling from his nose. "Listen." He said placing a firm grip on Jacks shoulder. "You just saved my life. That perp could have easily killed me. I was following a tip of a guy that just held up a liquor store in the last town we just past. At first when I saw you, I was thinking it was you. And that's when he hit me. But you stopped him. Listen, I can tell you're in some kind of trouble just by the look of you. I don't care what it is. I don't want to know what it is. Just take this money and get the hell out of here before I'm forced..." He pointed behind ... "to start asking you a lot of questions that you probably don't want to hear."

The officer pressed the door button. "Go and good luck." He said.

Jack snatched the money and stepped out on to the platform.

He took off the blood-stained jacket tossing it into a nearby trashcan. Setting his pack on the ground he grabbed a hooded sweat shirt and put it on. He stepped off an escalator quickly blending into the crowd. In the atrium he finally satisfied his hunger at Zebra's. He ordered two slices of pizza and a coffee. It was easy to hide in a crowd he thought. But still he needed to make a change.

After the meal had settled he focused his attention on getting back on track. He scanned the bill board noticing that the next train to New York City would arrive in thirty minutes. All the commotion upstairs was now dying down. He thought nothing more than to get moving. But, the first thing he needed to do was to change his appearance. He took the fresh hundred-dollar bill and walked up to a kiosk purchasing a razor, some deodorant, three packs of nature valley granola bars and the latest edition of the Daily News. He made his way to the rest room. It was unbelievably worse than the train tunnel he passed through earlier. Everything was dirty, and he was afraid to touch anything for fear of contracting some kind of disease. Again, he immediately tensed his body ready for a fight not knowing what kind of bottom feeders floated in this scum of primordial glue.

The mirror reflected a broken man scarred with the heaviness of potholed roads. Dried blood was stuck to the side of his face and hair line. It was the oddest feeling of not knowing if the blood on his face was his or someone else's. His stomach turned and he threw up in the sink when he realized it could be someone else's.

He looked like something the cat had dragged in. His beard was ragged, gray and old. His eyes were sunken in from lack of sleep and completely blood shot. He couldn't believe how gray his hair had become. The first sink had no soap, so he searched around until he found one with an active soap dispenser. Lathering up well he went about the task of shaving off his beard. The water turned red with the blood and he watched it as it flowed down the drain. Immediately he felt his knees shake and his whole body shuddered. He quickly splashed water in his face.

That man on the train didn't deserve what had happened to him. He was just an innocent bystander whose life force Jack was now washing down a drain. He stood there looking at his own reflection with tears in his eyes.

No one that came and went gave him a second look. Jack thought that the constant flow of people that looked homeless seemed to be just a normal everyday occurrence. When he was finished he was quite pleased with his new reflection. He looked younger and quite different than before. If the authorities were looking for a bum with a beard he no longer fit that bill, but he had to do something about his clothing. He decided he would address that when he arrived in New York City.

The PA system was muffled but loud and echoed off the leaded glass skylight, but Jack couldn't understand a word of it.

The train to New York City was right on schedule. Jack found a seat in a car that was almost empty except for a group of men and women all wearing Ranger's jerseys heading into the Garden for a hockey game. They were making too much noise and Jack had to move to another car. This time the ride seemed quiet for the most part and Jack paid his fair easing into the seat and closed his eyes hoping to get a least a half hour nap just about the time it would take to get into the city.

He tried closing his eyes, but sleep would not come. Too many images folded into his mind, too many unanswered questions fought him for his attention. All the happenings of the last few days played over again in his head like a broken record.

With his eyes shut he saw the image of his grandmother lying in a hospital bed, the bloody faced police officer, the car wreck. Then just as the image of the goddess Billie came into a fuzzy focus everything went black. He dreamt of talking to his grandmother and how he would explain his not answering her letters. He saw a small boy sitting on an old woman's lap under the shade of a great oak tree. They were both sharing a laugh. He saw the image of a woman walking alone in the woods. The images turned to darkness as the train car gently rocked him deeper into the abyss.

CHAPTER 14

NOT ON MY WATCH

Two police officers stood in front of Mike as Billie came back into the office carrying a tray of coffee placing it on Mike's desk. They went about helping themselves.

"Let me see if I got this straight." Mike went about lighting a cigar. "You're telling me that you found a set of finger prints in a wrecked car that match my parolee. And, you also found another wrecked car on seen with two deceased."

"Yes, that's exactly." The officer handed Mike an envelope. Mike poured out the contents onto his desk taking note of the suspects name and the horror show of black and white photos strewn about his desk. "Son of a bitch." He said stubbing out the cigar in an ashtray.

Mike pressed a button on the intercom "Billie get me the file on Jack Kahill. If this is your guy I saw him in here..." His voice trailed off. Mike pressed a finger to his head. Billie returned handing Mike a large red envelope. "When was the last time Kahill was in here?" He asked.

"Two days ago." She answered. Mike opened the file and found Jack Kahill's address.

"He's living in a flop house in downtown Elizabeth. He's..."

"He's not there." The officer cut him off. "We checked his last known address and he was not there. Looks like he left in a hurry too. He left too many personal items behind. And..."

This time Mike cut off the officer. "Maybe he's coming back."

The office shook his head no. "We don't think so. The door was locked but we found a back-room window wide open with a screen kicked out lying on the ground below. We also talked to a ..." the officer pulled out a note pad and thumbed through it... "A Mrs. Colandra who said she yelled out at a disturbance in the back-alley way. Sounded like someone crashed into the trash cans causing quite a ruckus. Any idea where you think he might have gone?"

Mike relit his cigar. "Well, the last thing I told him to do was to go see his grandmother at ST. ELIZABETHS HOSPETAL. She is terminally ill, and he promised he would go. "Could be, he's there."

"Did he go?" The officer asked.

"I don't know but he was pretty shaken when he got the letter I gave him."

"Letter?"

"Yea, a letter from his dying grandmother. She contacted us on many occasions over the last three years when Jack was locked up for accidental man slaughter. He killed two people drunk driving."

"Well it seems like we got the same situation here and now." The officer pointing to the photos on Mike's desk.

"No not a chance." Mike shook his head. "He passed the drug test. He's totality sober."

"Well we got two dead people lying in the basement of that very hospital who say differently."

This time Mike didn't hit the intercom he just yelled out to the next room. "Billie get my coat, I'm going to that hospital to check this myself. Nobody runs from Mike Shannon."

Mike opened the door and led the two officers out to the elevator and pushed the button for the lobby. "I'll check the hospital although I don't know what kind of shape she's in or if in fact that she's still there."

"Ok." The officer said. "We will go back and stage a look out at the apartment we will contact you if we find him."

The elevator door opened, and the three men steeped out.

"Agreed." Mike shook their hand and stopped at the news stand for a fresh cigar as he watched them walk away.

"Sorry Junior all I have is a twenty-dollar bill."

"Hello Mike." Junior said handing him change. "What's new?"

Mike thought for a moment and said. "What the hell it's worth a shot. Do remember two days ago a man coming through here ...ah." Mike caught himself, knowing what he was about to ask a blind man.

"Go ahead say it." Urged Junior. "Just because I'm blind don't mean I can't see." He said laughing.

Mike continued. "Well looking like a drowned rat."

"Yeah, you're talking about Jack Kahill." He answered handing Mike a book of matches.

"Yes that's him. How did you know?"

"Like I said I'm blind, but I could smell him a mile away. He smelled like a wet dog."

Mike lit his cigar. "Did he say anything, or did he seem odd at all to you?"

"Would you like some coffee?" Junior asked? "What's going on?"

"Well not more than ten minutes ago I had a visit by the police."

"Yes, I know, I saw them leaving." Junior laughed again.

"They seem to believe that he was involved in an auto accident and he fled the scene."

"You mean the accident he had three years ago?"

Mike was about to answer when he realized junior was a warehouse of information. "You know I think I will have that cup of coffee. Let's take a seat and you can tell me what I don't know about Jack Kahill."

Junior grabbed a pot of coffee, two cups and led Mike to an empty table.

Mike sat watching junior pore two cups of coffee and not spill a drop.

"You know." He said. "I find it hard to believe, I just can't see Jack being involved in this. Did he ever say anything strange or odd to you?"

"No, we talked about his past but the last time we were together he was very upset about his grandmother."

"Yea, I guess I'm responsible for that" Mike sipped at his coffee, perfect he thought.

"He must have gone to see her." Junior added.

Mike stood holding out his hand forgetting Junior couldn't see it, but Junior had a firm grip shaking it before Mike realized what had happened. "Thanks for the coffee. Well I guess I need to start there." Mike answered as he started to walk away.

"Wait a second." Junior called to Mike stopping him in his tracks. "I don't know if this helps, but Jack often talked about his time growing up in an orphanage in Maine."

"Thanks Junior I'll remember that." Mike took out a small pad and scribbled on it ...MAINE...?

When Mike arrived at the hospital, he walked through the entrance of the hospital avoiding the check in and went straight to the security office. When he came to the door he didn't knock. He open the door walking straight in, finding a young pimple faced man seated behind a desk in a security uniform reading a comic book. Startled, the young man jumped to his feet dropping the book to the floor. What now stood before him was a huge man with a military hair cut with deep eyes staring straight through him.

"Can I help you sir?" The man said through a squeaky voice that Mike had to strain to hear. Mike held out his identification under the nose of the young guard. But the only thing he saw was the U.S.M.C tattoo on Mike's forearm.

"There could be a fugitive here in the hospital." Mike said. "Call the nurses' station and find out on what floor and what room a Mrs. Kahill is located at."

"I'm new here and I'm not sure I'm authorized to do that." He answered picking up the comic book. "My supervisor will be back in twenty minutes. He went to lunch."

Mike's voice lowered an octave and he growled. "Listen sonny I don't have a lot of time." He reached over the desk grabbing the phone shoving the receiver under the man's chin. "Start dialing."

Mike paced back and forth. He checked his watch five minutes had passed since shoving the phone under the chin on the young security guard. The guard didn't hang up the receiver when Mike cut the silence. "Well what's the answer?"

"The head nurse said she is no longer here."

Mike clenched his teeth and reached into a jacket pocket producing a small leather case. He opened it and walking over to a trash can next to the desk cutting off a cigar end. He stood there twirling it between his fingers like a card shark.

"Well where did she go?"

No- the guard thought about saying- smoking. But quickly realized it was probably in is best interest not to get this man riled up any more than he already was.

"Sir I'm sorry she passed away some time this morning. Her body is in the morgue now waiting for transport. Do you want to see it?"

"No." Mike answered. "Transport to where?"

"The nurse said that she is going to be transported to Monson Maine."

Mike took out his note pad thumbing through until he stop at the page with the word circled in red as big as life…Maine.

He knew that there was no use in asking about Jack. With the grandmother now decease; he would have to look elsewhere.

"God dam." He said pounding his fist on the side of the guard's desk and walked out slamming the door behind him.

Chapter 15

DODGING QUESTIONS

Jack tasted paste in his mouth and this he thought was probably the roughest of mornings. Never did he think he would awake seated on a hard-plastic chair at New York Penn station. Not even the beds at the Maine state prison were as bad as this. It was a rough night of fending off various hobos, street people and homeless looking for a hand out.

Homeless that word sunk in. "Jesus, I'm homeless." He said aloud. But, at least the few patrolling police officers took no notice of him throughout the night. It was early morning and the crowds of commuters were beginning to thicken around the place.

Jack picked up his knapsack and headed for a sign with one flickering light that read public restrooms. The restroom was empty except a tall burley man staring at a wall tucked into a urinal. Jack walked into a handicapped toilet booth locking the door behind him. With his foot he kicked down the seat and placed his knapsack on top and went about changing into the last remaining clean clothing he had. At the sink he checked his reflection in the mirror. His image had changed with the shave but he thought he still looked like shit. He removed the bandage above his eye a dark scab was all that was left of the cut.

He had the taste of coffee on his lips and he wished he could share a cup with Junior Leeds now. He decided a hot cup of coffee was just what he needed and walked out of the restroom in search of caffeine.

With a fresh set of clothing on and the morning rush of people, he felt it safe to walk. He would be insulated among the crowd. He didn't look any different that the rats running through the maze all looking for their daily piece of cheese.

Ahead of him he saw a sign with an arrow that read exit street level this way. As Jack turned the corner he saw a small bagel shop and walked in. The smell of fresh brewed coffee was refreshing, and he took in a long deep breath. Four people were on line ahead of him. A young blond-haired girl was

144

waiting on customers. He approached the counter and ordered a large black coffee and a plain bagel with cream cheese. He hoped the extra calories would keep him going. He found an empty table placing his knapsack on the opposite chair and took a seat. The seat faced the street and it was a good way to keep an eye on the people coming through the door. He let out a sigh as he sipped the hot coffee and swallowing half the bagel in one bite. He couldn't remember the last time he had a real meal. He took another fast bite of the other half of the bagel again swallowing it in one gulp when he noticed the girl at the counter spying on him.

"Wow you must be really hungry." She said smiling.

"Yea I guess it's been a while." Jack answered sipping at the coffee.

He got up from the table and opened the drawstring of the knapsack. What the hell was the address of that book store? He thought. Unfolding the envelope, he read Sara's books New York City. He closed his eyes and rubbing them hard, biting the inside of his cheek.

"God dam it." He said in disgust. "This could be anywhere."

Seeing that there was no address, he turned to reseat himself at the table and found another bagel had been placed in front of him.

"This ones on the house." Said the blond girl at the counter.

Jack nodded and went about finishing off the offering. He turned looking at her. "Do you have a phone book? He asked.

The girl stood frozen staring at Jack with a blank look on her face. Jack could see her mouth the words- Phone book.

Suddenly she burst out laughing. "What the hell is a phone book? Nobody uses a phone book anymore." She stopped laughing when she saw the disappointed look in Jacks eyes. "Oh, I'm sorry." She said. "What are you looking for?"

Jack placed the envelope on the table. It was sealed but he thought of opening it, maybe it would have an address inside. He shook his head no when an image of old MR, Sampson flashed in his mind. He stood there in front of Jack.

"HONOR AND DUTY." He said.

"Here." He said handing the girl the envelope. "It only has the name of the book shop but no address."

Jack studied the girls face when suddenly she smiled at him. "You're in luck. I know this place sure." She said pouring Jack a refill of his coffee cup. Its Sara's Books and Mystic Shop. It's down in the village near Bleecker Street.

"Wow." She said. "What kind of eerie karma is this? It just so happens that I'm meeting some friends there tonight for a séance. I here that girl Sara is really good. What a great place for rare books. You looking for something special? If you want, we could go together but I don't get off until five."

Jack smiled back at the girl, shaking his head no. "I need to go now." He said.

"I'll write down the address and phone number of the place for you."

Jack folded up the letter and placed it back on top of his knapsack. He gathered up his belongings and made his way to the door.

At the door Jack turned back to the girl. "Thanks." He said. "I'm Jack. I didn't get your name."

"Margaret" She answered.

Jack felt his heart skip a beat. He could feel his eyes tearing up. The young girl having the same name of his grandmother tore a hole in his soul and he had to take a deep breath holding back the flood gates of emotions.

"Well Margaret I hope to see you there later and maybe after I can buy you a drink."

He waved as the door closed but he didn't hear the girl answer. "I'd like that." She said waving back.

The morning air was smog but dry. Looking at the directions he had six blocks to navigate. Even though his sciatica was flaring up from sleeping sitting up on a plastic chair all night, he chose not to hail a cab. He found the aspirin in his sack and along with the rest of his coffee swallowed them together in one last gulp. He was surprised he walked with a brisk step. Crowds of people sidestepped and dodged each other like a pinball machine along the way. The noise of the city was defining everything seemed to swirl like a wind devil in front of him.

There were some things he dodged he thought. He dodged the truth with his grandmother. And now he was dodging Mike Shannon and the law. He was dodging his responsibility for the accident yesterday afternoon and killing two people. He suddenly felt sick to his stomach and he quickly dodged into an alleyway between two store fronts. He couldn't hold it anymore and threw up, coughing and cloaking back tears. At the end of the block he slumped into a bench at a small park wiping back tears as they flowed down his face.

Jack felt like saw dust every bone in his body ached and he had a pounding headache. But he had to keep moving and honor a promise he made to deliver the letter.

It was early afternoon when he reached the store and he felt it odd that the store was in a basement and to gain access he would have to walk down some steps to get inside. Bending down he was able to peer through the window and see a few people milling about but couldn't see much more. He had no idea if Margaret was inside waiting for him or if she just blew him off. He shrugged his shoulder and told himself that it was better off that she didn't show and that he didn't really need to get involved with anyone.

He stepped down and missed the last step as his leg gave out and the sciatic pain shot up his side making him crash into the door. He wondered if he should just leave the envelope at the front counter or ask for the girl whose name on the envelope he was now fixed on. When he opened the door, it was as if a record had stopped. With the ringing of chimes above the door, everyone's attention was fixed on him. Jack wanted to turn and run back out the door and up the steps. It was as if the plague had just walked in. But as he was about to turn a voice came from the counter area stopping him in his tracks.

"Can I help you?" A girl spoke in a sweet soft voice.

"Excuse me." Jack answered. "I'm looking for Sara."

"Oh." The girl answered pointing at a table over Jack's shoulder. "She's over there. She's about to start a reading. Your welcome to join in but it will cost you twenty dollars to have a reading."

"Oh no, I'm ok." Jack answered waving her off. "If it's ok, I'll just stand over here and wait until she's finished."

"It could be awhile. "She smiled at Jack. "Please feel free to look around the store if you like."

Jack nodded and turned his attention to the group of people seated around the table.

Sara had her back to Jack and was busy speaking to the three-woman seated at the table. Suddenly she stopped in mid-sentence and turned to look up at Jack. She made eye contact and was just about to say hello when out of the corner of her eye her attention became focused on two figures that suddenly appeared at the window behind Jack. Could it be she wondered, but they looked like the two visitors she briefly saw the other night?

Jack turned wondering what the girl was staring at but saw nothing.

Sara looked back at Jack and suddenly she felt a cold shiver run down her spine. She didn't know what it was about the new stranger standing before her, but she was certain that he had an attachment and is the reason the new visitors had appeared again outside.

"I'll be with you shortly. Please have a seat." She said to Jack hoping he would sit so she could further get a feeling of him and just what was attached to him.

"I'm fine." Jack assured her. "I'll just stand if it's ok with you."

Sara nodded and returned her focus to the three ladies around the table who equally shared a puzzled look.

Jack watched in fascination as Sara spoke to the ladies of past lives and beautiful relationships they had. She spoke of pleasant things and wonderful futures for the three.

Jack watched their faces go quickly from puzzlement to smiles of contentment. He wondered if she could do the same for him but, chose not to spend the money he couldn't spare. What would she find doing a reading on him? How far could she look forward and into his past? No, he thought some deaths are best to keep buried and now was certainly not the time to stir up old wounds that would take a life time to explain.

Sara finished the reading with the ladies, thanking them for their participation and invited them to further explore the store. She turned to Jack inviting him to sit. Jack placed his knapsack on an empty chair and sat opposite her at the table. As he began to sit Sara offered a hand and Jack shook it noticing how soft her hand was. Her grip was tight, and she held it for a time staring directly into Jacks' eyes. A quick momentary flash of a small child seated on an old woman's lap snapped in her consciousness and faded.

"How can I help you?" She asked. Slowly letting go of Jacks hand. "You obviously know my name, what's yours?"

"My name is John Kahill, but everyone calls me Jack."

He unfolded the envelope and placed it on the table in front of Sara. She looked down at the envelope and then looked up past Jack. The two entities she had seen early, and the other night were back standing at the window. She was now certain that they had something in common with this new stranger seated across from her. But now something new came into the mix. What was this letter all about and who or better yet why was this man hand delivering it? She didn't know where to begin and sat there just staring at it.

"Listen." Jack said. "I really can't tell you much about that letter. I didn't open it and I can't tell you how I came to possess it. All I can tell you is it was given to me and I made a promise to deliver it to you." Another dodge another lied he thought. When will it ever end?

Sara felt a sudden nervousness come over her. Whether it was the old reporter in her knocking for attention or something else, she was certain that the stranger in front of her was lying and holding back information. She had too many years' experience following the smallest trickles of a lead to a story to know something more was being hidden now from her.

Sara touched the envelope; suddenly a terrible feeling came over her. A tragic accident scene flashed into her mind and she jumped back in her seat dropping the envelope on the table.

"Tell me this." She said. "You say you know nothing of what is inside this envelope and I believe you. So, let's start at the beginning. I'm going to make some tea; the store will be closing soon you look like you could use a sandwich, so I'll make us some tea and we can chat about what you do know."

Before Jack could answer she was gone into another room. Jack sat there thinking of just walking out, but the offer of tea and food sounded inviting and besides she was good looking so what would it hurt to sit awhile and have some tea besides he didn't have a plan yet on how to get to Maine.

Sara came back with two cups of tea and two ham and cheese sandwiches. Jack was half way finished before Sara had the opportunity to sit.

"Ok." She said sipping at her tea. "Let's play a game. How about fifty questions?" She was about to ask the first when the other store clerk broke her concentration.

"I'm sorry Sara but I just got off the phone with the group for tonight's reading they canceled. I'm going to close the store now." Millie said. "I'll lock up behind me. You kids have fun." She said rolling her eyes at Sara.

"Thanks Millie I'll be fine."

Millie was just about to close the door and set the lock when she saw an arm over her shoulder holding the door.

"I'm sorry were closed." She said.

"This won't take but a moment Miss." Responded a deep growly voice.

Millie spun on her heels to see two uniformed police officers and a man in a suit with a sharp crew cut standing on the steps.

"May we come in? We just have a few questions. Is the owner here?"

Jack heard the commotion first and jumped from his seat. Sara looked at him knowing that they were here for the stranger.

"Quick." She said. "The bathroom." She pointed to the back corner of the room.

"Trust me." She said. "I'll handle this and get rid of them."

Jack was already there before she finished telling him what she was going to do.

Sara quickly closed the door locking it and walked into the front room.

"I'm Sara and this is my shop." She said meeting the three men near the front counter. "How can I help you?"

"The name is Mike Shannon." Said the tall man with the crew cut hair.

Sara watched as he pulled a photo from his inside suit pocket. He held it out for her to see.

"We are looking for this man. We believe he's on his way here. Have any of you seen him or know of his whereabouts?"

Sara shook her head. "No, no idea who that is, never seen him before."

"How about you?" Mike turned to Millie showing her the photo.

Millie thought for a moment Sara's clearly lying and the fact that the man they are looking for is twenty feet away hiding in the other room there had to be a reason Sara was now protecting this man. But she knew Sara well enough to trust her instinct.

"No, no idea who that is, never seen him before." She echoed Sara.

"Well mind if we look around?" The police officer had a stern look on his face.

"Not unless you have a warrant." Sara answered.

But it was too late Mike was already in the next room standing near the séance table. Mike made a mental note that the table had what seemed to be a fresh setting for two people and the girl he encountered at the door was leaving. Odd he thought maybe it was a left over or maybe not.

"Hey do you mind?" Sara shouted.

Sara was now standing opposite Mike blocking his way into the back area and the bathroom.

"Ok lady." Mike said gesturing the two officers towards the door. "We'll leave."

As he came around the table he caught a glimpse of the envelope lying on the table. He shook his head for a second, not sure if he really had just seen an envelope with what clearly looked like blood stains on it. He stopped.

Sara quickly grabbed the envelope folding it into her pocket.

"Ok lady." Mike handed her his card. "If he does show up here give us a call."

As they walked toward the door Sara tried to fight back a gnawing feeling until she couldn't take it anymore.

"What is he wanted for anyway, and what makes you think he would show up here of all places?"

"We need to question him in the involvement of a double manslaughter. His prints are all over the scene. As far as him showing up here, we need to check all leads. It's just routine."

Mike didn't say any more, but he had a feeling based on what he had seen on the table, that she knew more than what she was willing to tell.

Sara led the three men to the door. She couldn't tell why Mike Shannon had given up so easily, but she was glad they were leaving. She felt there was a lot more to this story of an odd stranger along with two new entities and the police noising around her shop that she wanted to investigate. Who were the two new people and what did they have to do with Jack?

Sara turned the lock and followed the three men with her eyes, as they walked up the steps until she saw two dark shadows standing across the street. The new visitors were again standing there.

"Oh boy." She said making the connection that the two entities that she had been seeing are the two people the police were talking about. It had everything to do with the stranger hiding out in her bath room, but what about the blood-stained envelope. She didn't have time to look at it.

A banging sound came from the bathroom followed by Jack yelling out.

"Hay let me out of here."

"Millie would you do the honors?" Sara pointed to the bathroom door. "And Millie thanks for that back there."

Millie smiled. "Not a problem boss. I know you too long not to fallow your lead."

Millie unlocked the door.

"Shush. You keep it down they might hear you. Now listen." Sara pointed to the table. "I just saved your ass so you're going to park it over there and spill the beans and were going to get to the bottom of this right now."

Millie walked back to the door. She waved over her shoulder as she left.

"Good night Millie." Sara waved back.

Jack dropped his bag on the table shook his head yes. There was nothing more he could do. She did save his ass, but why? She could have easily given him up and been none the worse for it.

Jack sat at the table as instructed. He wanted to know why she had lied for him and why she would go out of the way to protect a total stranger.

"Ok let's get back to this little game I like to call 50 questions." Sara held the envelope. "You know you can start first. You obviously know my name. So" …. Sara didn't finish.

Lights, memories and images were flashing like a picture show on steroids moving in a time warp in Jacks mind. He wondered what enough information was and what he should hold back.

"Like I said before." He answered. "My name is Jack."

"Well ok, Jack." Sara waved her hand it him. "Come on." She said.

"Well as you can easily figure out I guess I'm a fugitive."

"What the hell was that all about?" She asked.

"Well I had an accident a day ago and two people died but I swear to you it was not my fault."

"Let me guess, you ran."

Jack shook his head yes.

"I couldn't go back to prison. I'd just as soon jump from a bridge."

"And you shouldn't have been driving?"

"No." Jack answered. "It wasn't even my car."

"Why should I believe you?"

"A better question is why you didn't give me up?"

Sara didn't know why other than the fact that she now a strong feeling that she somehow had a connection to this man or maybe the attachments he had with him. She was now more than ever determined to get to the bottom of it.

"Ok Jack." She held the envelope. "Where did you get this?" But she had a slight feeling what his answer was going to be.

Tears welted up in his eyes and he took a long deep breath before he answered.

"I held his hand as long as I could." He started shutting his eyes and seeing the images of the other day in his mind. "I felt the life passing from him and before he died he gave me that envelope making me promise to deliver it to you."

"Did he say anything else?"

"Only that he knew that he ran the traffic light and the accident was not my fault."

Feeling curious and apprehensive at the same time she knew what she had to do. She tore open the envelope.

Dear Sara as you read this please note that I am dead. I don't know if you remember me as it has been many years since I saw you last as a little girl. I am your grandfather Miles Parker. I don't believe you would remember me, you were quite little when I saw you last. There is no one left in my family but you. And I want to tell you of a fortune that all you need do is go and get it......

Sara stopped reading and looked up at Jack with a puzzled look on her face.

"Hay what the hell is this?" She pushed the letter at Jack. Is this a joke?"

"I really don't know anything about it other than what I already to you." Jack pushed it back to her not looking at it. "Only that I was given it to deliver to you. Maybe you should finish reading it to find out."

"This is crazy." She answered. "Ok I'm game I like a good mystery. It says here that some guy who I really don't remember claims to be my grandfather and has left me a fortune and all I need to do is go get it."

"This is really none of my business and you don't have to tell me…." Jack stopped in mid-sentence. He shook his head.

She saw his action like a hawk on a fat rat. "What's wrong?" Sara asked.

Jack thought for a moment. "Nothing." He said.

She didn't believe it for a second. There's more to this she was sure.

Another lie he thought. What's going on here? Why is all this so eerily similar? He found the envelope his grandmother had left for him, but he left it hidden.

When Sara had finished she sat there with a stunned look on her face. "This is going to be a long night." She whispered.

Jack nodded.

CHAPTER 16

ERASING HISTORY

A Loon belched out an eerie cry from somewhere on the lake. It laughed in hysteria of being the witness to death. A light mist hung low in the clouds hovering just above the water. Montgomery walked briskly tucking his chin into his jacket trying to shake off the chill. It was no use as the wind off the lake blew strong at his back. Again, the bird let go a scream of horror. It sent a chill up his spine and he felt the hair on the back of his neck stand at attention. He laughed along with the haunted echoes reflecting from hillside to hillside. He followed it along the trail until it faded and died. He frowned; it was such a beautiful melodic sound. Fifty feet ahead he came to a clearing and could see the commotion now happening was responsible for frightening the bird away.

Two police officers were pacing back and forth at the edge of the lake. They wore long trench coats and in the darken light they looked like two giant vultures bouncing along the ground about to dine on a carcass.

A recovery dive team was just coming out of the water carrying the lifeless body of a hiker that had gone missing earlier in the week. It was around two in the afternoon that he received a phone call from Officer Johnson to come to the lake. They were sure they located the body and the recovery wouldn't take long.

The lake was about a quarter of a mile away from where he had to leave his car, but the trail was rock less, flat and an easy walk through a pine forest along a small brook. The sound of the water flowing along the brook reminded him of falling rain and he stopped there for a moment closing his eyes imagining it was night and raining. His favorite distraction. Even though the walk should have been easy, it had rained the evening before and the trees had dropped leaves making the trail muddy and slippery. He carried only a body bag and would need the help of the other men to navigate the wet terrain and carry out the body.

"Hello Montgomery." The officer held out his hand.

Montgomery hesitated for a moment but shook the officer's hand. How he despised touching people with all their germs.

The officer's hand felt like wet raw dough. He quickly shoved his hand into his pocket wiping away the moisture.

"We had to call you because our coroner is out of town and the only place we can store the body is with you until he comes back. Hope it's not too much of an inconvenience."

Montgomery feigned a smile. "No, not at all always glad to help." It was a lie; he hated having to get involved especially when there was no profit in it. But what upset him the most was knowing that he would be denied the fun that went along with it. He would be denied the opportunity to create another trophy. He would have to hold the body long enough until the coroner could take charge.

He watched as one of the officers stepped to the side and heaved over throwing up. The stench of a dead body was something Montgomery was accustomed too. A body left rotting for a week in a swamp was something altogether different and Montgomery gagged as he laid the body bag alongside the body now lying on the grown. He now wished he had brought a larger body bag. The one he was now forcing the body into became difficult because the body was bloated from deterioration and water logged. Yet he could tell that the young man now being zipped up was muscular and in good shape. It was odd that he wound up in the lake but if a person is cramped while swimming this was most of the time the results.

165

Officer Collins approached Montgomery "Let the boy's here change out of their wetsuits and we can all help to get out of here."

"That will be fine." Montgomery answered as he walked away toward the lake. He stood at the edge hoping the Loon would return and begin its serenade to the dead.

He looked out over the lake to a large clearing on the hillside; trees were beginning to change color. It reminded him of the project he set in motion earlier that morning. He wondered how it was coming along. He was certain that no one would ever notice.

It had been nearly seventy years since anyone had been buried in the old part of the cemetery. It was now well overgrown. He felt certain that not a living soul in town was alive long enough to remember that it was there. Montgomery hoped the contractor he hired from out of town would leave no trace.

He turned away from the lake now hoping that everyone was ready to get back to town. He was anxious to check on the contractor's progress. The drive back to the funeral home seemed long and although the deceased was zippered tight in the body bag he caught an occasional whiff of rotted vegetation.

When he arrived at the funeral home he found Lou Mancini waiting for him pacing back and forth under a small lamp in the entrance way of the funeral home. The subdued lighting made the figure appear as if there was more than one person standing there as he moved about.

Montgomery walked up to the entrance and as he did they all seemed to slowly vanish except for one.

"You're late." Lou Mancini said in a low grumbly voice.

"I know." Montgomery answered. "It couldn't be helped I got called away to pick up a body found in the lake." He pointed over his shoulder to the hearse.

Montgomery pushed past him unlocking the door and pushed it open with his boot. Immediately the dry smell of death hit them both and swirled around clinging to attach itself like hound's-tong.

Lou flinched, stopping in mid- stride. "I don't know how you do it."

"We all have of demons to deal with."

"What?" Lou asked.

Montgomery stood there towering over the small man like a vulture perched to attack. "Let me put this into terms a simple mind can comprehend .Our cross to bear." He answered. He was obviously insulting the man, but Lou Mancini said nothing.

"Please follow me."Montgomery waved Lou on.

He led the way into a darkened room adjusting the light just enough to see. He led Lou to a small desk next to a row of open caskets. "Please take a seat I'll be but a moment and I'll return with your cash."

Montgomery took the elevator to the basement open the garage door and went about pushing a gurney toward the hearse to retrieve the package. When he got to the hearse he opened the door pulling at the body bag and began placing it on the gurney. Suddenly he felt the air change and he turned to find Lou standing behind him.

Montgomery was about to question him as to why he was standing there when Lou cut him off.

"Can I help you with that?"

Montgomery had the body bag half way onto the gurney but answered. "Sure, why not? We can talk business along the way."

Lou grabbed a handle and followed Montgomery as he pushed the gurney through the open door and into the body holding area. He shivered in the cold darkness.

"I trust everything went as planned." Montgomery adjust the lighting just enough to see.

"Yea, you wanted it to look like freshly plowed farm land that's what it looks like now. As far as the old stone, I dug a big hole and deep sixed them. It's none of my business what you do with your land as long as I get paid for my work." Lou held his hand up rubbing index finger and thumb together.

"Yes, and too that. If you would be so kind to wait a moment as I gather just that for you. I will return presently." Montgomery slipped out into a darkened hall way and into another room. He grabbed a bottle of brandy two glasses and placed them on a cold medical tray. He opened a cabinet and grabbed a syringe. Ah... this will do just fine he though and carefully slid it into his pant pocket. He walked over to a desk and opened the top drawer and pulled out a large envelop full of cash. He placed it on the tray next to the bottles. He stopped for a moment when passing a mirror, adjusting his tie smiling at his reflection.

He returned to the room placing the tray on top the body bag.

"If you don't mind pouring us a drink to our good fortune." He said handing Lou the brandy bottle.

"Don't mind if I do." He answered popping the cork and went about filling the two glasses with brandy.

Montgomery watched with a hawk's eye. He was quite accustomed working in the dark. Slowly his fingers wrapped around the syringe and in a split second plunged it into the chest of Lou Mancini, injecting air into his heart. He watched the pupils of the man's eyes widen as the realization of what was now happening to him became realized. Montgomery smiled deeply as the man's pupils shrunk quickly from a lively sky of blue to a darkened gray quicksand. He grabbed the brandy glass in midair as the man clutched at his chest and began to slump.

Montgomery grabbed the back of the man's head and brought his face within an inch of the dying man's face. He stared intently into the man eyes. He hoped to get a glimpse the instant death came to snatch away the man's soul. He hoped to see the last flicker of life fading away. He licked his lips in anticipation. In the deepening gray of the man's eyes he saw an old woman in a kitchen cooking a large meal and a young child running around tugging at her apron. He saw her place a finger to her lips shushing the little boy quiet. The image quickly changed to a scene of people seated around a large table with the old woman carrying a large pot to the table. The image started to fade in a haze of darkness. Montgomery grabbed the man's eyelid forcing it open more but it was over the man's pupils were now completely black, dead. He let go of the man's head allowing the body to fall to the floor. He felt exhilarated with life. This time was one of the best final glimpses he had the pleasure of witnessing of a dying person last moments.

Montgomery stood above him like a gargoyle smiling as Lou grabbed at his chest lying on the floor.

"Cheers." He toasted swallowing the brandy in one gulp. "You're going to be the first to visit the new land."

Back at his office Montgomery quickly gathered up all the correspondence he filed from Lou Mancini. He held it there up to the desk lamp...clear all land level, place all head stones in large pit and cover.... $ 6000.00 dollars.... He tucked all the paper work into a folder. He made his way back to where Lou was lying on the floor. He rolled the body on to its back and unzipped his jacket placing the file envelope on Lou's chest and zipped up the jacket. Need to keep thing tidy he thought, and burry it all together. He then walked over to a cabinet and pulled out a large body bag placing it on the floor and went about zipping up the newly deceased. He rolled the body along the floor until it came to a stop next to the cold lockers and with a great deal of effort stuffed it into a bottom slide. That will hold you just fine until the opening ceremonies.

The other body from the lake was much easier to tuck into a locker as the gurney was at the height needed to roll it on to a slab.

He then returned to his trophy room but this time he was feeling pissed off. Two new bodies tucked away down stairs and not a one single dollar in profit to show for his efforts. One a free ride held in limbo and the other leaving no trace.

CHAPTER 17

MIXED PLANS

It was late evening Sara had a splitting headache and was exhausted. She had too many questions that needed to be answered before she could rest. When she had finished reading the letter, she shared with Jack the contents. She told him of having a grandfather who she never remembers having met and that she was the only family the old man had left. The old man spoke of a fortune he believed buried in a coffin of a baby who was her step brother who died at child birth. He spoke of how his first wife had stolen from him and where to go to look for it.

Sara was already tracking out a route on a map. When Jack finished reading the letter himself a cold shutter ran up his spine. He couldn't believe what he had just read. If he told her now, what he knew he felt certain of, the fact that he was in possession of a letter from his grandmother when placed side by side could be twins. He wasn't a hundred present sure just yet, but could she be the girl mentioned in the letter from his grandmother. Is she his step sister? This question he would need to take his time answering. He didn't want to scare her off when he had too many questions of his own that she could possibly answer. Some strange force was at work here and he didn't understand how any of this could be happening now.

"That's it." She said startling Jack. "We are going to Maine." She folded the map handing it to Jack.

"What are you crazy? I'm traveling alone. I don't need you mixed up in my problems. And besides you got a business here."

"Millie can run it while I'm gone and it's not like I'm going forever." She took back the map folding it carefully.

"You said you need to go to Maine to see an old friend at an orphanage. Well it just so happens where I need to go is in the same town even close by. While I'm there, it will give me a chance to investigate a story I read a few days ago about a crooked funeral home."

Jack looked at her shaking his head. "What are you talking about funeral home?"

"The Montgomery Barry funeral home in Monson Maine. Hold on a second." She walked over to a desk and retrieved a news article and handed it to Jack.

Jack thumbed through the article. "WOW." He said. "I know this place. It's up on a hill on the other side of town next to the old graveyard."

"We got a problem." She added. "How are we going to get you out of here in the morning when we got the police and a Mr. Crew cut looking for you?"

Jack laughed. "Did you catch the name of Mr. Crew cut?"

"Ah wait, he gave me his card. Yeah here it is." She pulled it out of her pocket and handed it to Jack.

Jacks eyes widened, and his hands started to tremble. He felt a panic attack awakening deep inside. He dropped the card on the table. "Mike Shannon." He whispered.

"You know him?" She asked.

"Yea he's my parole officer. How the hell did they tract me here."

Sara could feel her heart racing. "He said it was routine, but I suspected he was lying and he knew more than what he was willing to give out. I could tell by the look on his face. He saw that envelope with the blood stains on it. I'm sure of it."

Jack could see the worried look on her face. He sat there biting on the inside of his cheek. Immediately tasting blood. "But he didn't say anything?"

"No." She answered.

Jack felt the room begin to spin. His heart was thumping in his ears. He wants to run out of there. He felt his hand shaking and he couldn't hide it.

Sara immediately took notice of how the look on his face changed. He looked pale and she could see beads of sweat forming at his temples.

"What's wrong are you okay? Can I get you a glass of water or something?"

Jack shook his head. "I'm having a panic attack."

Sara slowly got up from her chair and came around the table standing behind Jack.

"I can fix it if you'll trust me. Millie would get them all the time. I learned a trick from my old newspaper editor years ago when I saw him perform it on Millie."

Sara grabbed the back of Jacks neck pressing her thumb and forefinger into his neck just below his ears. Jack flinched.

"Relax." She said. "I swear it works." Around his right side she held her hand in front of him.

"Here grab hold of my hand."

Again, Jack hesitated but folded his fingers into hers.

"Close your eyes and imagine you're at your favorite place." She wanted to help him remembering seeing how upset Millie would become when she had an attack.

Jack close his eyes and immediately saw himself seated on his grandmother's lap at her cabin in Maine. She was smiling and laughing at how far she was able to spit watermelon seeds. Together they watched a curious little chipmunk dashed back and forth from tree log to rock out crop cautiously grabbing seed after seed scurrying in and out hiding seeds to retrieve them later. He let out a laugh.

Sara felt pins and needles race up her arm and a numbness slowly trying to enter her body. She fought it back.

Sara closed her eyes. Immediately she saw through a damp gray afternoon a hazy fog of images drift in and out of focus. She saw two cars rapidly approaching each other until they hit each other in a deadly tangled mess of twisted metal and blood. In one car a man struggling to get out of the wreckage and in the other one a man entrapped in the wreckage and a woman some distance away. She and been thrown from the car. And as she approached she suddenly saw the two entities standing on a side walk. She realized that they were watching themselves entangled in the wreckage. A great feeling of sorrow came over her and she wasn't sure if she was now crying. But she knew why she was there. If she didn't help them now to cross over they would be stuck there forever.

"It's ok." She said not sure if she was speaking aloud to them.

"What?"Jack asked.

Letting go of Jack's neck and hand Sara broke the spell. "You are safe you can go." She called out and watched as they slowly faded away.

"Go where?"Jack said as the image of his grandmother faded.

Sara wiped her face in her hands and came around to stand in front of Jack facing him. "Maine." She said.

Jack smiled. "I don't know what you just did but I never felt better."

Suddenly Sara felt exhausted and began to slump. Jack caught her and helped her into a chair next to him.

"Are you okay?" He asked.

"I'll be fine." She answered. "This sometimes happens when I help those who are stuck cross over."

"Just now?" Jack asked with a surprised look on his face, pointing a finger in the air.

Sara nodded.

"Well the police must think you're here, but they couldn't do much without a warrant, but they'll be back. What size are you?"

"What?"

"I've got an idea to get us both out of here. Just hear me out before you tell me it's crazy and it won't work. Have you ever been a woman?" Sara laughed.

"Oh no, I'm sure."

"It will work." She answered. "I'll call Millie to bring some clothing and a wig in the morning. You'll stay here on the couch tonight. I've got a cot in the back. First don't get me wrong I like it but you're going to need to do something about that beard coming in on your face."

Jack protested. "This is never going to work." He said but gave up quickly as Sara pointed to the bathroom.

"You'll find a new razor in the cabinet."

Bloodshot eyes stared back when he looked in the mirror. He wiped his face with his hands. He didn't have more than a five o'clock shadow but it was enough for anyone who got a good look at him to tell he was not a woman. He lathered and went about shaving.

Sara scurried about the room gathering up maps and a few personal items and stuffing them into a plastic bag.

"As soon as Millie gets here in the morning we are out of here." She called out over her shoulder. "They might be watching they might not. Pack up your things and I'll pack them into my car. Let me see you."

Jack poked his head out of bath room.

179

She laughed. "You're going to make a wonderful bride."

"Listen let's try to get some sleep. I don't want an argument from you. I'll take the cot and you take the couch."

Jack was about to protest but it was too late. Sara was already lying on the cot.

"Listen." Jack said as he nestled onto the couch. "Why do you want to help me?"

"It's easy." She said. "We both need to get to Maine. You said you wanted to look up an old friend and I need to investigate some family history and investigate the shenanigans of that funeral director."

"Be careful with that." Jack added.

"I'm careful about everything." She winked.

In the darkness Jack heard, the slamming of the cell doors and he smelled the rotten stench of decay. He reached out a hand and felt time peeling away slowly along the cold gray wall of his cell. Screams echoed around the walls. At one moment they seemed to get louder then quickly fade away. In the darkness he saw images come into focus and then fade.

He awoke with a startle and smelled toast. What was it he asked himself? Obviously, Sara was up before him and already prepping to leave. He wondered just how this was going to work and can they get away with it? Sara must have heard him getting up. "You want coffee?" She asked.

"About a half a gallon would do me find." He answered. "What time is it?"

"Its 6 am." She answered.

"Ouch." He said. Combing his fingers through his hair and stretching.

Sara was already packing a bag with her belongings. "Millie should be here soon and well get you all dolled up and then we are out of here."

Jack walked over to the coffee pot and refilled his cup. "You ever been to Maine." He asked.

She shook her head no.

"Well it's amazing. It's one of if not the most beautiful places I've ever been to. I've spent quite a bit of time there. I remember once being on a dark road as a child heading to Baxter St Forest. We drove with my grandmother in her old Chevy impala station wagon on a long road in the middle of the night maybe 2 a.m. It was as dark as nothingness you couldn't see your hand in front of your face. Yet what I do remember was seeing this ongoing flashing reflecting in the cars head lights as we drove ever closer to Katahdin.

After a time, curiosity got the best of us and we stopped to see what it was we were experiencing. And when we got out of the car the sound around us was deafening it was as we were standing in a tunnel and someone had turned up the volume on some strange cosmic amplifier. The forest was alive and over generated echoes' of all that it surrounded. The tiniest of its inhabitance were screaming to let you know they were there ready to eat you alive.

And when we emerged from the protective cocoon of the car we stumbled there in the darkness until our focus became fixed on the reflections of the cars head lights. We stood there sharing in the belief of what we were experiencing together at that moment, our accidental participation in the extinction of an innocent species. There with our mouths agape, we were the cause of the direct death of millions of migrating frogs who wanted nothing more than to go about their natural life cycle of gathering in and orgy of cosmic indulgences only to be wiped out by pure innocence.

What we saw in the darkness there at that moment was our destruction of migrating frogs run over by our car along the road as far as the eye could see up and down the road. How could it be that I was responsible for the destruction of an innocent species?"

Jack stopped and thought about what he had just said. Now he was responsible for the destruction of four lives. He forced himself to continue.

"When at that very moment my grandmother came up to me and put her arm around my shoulder and said what later took me years to understand. Life and death, you can't control. It just happens no matter how hard you try.

And we drove on until we came to the gate leading to Mount Katahdin. But, the forest ranger wouldn't let us in, we were there too early in the morning and they would not be open until seven the following morning. He welcomed us to park our car there along the side of the road and sleep if we wished until morning. And that we did until we were eaten alive by the no see-ums. I couldn't understand at first what was attacking us, but soon we were traveling at sixty miles an hour down the road leaving a trail of bugs streaming out the windows behind us.

It was shortly after that while slowing down and enjoying the morning sun that a cow moose and her calf came out of the woods and jogged along the side of the road keeping pace with our car for about two miles. I was in awe of the beauty of it all.

It was beautiful watching as they glided along the road with us until they shortened their stride and then disappeared back into the forest. We stopped the car getting out on the road smiling at each other taking in the fun that we just experienced. My eyes were as wide as could be with the fun of life and breathing in all the enrichment it brought forth.

Mother Nature had another surprised in store for us that day. As we left the comfort of the car, we stepped into the full bloom of wild strawberries growing along the side of the road. They are smaller than strawberries purchased in a supermarket, but what they lack in size is most certainly outweighed by the most amazing flavor I've ever experienced. They are small about the size of your finger nail but the concentration in flavor is over the top."

Sara placed two cups of coffee on the table and a plate of toast. "Here" She said. "It's not much, but you better have something."

Jack smiled." It might just be the best breakfast I had in a few days."

Suddenly a sound of a lock turning could be heard and Sara met Millie as she pushed through the door carrying two large bags.

"Here let me help you with that." Jack came up behind Sara and grabbed the bags from Millie and placed them on the table.

"Did you notice any one out there?" He asked sipping at his coffee.

"No, it looked quiet, but you never know who's out there watching."

Sara shuttered. A cold chill ran up her spine. She knew how true that could be.

CHAPTER 18

LOOSE LIPS

When Mike Shannon turned the car off it was near 6 am. Rolling down the window, he felt the air outside cool and a light fog hung low in the morning light. The sun was just about to break over the horizon. Birds broke out in song welcoming the day. Mike stuck his head out the window to breath in the fresh air. It was odd depending on which way the breeze was flowing, he caught whiffs of pine one moment and then bacon the next. He heard a loud grumbling and quickly scanned the area looking for moose that he heard about but never had seen except in a

185

zoo, but he saw nothing. The sound came again, hunger pains from his stomach called out for attention.

The drive had taken a little under eight hours nonstop from New York City. Billie his secretary didn't even question him when he told her that he was going to Maine to look for Jack Kahill. She knew that trying to talk him out of it was of no use and that once he put his mind to it there was no stopping him. So when he told her he was going after Jack she responded. "Be careful, I'll forward your calls and check in when you can."

It had been a long drive and he knew that he needed a shower. Being awake for nearly twenty-four hours he felt his eyes burning but it was nothing he told himself. It was nothing when lives are in your hands.

He had been awake in a fox hole in the jungles of Vietnam with three other men for three days fighting for his life and the life of his comrades. Low on ammunition and rations in one hundred degree temperature and humidity, facing an enemy coming at him from all angles, he fought off hunger, thirst and death.

As he emerged from the car he had to shake out his legs to get the blood flowing and stop them from vibrating.

The sign on the door read Green Lantern, Monson's best breakfast open 5AM. He could smell bacon frying and he heard his stomach growl.

He made a quick assessment of his surroundings. An old faded Greyhound bus sign hung askew on one chain from a lamp post banging in the breeze on a top corner of an old phone booth. Mike could see what he thought might be a payphone still in the booth and an old phone book lying on the counter. He walked up to the booth pushing open the folding door. It fought back on rusted hinges and he had to kick at the bottom panel. It was obvious that no one had used this phone booth in a long time. Inside he found the phone missing only the casing remained. He grabbed the phone book and placed it on the passenger seat of his car. This was a good working library of information if need be.

There were two other cars in the parking lot and through the dirt stained café window he could see the silhouette of four people seated at tables near the door and two seated at the counter. Behind the counter all he could see was a large blur moving back and forth. He looked up and down the street and saw nothing other than an old filling station that looked like it might be abandoned except for an old tow truck parked in front. Except for three roads that split from the main road, the road seemed to go on forever into nothing in both directions.

He sucked on his teeth. Well this is it he told himself. It's this or nothing.

The bells on the door announced his arrival and at once he felt out of place. There were only two tables to sit at near the door and they were occupied by two couples with backpacks that looked like they hadn't showered in days.

The counter had a dozen seats to choose from and there was what looked like two dirt farmers sitting there. One was a very tall man and quite slim. Mike thought he looked malnourished. And the other was short and stumpy looking like he was eating for the both. As the door closed behind him all of a dozen eye balls fixed on him.

He smelled a real funk coming from the table of the four people seated near the door as he walked past. An odd mixture of wet mud and fresh cut grass hung in the air among the table it was the unmistakable smell of marijuana that stuck out most. He could see eyes divert quickly as he passed.

Reaching the counter, he paused for a moment thinking this might be a bad idea. And as he stood there he realized he must look like a sore thumb dressed in a suit and tie. He locked eyes with the cook standing behind the counter giving him the once over.

"Have a seat pal. No need to be shy here. Can I take your order?" Said a man wearing a filthy apron as he walked by carrying a pot of coffee.

Mike found himself looking at a human grease ball. There before him stood a big burley man with an apron on that was covered in a canvas of multi encrusted new and old stains. The apron barely fit around the pot belly of the man and he wore an overly exaggerated paper hat that he obviously made himself from used grocer bags. It had burn holes in it at different places. Under the apron he wore overalls like the two dirt farmers at the end of the counter.   Except for the hat he looked more like a garage mechanic then a short order cook. This is probably going to kill me he thought.

How bad could eggs and toast be? He asked himself.

Mike sat at the counter the eyes of the room were still on him.

"How's the coffee?" He asked.

The man filled a cup placed it in front of Mike and then disappeared into the kitchen.

"Best around for a mile." The man shouted out from somewhere in the kitchen. "Don't be shy just yell out what you want." He added.

Mike took a long hard gulp of coffee. Not bad, he thought before he noticed the cup had many chips along the rim and he wondered if he should continue drinking.

"I'll have a couple scrambled eggs and some toast." He yelled back.

He thought about asking for another cup, but looking up at the shelves along the back wall, he could see that none of the chinaware matched any of the others and most if not, all had chips in them.

He was just about to call out to the kitchen when an argument broke out between the two dirt farmers seated at the far end of the counter.

"You cheated last time." The bigger man said as he poked a finger into the chest of the other man.

"Well you want a rematch let's do it." The small man answered pushing his way past the taller man and coming to a stop directly behind Mike.

Mikes ears went up like a Doberman. His eyes widened, and adrenalin pumped through his chest. He could just make out the figure standing behind him in the reflection of the dirty mirror on the wall behind the counter. He never liked someone standing behind him. It always made for a bad situation.

Mike immediately tried to swivel on the seat, but it didn't move. He knew the last place he wanted to be was in the middle of a fight if it was to break out.

He turned about as quickly as he could and when he stood he towered above the man standing there by a foot. He had to look down to see the small man standing there holding a pool cue.

"Listen friend just take it easy." Mike felt for his waist revolver.

The little man followed his movements with his eyes. He caught the reflected light off the silver handle of the pistol. His eyes widening and then squinting like a cat.

" Whoa... hold on their mister no trouble here we're only playing pool." He pointed over his shoulder.

Seeing what was about to happen, the backpackers abruptly got up from the table and without finishing their meal left money on the table making a beeline for the exit.

"I was just going to ask you if would referee our game."

"Why me?" Mike asked tapping his fingers on the handle of his revolver.

This time Lester but in. "Well you look like someone who could be trusted. But to be honest with you, you're kind of like the only one here."

Mike shook his head no.

Lester could see the frown on the big man's face and decided to say nothing more.

This could have gotten ugly real fast. Mike thought. He had killed people for less of a movement in the dark jungles of Vietnam.

"No, no thanks. I'm just going to try to have some breakfast." He said pushing past the two men. "Point me to the rest room."

Ernie pointed to the far end of the counter. "It's just around the corner there."

Mike opened the door of the rest room and was hit with an aroma of fresh lavender. A soft music played from speakers in the ceiling. The room was immaculate in cleanliness and could have easily been mistaken for one found in the finest hotels in New York City. He wondered if he had walked through a portal and into another reality. The floor sparkled and the knobs on the sink shown in a gold brilliance. He couldn't see a speck of dust anywhere. How the hell can this be when the rest of the place looks like death warmed over?

He checked his reflection in the mirror. His eyes were blood shot and he looked tired. He pulled the gun from its holster and placed it atop the sink shelf. He quickly turned the lock of the door and went about washing and drying his face with a fresh towel. He picked up his revolver from the counter opened it went about checking the chambers, counting six bullets. "Hello old friend." He said clicking it shut and securing the safety. He put it back it its holster glad he didn't have to use it. When he reappeared at the counter he was met by the cook placing a plate of food in front of him.

Ernie and Lester were heavily engaged in the pool game arguing with each other and paid no attention to him.

"Listen you two leave the man be." The cook placed the plate of eggs, toast and spam in front of Mike.

"Lester you and Ernie go about your game and let the fellow have his breakfast. Pay them no mind mister they're always fighting over a pool game."

Mike took a bite of the undercooked eggs and poked at the gray square blob on the plate pushing it to the side. Not since Vietnam had he eaten spam and after eating it for months he despised it.

He took a bite of the toast when the word... pool table...registered in his mind. Pool table? He spun in his seat just in time to see Ernie breaking a set of balls on a long table. And surrounding the pool table he could see long folding tables with dust covered wood carved figurines of moose in every kind of stance. He instantly felt mad with himself. How could he have missed seeing this when he walked in? It stuck out there like a sore thumb on the left side of the room. Need to be more careful he thought. Being unobservant just in the slightest was enough to get himself or his buddies killed. But that was a long time ago in a different place and a different time. Yet he prided himself in being fearless in the face of danger and ready to act if the situation warranted.

"More coffee?" The cook stood holding the pot watching Mike as he fished out a note pad from his inside suit pocket placing it on the counter.

"Yes please." Mike held up the chipped cup.

Mike sat at the counter and opened his note book thumbing through a few photos pulling the one of Jack Kahill out and turned it, so the cook could see it.

"Let me ask you something, have you ever seen this man?"

The cook fished out a pair of glasses hanging on a long chain he had tucked in his shirt and placed it on his nose. The chains dangled near his ear lobes.

"You a bounty hunter?" The cook asked pushing the glasses further up his nose.

"Nope." Mike added nothing more studying the cooks face for a reaction.

"No, I don't think so. You want me to ask Ernie and Lester over there?"

"No." Mike answered taking back the photo.

"Wait a second let me see that again. Yeah that's it. The name, I know that name well, at least the last name is familiar. Yea Kahill there was a lady who used to come in here. I haven't seen her in years. She had a small cabin up near the trail near Blanchard."

Mike wrote it all in his book.

"She would come in here with a little boy. Is that him?

"I don't know."

"I understand that there was an orphanage around here."Mike asked.

"Yeah but it's been closed now for years yet I think there is still a care taker there. It's on the other side of Monson pond.

Mike turned a page in his book. "And there is an undertaker here that has a long family history to the area."

"Yeah, Montgomery Barry second generation. They have been here almost a hundred years. Taken care of everyone's funeral and yours truly when the time comes. "Like my father said, life causes death, so you need to be careful." He laughed. "But if you don't mine my asking what this is all about?"

Mike looked him straight in the eyes and he felt a coldness run straight into his bones he knew he was at the end of the line and shouldn't ask any more questions.

"All I can tell you is its important I find this guy. The sooner the better."

"Well pardon me; I got something to check on in the kitchen. Take your time and if you need anything else just shout it out."

Mike waved him off. He heard the doorbell chime and turned to see the two pool players leaving still arguing about their earlier pool game.

In the kitchen the cook dialed the phone that hung on the back wall. His hand shook as he punched the numbers as quickly as he could. It was into its tenth ring and he was about to hang up when he heard the unmistakable low growl of a hello.

"Hay Monty it's me Pete from the dinner. Listen I got a guy here looks like a detective with a thick New York accent asking a lot of question hot on the tail of a fugitive. He mentioned you and your family just thought you should know in case he comes snooping around."

"What type of questions?" Montgomery's ears perked up.

"Well he seemed especially interested in finding a guy named Jack Kahill."

"Kahill you say?"

"Yeah I don't know the guy but the name Kahill rings a bell. I kind of remember a lady who used to come around years ago. I think Maggie or Mary Kahill. If my memory is right she had that little cabin near Blanchard."

"Thank you, Henry I'll handle, it." He answered.

"Oh, and thank you again for handling Helen's funeral."

It had been eight months ago that Pete's wife had passed away after a long battle with cancer and Montgomery's funeral home was hired to handle the arrangements.

"Oh, you're welcome Pete." Montgomery answered hanging up the phone.

Montgomery couldn't hold it in any longer and he burst out laughing. "Jackass." He said. It was almost eight months ago to the day that he sold Helen's body to a cadaver school in

Portland for thee thousand dollars claiming she was an unknown. He then went about gathering horse manure from Lester Mansfield's farm and filled the coffin with it to give it the proper body weight. He was most proud of the fact that he charged Pete seven thousand dollars for the funeral. Her picture hung lonely staring at the other victims on the cold dark walls of the dead gallery on Montgomery's wall of death. A beautiful gold broach hung from a tack below her picture that Montgomery cut with wire cutters from her neck before changing her into ragged clothing when the school picked up the body.

Mike took back the photo and slid it between the pages of his note book placing it back into his pocket.

"Is there a hotel around here maybe a place where a fellow can get a shower?"

"Na… the closest place is down in Bangor about sixty miles south. But if you don't care too much about comfort you can get a night's sleep at that hiker hostel those backpackers were headed to. They got a shower there. It's pretty much the only game in town. It's an old church at the far end of town hidden back some ways from the road. It's called Ken's place. If you like, I'll write down the directions."

Mike agreed. "Well what do I owe you for breakfast?"

The cook handed him the directions. "Eggs and coffee that's five bucks."

Mike placed a ten-dollar bill in the counter and folded the directions into his pocket.

"Thanks, keep the change." He said over his shoulder as he got up and walked out.

Outside the fog had lifted and the sun was shining brightly in the sky. The air was crisp and clean. Mike took in a deep breath. It was a wonderful smell of fresh pine.

Seated in the car he immediately started thumbing through the old phone book first looking up the name Kahill but found nothing. He knew from experience that just because the name was a dead end in the phone book didn't necessarily mean that there were not family members still living in the area. Then licking his finger, he quickly turned pages, stopping at an ad for the Montgomery Barry funeral home and tore out the page. If what the cook had said was true and the Barry family had been in the area for nearly a hundred years the information they knew about the Kahill Family might come in handy. In his pad he wrote: start with SUNNY SIDE ORPHANAGE. #2 MONTGOMERY BARRY FUNERAL HOME, #3 TOWN HALL RECORDS ...if this town had a town hall and records. But that was a last possibility. He wasn't ready to announce his intentions to the local authorities especially since he was way out of his jurisdiction.

He let out a sigh and wiped his face in his hands, his eyes were getting blurry and he suddenly felt drained. He started the car fishing out the directions from his pocket for Ken's Place.

Two miles up the road he stopped. There in front of him stood an old dilapidated church at the end of winding dirt drive way. The path in had more pot holes to navigate around then bombed out roads he remembered seeing in Vietnam. Window shutters were missing slats and paint was peeling off the building. It looked like it was listing to two sides at once and at any moment would burst at the seams like a cracked egg giving up on life. Yet around it the area was filled with life. People were moving all around it like a giant swam of ants. Hammocks were being strung between trees and people were setting up tents on the grassy flat spots if front.

He eased the car into a spot under a pine tree at the far end of the property away from the swarm of activity.

He reached grabbing a small duffel bag he had packed earlier from the back seat and made his way to the front entrance of the church. No one paid him any mind as he walked by.

Mike stood there for a moment gazing at the elaborate ornate arched doors. They were massive in size. He guessed maybe oak, a half foot thick and ten foot tall. Surely, they would out live the decaying church. Mike used very little force to push them open and was surprised how easily they opened for their size. They made no noise. Once inside he could see that time was no kinder to its passing of inside then it was of the outside.

Many of the old church pews were missing or perhaps taken out on purpose as the back of the church now could accommodate a dance floor. Mike counted three rows of pews, but the oddest thing was that there seemed to be temporary dividers of shower curtains or tarps of various sizes suspended from cords strung between the beams along the ceiling as to make small individual rooms. Ceiling fans hung low from the rafters none of them were moving. One hung low falling on its side looking like a propeller he had seen on an old prop plane a long time ago. All were covered in a paste of crocheted cobwebs. Two people at the far end of the room were unfolding chairs and placing them facing each other about the room.

He walked towards the sanctuary the echo of his footsteps followed him, reverberating magnificently in the half empty vestibule. It was empty of it's alter and replaced by four folding chairs. A door was strewn between them and a sleeping bag lay on top the door. All of it was worse looking than any of the military refugee camps he had seen in Vietnam.

Mike turned around and fifty feet away he could just about make out seeing a man with a long beard standing there in the subdued light.

"Hello there." He shouted." His voice echoed back from three different directions.

"I'm Ken, and welcome to Kens place." The man with the beard said in a heavy New England accent. He held a hand out as he walked toward Mike. Mike had to strain to understand what the old man was saying.

"A man ...ere going to be sleeping ...ere with his wife." He pointed to the four chairs with the door suspended between them. "We gona give them some privy when we finish stringing this...ere shower curtain."

"Well what I could really use is a shower at the moment."Mike said extending his hand.

Ken griped Mike's hand firmly it felt like a bear claw surrounding his small hand. Mike saw a tattoo that he recognized at once.

"SEMPER FI" Mike said as he let go of the man's grip.

"Yeah Korea." Ken said smiling.

"NAM, Hanoi Hilton." Mike answered pulling up his sleeve showing Ken his tattoo. "We'll have to get together and compare notes later."

"Sure, sure. Now the showers are in the back... der. A dollar fifty and you'll find a clean towel in the cupboard next to it. I'm afraid all the cots are taken, backpacking season ya know. For a dollar you can crash out on one of the pews if you wish."

Mike handed him a five-dollar bill and told him to keep the change. He placed his bag on an empty pew at the far end of the room staking out his claim. He opened his bag and pulled out a change of clothing and walked toward where Ken had pointed he would find the shower.

"Hey partner, making ca...der for the evening meal join us later if you like. I only charge a buck a cup."

"I think I'll do that." Mike answered as he stepped outside first finding the towel locker in a small room next to the shower. He pulled the clip holster from his waist band wrapping the gun in a towel and shoving into a far corner rafter space.

When he got outside he found two old stalls that reminded him of the shower arrangements in camp in Vietnam. They were nothing more than four walls of plywood nailed together at the corners, a pallet board to stand on and copper piping plumbed in with hot and cold faucet knobs and a shower head. One had a man inside bobbing up and down and spinning slowly in circles with long Rastafarian hair singing loudly what Mike recognized as an old bob Marley tune. In the other was a beautiful blond-haired woman wrapping a towel around her and shutting off the water.

He smiled as she open the door and walked past him leaving behind a trail of fresh honeysuckle.

Just my luck he thought as he stepped inside the small booth. It had just enough space to hang clothing on without getting them wet. He wished he had kept the gun on him, so he could shoot Bob Marley in the next booth to make him shut up.

Mike welcomed the hot water on his aging bones and he wished he could just sand in the stream for an hour. But he was worried if someone was to find the gun. He toweled off quickly and put on a polo shirt and kakis. Leaving he found a line of backpackers waiting to go in. He was glad to find the gun where he had left it undisturbed and clipped it back onto his waist band pulling his shirt over it. Coffee was on his mind and he went back into the church to find Ken.

It took some time for his eyes to adjust and he was glad he didn't walk forward into a closed door. He opened the door and smiled recognizing the trail of fresh coffee brewing. He followed the trail and found Ken in a small modern kitchen. He could see pots on a stove and Ken chopping vegetables on a table next to them.

"Hope you don't mind but I couldn't resist. This old soldier loves his coffee."

"No not at all there is a cup on the counter behind you help yourself to a cup of Joe, cream and sugar… deir, Coffee around here is free for vets." Ken pointed with the knife out the window. "Those hippies outside don't want anything to do with it. They want me to get one of those fancy schmancy latte machines you know what it tell them …fuck off."

Mike laughed. "Black is good." He said filling the cup. "Mississippi mud." He knew the old vet would know exactly what he meant.

Ken nodded. "Yep likewise." He stopped cutting vegetables and came up next to Mike grabbing a cup and filling it with black coffee. "Well I've been thinking about this. You don't look like a backpacker. So, what brings a man up here from New York?"

"My heavy accent gave it away?" Mike asked.

"Well …a little now that you mention it. But no, I saw your car as you came up the drive. We don't too many people driving in. I saw the plates. You a cop?"

"Not exactly." He answered. Letting the question die.

"Well you look like a cop. But it's none of my concern."

"What I can tell you is I'm looking for someone who's on the run." Mike pulled out the book from his back pocket and handed Ken the photo of Jack Kahill. "I know he has or had family in this area and there is a good likely hood that he's going to show up here in town."

"I've been in this town for eighty-five years and if there is one thing you get to know is the name of the people around you. Now I'll tell you the first name and the photo of the man I don't know, but the second name I know it well. Kahill... yea use to be a woman come around town. Lived up near Blanchard a small cabin there. She was kind of sweet back in the day if you know what I mean but she didn't want anything to do with an ex GI with no money and not too many prospects." Ken held his arms open wide pointing at the four walls around him. Ken studied the photo.

 "So, this is the guy you're looking for?"

"Yeah." Mike answered taking back the photo. "Well I'm going to take a ride out there and see what I can find. Think I'll check out the orphanage fist. Maybe you like to come along and show me where I can find this cabin."

"I'm sorry but if I left this place now them hippies outside would overrun the place. It's not much but it's all I got. I wouldn't bother with the orphanage it's been closed now for years only an old caretaker out there attending to the place. But I can draw you a map."

Ken got out a pen and some paper from a cabinet and drew out the directions.

"The road is not far about a mile out of town you'll see the BARRY FUNERAL HOME on a hill take a right on that road and go past the cemetery about a mile past you'll see a really old looking second cemetery. My father is buried there. Once you past that there will be and old dirt road on the right take that road about a half mile and the cabin should be set back in the woods you can't miss it." Ken handed him the map.

"Thanks, mind if I take a cup of Joe for the ride?"

"I'll give you a paper cup with a lid, so you don't spill it all over yourself. Last I was up that road it could rattle your denatures loose."

CHAPTER19

TRUTH'S BE TOLD

When Jack came out of the bathroom Sara and Millie burst out laughing. "You're going to make a lovely bride." Sara said wiping away tears from her eyes.

Jack tried to turn around, but Sara caught his arm. She could see the smirk look on his face. "Now take it easy, this has got to work if were to get you out of here."

"I'm not putting on a bra." He said.

Jack stood there wearing the dress Millie brought and tried to adjust the wig on his head, but it kept blocking his vision.

"Here let me fix that." Sara stuck a Bobbie pin into the wig, nicking Jacks scalp.

"Ouch."

"Hold still." She said pushing back the hair from his face. Stepping back, she saw that the dress was just long enough to cover his boots. "There, that's perfect." She said.

"You two be careful out there and check in with me when you get to Maine. I'll hold down the fort here until you get back." Millie grabbed the bag with the maps and placed it near the door.

At the door Sara turned to Jack. "I'll go out first and you follow behind me. My car is just around the side of the building. I'll get the car and bring it in front of the building and then you come up."

Jack nodded his head yes.

Sara grabbed his pack and the map bag and walked out the door pausing momentarily at the top step. Looking left the right she saw no one there. She motioned for Jack to follow along.

Jack came up the steps and as he reached the top step the dress caught under his boot. He tried to stop but his forward motion relented to the force of gravity and he fell forward into the back of Sara knocking her to the ground sending them both rolling like a human ball into the street.

Sara bit her tongue as she forced herself not to scream out in pain when she landed on her elbow. Blood quickly filled her mouth.

Jack quickly scrambled to his feet and grabbed Sara around her waist righting her on the pavement.

"You ok?" He asked gathering up the bags.

"I'm fine." She answered dusting away the dirt from her knee.

Fear started pumping through Jack's veins. He could see a patrol car turning on to the street, not more than three blocks away. He froze not knowing what to do.

Sara caught the panic look on his face and turned to see the approaching car. She squeezed Jack's hand pulling him in the direction of her car.

"Come on Jack focus, we can do this there is still time."

At that moment she saw lights turn on and heard a siren began to whale.

Ten feet from the car she hit the key bob and the trunk popped open. Jack tossed the bags into the trunk from three feet away spilling the bags contents into the space. Sara turned the key in the ignition and the car immediately fired up. She clicked the gear shift into drive and pressed the accelerator to the floor. Jacks head shaped back against the head rest and he dug his nails hard into the seat to hold on. The car kicked up rocks as it left the alleyway and fishtailed onto the street. Sara could see that the light up ahead had just turned red and the cop car with is light flashing and siren blaring raced through it. She slowed to a stop thinking to go through the red light. Jack froze in his seat biting down on the inside of his cheek. He could feel his body tense and the beginning of a panic attack fighting him. Hold it together he thought. He split the image in his mind one eye straight ahead on to what he hoped was the open road and the other on the approaching end of the line, hand cuffs and another lengthy prison sentence.

Sara tapped her hand on the steering wheel "Come on, come on." She said. "Light change let's go." But time slowed to a crawl. Jack watched it all in slow motion. "Hold on!" She shouted.

"NO!" Jack yelled back.

Through the window Jack could see the patrol car as it pulled up to their driver side window. The officers face almost pressing up to the glass and the officer mouthing some word that didn't seem to register.

Then suddenly in front of him through the one eye focused on the future he saw it. There a burr quickly came into focus. The light changed Sara was about to go. When Jack was able to yell out... "Car!" Through the red light a car spinning almost on two wheels, came around the corner clipping the tail end of the patrol car and pushing it into Sara's, denting her door. With one eye on the rear-view mirror, Jack watched the car continue racing down the street like a bat out of hell.

Sara now had the green light and was about to go. Jack cleared the two images out of his mind and focused his attention now on Sara.

"Waite!" He yelled. She turned toward Jack with a puzzled look on her face. "WHY?" She asked.

"Just wait a second, you'll see." Jack grabbed her wrist.

Two seconds later a patrol car with lights flashing and siren blaring came screaming around the corner in hot pursuit of the first car.

"What the hell?" She screamed. "Holy shit, how did you know?"

"I don't know it's just sometimes I can feel what's going to happen before it happens."

The officer next to their car rolled up his window not giving Jack or Sara a second look and took off in hot pursuit on the tail of the feeing cars.

"Why do you think they were asking if we were okay and not getting out of the car to take us into custody?"

Jack flipped the hair back from the side of his face. "I guess they just wanted to see if we gals were okay." They both laughed as the traffic light turned green and Sara gently tapped on the accelerator.

"This is going to be an interesting ride." She said.

Jack nodded his head. The wig blocked his view. "When can I take this dam thing off?"

"Wait until we're across the George Washington Bridge. If they don't follow us by then they are not going to."

Jack fought to focus all his attention on the road ahead of him and not the panic attack. The sun was peeking out between swift moving clouds among a changing front line. "Looks like rain soon." He said. The ride across the bridge was smooth and traffic was light.

"Sunday is a good time to drive." She said.

Jack had his eyes closed crossing the bridge. This was the first time he had no control of where he was going and especially how he was going to get there. But, he felt confident in Sara's ability in driving the total distance. The way she handled the car not long ago was a good indication.

"You can take that wig off now." She turned to Jack seeing that he had his eyes closed. "You okay?" She asked.

Jack took a deep breath. Pulling off the wig and tossing it into the back seat.

"Let's just say I'm not a big fan of high bridges." He reached under the seat and pulled the seat lever pushing the seat back as far as it would go with his legs.

Sara watched Jack in the cramped space of the passenger seat contort into something resembling a circus act. He looked like a butterfly morphing out of its cocoon as he went about trying to birth himself out of the dress.

"When you want, let's find a place for some coffee and we can check the maps." He said.

"Should I stay with the highways or should we detour onto the back roads?" She asked.

"Well I don't think that anyone is following us and seeing as how we got five hundred and fifty miles to go I'd say let's put some miles behind us." Jack reached for the radio controls. "What will it be music or news?"

"Neither, how about we finish some of the questions we started last night before all this went crazy?"

Jack adjusted the seat back to almost a lying position. "Okay with me." He answered. "I'll try to tell you what I know, if you don't mind doing the same."

Sara nodded yes.

The road ahead was wide open, and the weather changed for the better. Sara smiled seeing the blue sky with light puffy white clouds. Jack sat across from her and began to whistle BORN TO BE WILD.

"Wow that's horrible." She laughed and started singing the song. Jack stopped whistling and quickly joined in.

Jack gazed out the window seeing the sign: WELCOME TO CONNECUTE. The song slowly faded as Sara turned off the high way and into a rest stop. "Pit stop time." She announced with a frown realizing that they never got to the part of answering any questions.

She eased the car slowly through the parking lot. At the front entrance Sara could see a large man standing there in full state police uniform looking like SMOKY THE BEAR. "Let's try the side entrance." She said.

"Sounds good to me." Jack agreed.

"Do you think they could have sent out a what do you call it....?"

"A... APB." Jack finished. "Let's split up I'll go in fist. You get the maps out of the trunk. Inside pretend you don't know me. Get what you want, and we'll meet back at the car in fifteen minutes."

Sara was heading out the door when Jack grabbed her arm. "If any happens just keep going." Sara nodded, shutting the door and walked to the back of the car. "Be careful." She said, but Jack was too far away to hear her.

Jack could see a set of double doors ahead and he kept his head down as he approached. The first door was heavy, and it took some force to open. When his hand reached out to open the second door he missed the handle as a large figure appeared from the other side pulling the door open. Jack had to wait as the man backed up making room for him to pass. He felt his heart skip a beat. He didn't have to look up. He recognized what he was looking at. He had seen it a thousand times before in lock up. He saw his reflection in the highly polished shoes and there was no mistaking the crisp razor sharp pleated pants belonging to a police officer. He felt a lump in his throat and swallowed hard, turning to look up.

"Good morning." The Marine said holding the door for Jack.

Jack stood there frozen every bone in his body tensed up and he couldn't move. He burst out laughing he was sure he was done for. He could see the Marine's eyes widen and an expression of confusion on his face. Quickly Jack split the image in his mind. One eye he kept on the Marine and the other he scanned the room. The only thing he saw was a small lunch crowd and another Marine seated at a table next to the door.

"SEMPER FI" Jack said. The MARINE nodded smiling back at Jack. "Follow me. Let me get you guys a cup of Joe."

"Thank you, sir." The MARINE'S followed Jack to the STAR BUCKS.

What better way to hide, thought Jack then to hide in plain sight. Who would think to take a second look at him surrounded by Marines?

From the far side of the room he could see Sara making a purchase at a bagel shop. She turned making eye contact with him. She had a startled look on her face. Jack winked but wasn't sure if she saw it. But she gave a slight nod in response. He could see that she had finished her purchase and was now heading back to the car. He wanted to call out to her but kept quiet. He hoped that she didn't misunderstand what was taking place and get in the car and take off. He guessed the time that had passed was not more than ten munities and if he hurried he still had time to relieve himself. He purchased three cups of coffee handing two to the Marines. Thanking the Marines for their service, he took leave of them and went about finding the rest room.

Stopping at the sink he turned on the cold water faucet and splashed his face. Looking up at the mirror he was aghast at his reflection. He looked horribly thin and older. Crow's feet had taken up residence near his eyes and the hair at his temples was now full on gray. CHRIST, I look like a homeless person he thought. He quickly washed his face and ran a comb in the stream fixing his hair.

Leaving the rest room, he was surprised to see the two MARINES standing there speaking to a state police officer. Jack froze he could hear the seconds ticking off in his head. He was sure that he wouldn't get past the officer. He slowly glided along the wall in an attempt to get away.

"Sir." Jack heard it loud and clear.

He thought about running but instead came to a dead stop. Then he heard something else coming from a distance.

"Come on honey we have to go."Sara called out.

Jack split the images in his mind and moved his right eye slightly like a chameleon to make out the image of Sara standing buy the door waving him in.

218

Again, he heard "Sir. Just wanted to thank you again for the coffees."

The Marine held out his hand. Jack shook it and said nothing. The police officer paid no attention to Jack. Just then he felt a hand grab his arm and pull him.

"We got to go now dear." Sara said smiling at the men as she led Jack toward the door.

Sara fired up the car and slowly backed it out of the parking spot. She eased onto the highway as two police cars went flying past her, lights and sirens blaring. She handed Jack the maps and a bag with a bagel in it. "What the hell was that all about back there?"

Jack took a bite of the bagel. "I was hiding in plain sight." He mumbled.

"Yeah that seemed to be working out well." She rolled her eyes.

"I thought I told you to take off without me." He said. "What happened?"

"Well seeing you standing there frozen like that, I had to do something."

"I'm glad you did." Jack said smiling at her.

"Besides you never asked me what my plan was. We do this together or we don't do it at all now shut up check the directions and eat your bagel."

"Yes, ma'am." Jack answered, taking another bite of the bagel and unfolding the map.

Traffic picked up and Sara slowed the car to adjust. A mile more and the traffic came to a crawl. Cars were backed up as far as she could see. Slowly they inched forward and saw a state trooper standing in the road pointing cars onto the shoulder. Ahead a car was on fire in wreckage with a tractor trailer. Police and fire crews were running about the area.

Jack closed his eyes as they passed he had already seen too much and instead tried to focus his mind on the beautiful blue sky they had been experiencing. He choked on the smell of the fire as they drove by. Black smoke, smelling like burnt rubber, filled the road.

Sara looked at the wrecked car as they drove by. Suddenly, she saw two children standing there. Their clothing was completely burned. "Why is no one helping them?" She yelled startling Jack.

"Who are you talking about?" Jack looked seeing no one there.

"The two children standing there." She answered.

"What children? What are you seeing?" He asked.

"The two... oh..." She stopped. This was a new development. Entities came to her all the time, but she had never experienced them at the exact moment of their death.

Sara didn't answer and drove on until she found a road side rest area a mile away with picnic tables and benches. She parked the car and got out not waiting for Jack and went to sit at one of the tables.

When Jack approached he found her shaking and sobbing uncontrollably. He sat down next to her and put his arms around her holding her close.

"I've seen a lot of things." She began. "But I've never seen anything like that before. They were burnt beyond recognition. We need to go back."

"What why?"Jack shook his head.

"They will be stuck standing there forever if we don't. I've got to help them cross over." She started to get up and Jack pulled her back.

"We can't."Jack answered. "There is too much traffic, besides how are you going to explain to the authorities standing there

221

that you wanted to get out of your car and conduct some kind of voodoo magic in an effort to help the people cross over. Do you know how crazy that sounds? They might let me go but they will lock you up for sure. Please trust me on this Sara you can't put this on your shoulders. You can't have the responsibility of having to help everyone. There are, and always will be, situations that are out of your control."

"But, they are so young." She cried.

"It's out of your hands." He said. Jack went back to the car and grabbed her coffee handing it to her that now had become cold. "Drink this." He said.

"I helped you." She sobbed.

"Yes, I know." He said.

Shaking her head. "No, you don't. I'm not talking about the cops. I'm talking about the two people you had attached to you when you showed up."

"What are you talking about? What people?" Jack's eyes widened.

Sara could see the confused look on Jack's face.

"The other night before and after the séance two people showed up standing outside in the shadows. They looked like they were in an accident. They had on ragged clothing and were completely covered in blood. Their presence became stronger when you showed up. I crossed them over. Did you know them?"

"Yeah." He answered. "I mean no. I did not know them. They could be the people from the accident the other night. But, why would they follow me?"

"Sounds about right. Sometimes they attach to the last person they see. Why? I'm not sure of yet. But they followed you and if I didn't cross them over they could have followed you forever. You might or might not have ever noticed it. "

"That would be the last thing I need. The horror of seeing it all and living through it imprinted an image in my mind that will play like a bad movie forever haunting me."Jack wiped his face in his hands.

"Wait a minute." She said. "That was the man who gave you the envelope to give to me." Sara had a puzzled look on her face.

Tears welted up in Jacks eyes and after a long pause he swallowed hard. "Yes." He answered. "I'm sorry."

Sara got up and paced back and forth. She walked back standing in front of Jack with her hands in the air. "How the hell is this possible?" She asked. "I'm certainly sorry for the people in the accident but I'm glad I crossed them over. Truth be told, I don't know how I feel about it. I never knew the man. I think we need to compare our notes and finish that conversation we started the other night."

Sara seated herself across the picnic table from Jack. "If we are going to do this we put all our cards on the table, nothing held back." She stuck her hand across the table and Jack took hold of her hand.

"You saved my ass twice. I owe you that much. Agreed." He said. "What I told you the other night was the truth. I never saw those people before. The old man before he died gave me that envelope to give to you. That's all I know."

Sara took out the envelope from her jacket, opened it and spread it out between them on the table.

Jack copied her and placed his letter next to it.

Sara burst out in tears when she saw that the two letters both were stained with blood. "What happen to the people who penned this letter and what was their life like?"

Sara picked up her letter handing it to Jack. "You better read this again."

Jack picked up the letter and if it wasn't signed and addressed to Sara he could swear that it was the same letter penned by his grandmother.

When he finished he sat there for what seemed like a long time just staring at Sara with his mouth agape.

With tears streaming down her face Sara rocked back and forth on her seat repeating over and over "How can this be? Strange forces are at work here. I felt it the moment you walked in."

Jack folded the letter stuffing it back into the envelope and pushed it across the table to Sara. He pulled out his wallet and fished out an old cracked black and white photo, its corners bent. "Other than that letter this is all I have to remember my childhood with my grandmother." Jack handed the photo to her.

Sara's hands trembled as she studied the photo. "Where did you get this?" She asked.

"What do you mean?" Jack took back the photo studying it.

The photo showed Jack seated on his grandmother's lap on the porch of her cabin in Maine. In one arm she's caressing Jack and in the other she held a book she was reading to him. But, there was something more that Jack never paid any attention to. In

225

the background, a small figure of a little girl stood watching the whole thing from the shadows of the cabin doorway.

Sara got up and came to sit along-side of Jack on the bench. She tapped at the photo. Choking on her words she managed to say. "That's me."

Jack dropped the photo on the table. "What are you talking about?"

"I remember that cabin. My father would take us there to stay with this kind old lady when he had to go on business trips. I remember this little boy crying hysterically as men in suits came one day and took him away. I never knew why, and I never seen him again. My mother died sometime after that and I lived with my dad and his new wife growing up in New York City." Jack put his arm around her shoulder. "It's too late now to ask them anything. They died some years ago sub- coming to cancer."

"How do you remember any of this you were so young? I, on the other hand remember nothing and if I didn't have this photo and the stories from my grandmother I would know none of it."

Sara reached out and grabbed Jacks hand squeezing it tight. "Our grandmother." She whispered.

Stunned, Jack sat there and shook his head up and down. "My letter says of my having a sister that I never knew. You don't suppose?"

Now Sara shook her head up and down with a Cheshire cat smile on her face. "You're looking at her." She said waving her fingers in the air above her.

"But what about the little boy?" The letter from my grandmother says that she put a key in the coffin and that it was buried with him. Jack swallowed hard. "You know what we have to do."

Sara shrugged her shoulders. "I don't know anything about him, nor do I get any kind of feeling."

Jack was about to question her when he realized what Sara had meant. "Oh, that voodoo stuff." He said.

"I wish you wouldn't say it like that."

"I'm sorry." He said. "It's just that this it too much to take in. I'm sure that if we go to her old cabin maybe there we can find the answers to all of this."

Sara was already ahead of him when she called back over her shoulder. "Only way to find out is we got to get to Maine.

Jack closed the car door as Sara pulled back onto the high way. "You know what we have to do." He said.

Sara felt a cold chill run up her spine. "Yeah." She answered. "Buy a shovel."

Four hours after comparing notes Jack found himself waking cramped in his seat. He adjusted the seat to the up-rite position grabbed a water bottle from the cup holder and splashed a little on to his hands wiping his face.

"Where are we?" He asked

"Near Portland." She answered.

"Wow how long have I been asleep?"

"You've been snoring for well over four hours."

"At the next opportunity let's stop. I need to stretch, and we can get some food."

"Yeah we need some gas and according to the maps we are going to turn off the highway a few miles ahead and I was thinking it would be a good time to switch up."

"Switch up? What do you mean?" Jack asked with a panic look on his face.

"I need some rest from driving. So, you can take over."

"Are you crazy? Jack frowned.

"Take a good look around." Sara pointed out the window. "Its mid afternoon and the only thing I've seen for the last hundred miles are woods and mountains."

Jack looked out the window and as far as he could see around him was a birch and maple forest, thick and dark. He rolled down the window the air was crisp and fresh.

Irrational or not, he had the constant fear that just around the next turn would be a waiting police car just itching to pull over out- of -towners to pounce on like a tiger eager for its next meal victim.

He bit on the inside of his tattered cheek holding it there between his teeth. He ran his fingers through his hair and felt the stubble now thick on his face. A hot shower would be welcoming but that felt like a million miles away.

The only thing he heard was the droning of the tires echoing off the pavement as they drove along. The road was lifeless except for an occasional tractor trailer passing southbound full of fresh timbered logs headed to a mill. The road followed along route 2 northbound and at times coming close to the Kennebec River.

When they reached an overlook at the top of a hill Jack urged Sara to pull over and stop so he could urinate. Sara guided the car over the double line in the middle of the road stopped the car pulling under a tall oak tree at the edge of the overlook. Jack got out and ducked into the thicket of weeds and overgrowth. When Jack came back out he found Sara not at the car. He quickly looked left and right and found she was nowhere around. Suddenly he saw a dark shadow move through the glare of sunlight in front him.

"Jack come here." Sara yelled, waving her arm in the air. "You got to see this."

As Jack got closer he could see Sara standing on an outcrop of granite boulders perched twenty feet out over the ledge. Stopping ten feet in front of her, he felt his head get dizzy as he approached.

Sara urged him forward. "I'm fine right here." She pointed. "It's so beautiful. I've never seen anything like this."

Jack inched forward ever so slowly. He wanted to stop and turn around, but he couldn't let her see how fearful he was. He didn't want, what she was obviously seeing as beautiful, to end in tragedy of her saving him from a panic attack or worse yet, him falling off the cliff.

"Come on. I won't let you fall." She urged. The moments passed at an agonizing pace, but he finally found himself standing next to her, arm around her waist. "There." She pointed at the river gap.

Jack was wondering why she wasn't looking at the horizon and what seemed to be never ending mountain tops after rolling mountain tops.

"No- there." She grabbed his chin pulling it down.

There as far as he could see on the river were floating logs. Thousands upon thousands of logs rested next to each other like a giant puzzle box of toothpicks, floating down the river. The logs were so thick as to obscure the river at times. As he looked towards the distance he could make out small figures of men hopping back and forth on the logs. They looked like Shaolin Ninja Monks, spear in hand, as if fighting off an invisible monster and impending death there among the logs. They hopped along effortlessly form log to log. If they had wanted, he figured they could walk up the river for miles until they disappeared into the unknown. It was quite a sight to behold and he was glad Sara called him over to witness it.

CHAPTER 20

IN THE DEVIL'S CLUTCHES

When mike Shannon unfolded the directions, he took his eyes off the road. The car hit a pothole in the road and he lost control of the vehicle just long enough for the steering wheel to come out of his grip. The car went slipping off the road into a culvert.

Mike adjusted quickly turning into the slide and accidently hit the accelerator hard. His footing finally hitting the breaks, he was sure the car would flip offer and trap him in it upside down. On the other side of the road the nose of the car hit the embankment sending dirt and grass into the air covering the windshield. He could hear the crunching of metal against the turf and fought hard for the possession of the steering wheel. He felt the car take flight as it came up the embankment. It hit hard landing on all fours like a cat that just realized one of its life's had flashed in front of its eyes and passed away. The car came to rest on gravel leading to a gate of a farm, its engine still running.

Mike felt pain immediately in his wrist and could see the windshield cracked where it came in contact with his head. He was glad that the air big hadn't deployed and left him with a broken nose.

Outside the car he quickly took stock of his situation. The car although battered and bruised was still running and he was certain it would go. He moved his finger on his left hand. It wasn't broken but it hurt like hell. In the car he found an old rag and flipped off the lid from the cup of soda now lying of the passenger floor. He dumped the ice into the rag and tied it into a knot placing it around his wrist. When he checked the mirror, he found a large welt forming on his forehead. He got back out of the car and walked around it and found for the most part it was still intact except for a side mirror now lying in the dirt across the street.

Mike edged the car slowly forward back onto the dirt road. He was sure he was on the right road but the map he held in his hand became useless as it absorbed soda lying on the floor before he had the opportunity to rescue it. He thought of turning around but the Marine in him would never accept an easy retreat.

He lit a cigar and clenched down on it with his teeth and cursed away the pain. He came too far to turn back without obtaining his objective. And now he was mad as hell at Jack Kahill and wanted nothing more than to see his ass behind bars. As the road turned to the right he could see the funeral home just as Ken had described it.

The road became worse with potholes turning into small streams that crossed the road. With every bump in the road, he felt his brain swimming in his skull. But at least the ice was numbing the pain dull in his wrist.

The mansion was a Victorian home with need of desperate attention. It had become overgrown with wisteria and other weed plants. Its name was partly obscured from overgrown hedges. The driveway was empty as he passed by so stopping there first was out of the question and he drove on. Immediately behind the house he saw the beginning of a large cemetery. It was odd that a cemetery was next to a funeral home.

As in most cities' he was familiar with, cemeteries were always next to a church. Ken's place was the only church around that he was aware of but there was no cemetery anywhere around it.

He stopped the car for a brief moment and got out climbing up the embankment to see how large the cemetery was. His legs ached as he climbed, and his soft leather shoes slipped easily in the mud. Close to the road, he could see that the grave markers seemed new and a few of the headstones had dates on them of the departed not more than a few years old. As he gazed further into the distance he could see huge statues and massive vaults that looked quite old. He recalled what Ken had told him that he needed to go past a second graveyard down the road much older than the first.

Back in the car he drove further on, the road becoming worse. On the right side of the road the land opened into a cow pasture enclosed in barbed wire. On the left he followed along a rock wall for a mile until it ended abruptly at a line of trees that separated the property. When he got to the line of trees he stopped the car again getting out trying to get his bearings. Just past the line of trees all he saw was a freshly tilled farm land and on the other side of the road the cows had gathered in the corner along the barbed wire seemingly mocking him with stares, tongues hanging and belching an occasional haunting low grumble at his presence. He was sure that by now he should have seen the second older graveyard. There was nothing there other than freshly tilled farm land that rolled up over a hill at what he guessed to be a half mile.

Was it possible that he missed it along the road or hadn't he driven far enough? Looking up the road he could see thick forest growth along both sides of the road. He wiped the gathering sweat from his temples and walked up the road leaving the car where it stood.

A half mile up the road he stopped walking. He suddenly heard something coming through the thick woods. He stood there waiting as the thumping sound grew louder. He turned toward the noise reaching for his revolver but came up empty. "Oh shit." He said, realizing that the gun must fallen from it holster when the car hit the pothole. His eyes widened, and he felt his heart thumping in his chest as a mass emerged from within the darkness. A moose ten-foot-tall along with a yearling calf took up his entire vision blocking the sun. Slowly he backed away giving it distance as they made their way out into the road. He made sure to make no noise in fear of startling the mother and sending her into an attack. He backed away until he was nearly standing in a ditch on the other side of the road. The moose and calf paid no attention to him as they walked up the road a hundred feet disappearing back into the forest.

Mike felt exhilarated and frustrated at the same time. He was excited at having survived the road and the encounter with the moose. It truly was a once in a life time experience. Yet he was completely frustrated that this road led him to a dead end in his finding Jack Kahill or anything that could possibly lead him to Jack.

When he got back to the car he found the cows right where he left them still mocking him. Opening the door, he found the gun lying on the passenger floor, its safety still on. He pointed the gun at the cows wanting to take a shot. But they were just innocent bystanders witness to only the passing of time. Driving back, he rolled down the window noticing that the cows were now pacing along the fence line with him mooing at the wind. Seeing that, he flip them the bird. "Shut the fuck up." He yelled out the window.

He drove past the funeral home again seeing a car was now parked in the drive, but he decided he needed to get back to Ken's place regroup with fresh directions and try again in the morning.

Pulling up the driveway he saw a group of people who looked similar to the group from the Green Lantern earlier in the day. They were carrying logs and placed them in a stone circle on top of each other in a cross pattern. More people were pitching tents on any open flat land they could find. And, it looked like the place would soon run out of room. The total gathering had now enlarged to more than a hundred people. He found Ken still in the kitchen attending to a large pot.

"Cha...dder's almost ready." Ken said stirring a big ladle. "Your back early how'd you make out?"

Mike stood there shaking his head. But Ken didn't see him over the large pot. "Well that all depends on what cow you ask."

"What?" Ken asked stopping the stirring and looking up.

"Nothing." Mike said making his way around the table. "You still got any coffee left?"

"Coffee is always on. Help yourself." Ken handed him a cup.

"I'm sure I was on the right road until everything went south."

"What happened?" Ken now stood on the opposite side of the table coffee cup in his hand. "Didn't you see the old graveyard?" Ken could see a frustrated look take over Mikes face.

Mike scratched his head. "You got any ice." He held up his wrist in front of ken.

"Wow what the hell happened out there? That looks pretty swollen. "And you got a knot on your head." I'll get you some from the freezer."

"That is not a road. That is a death trap straight into hell."

"I knew that road was bad, but I guess it's worse now. It's been some time since I've been up that way." Ken said "Sorry, here this ice wrap should help."

"I'll be fine." Mike took the offering and wrapped it tightly around his wrist.

"But, I've got to tell you, I saw the funeral home fine and all. I saw the first graveyard. I even got out taking a better look but

238

when I drove further down the road not seeing the second older graveyard that's when I realized that something's wrong. I must have made a wrong turn. And in the melee..." Mike held up his swollen arm. "I destroyed the map you gave me."

Ken moved from around the table and placed his hand on top Mike's shoulder. "There is no way you could have missed anything." Ken had a puzzled look on his face. "You didn't see a second graveyard?" He asked.

"No, I drove along a short stone wall until it ended at a row of trees separating a field that looked like it was freshly tilled over for planting. I saw nothing more."

Ken dropped his hand from Mike's shoulder a look of horror came over his face. "What are you talking about? At that point you should have seen a graveyard. I know, like I said, my father is buried there."

Mike took another sip of his coffee it was he this time that put his hand on Ken's shoulder. "All I saw there was a dead empty field."

"Something's wrong. Something, my friend, is terribly wrong here. I can't go now because of the festival tonight. Fist light, I want you to take me there so that I can see it for myself."

Mike smiled sticking out his good hand and Ken shook it. "I was hoping you'd say that. You got a deal."

Ken went back to stir the pot on the stove.

"That smells good."Mike said.

"It's my famous clam cha...dder for the festival. I'm afraid it's going to get a bit lively around here soon. Here try this." Ken spooned out a good portion into a bowl and handed it to Mike. "You'll find a spoon in that top draw over there."

Mike took a big spoon of the chowder. "Well you got enough people gathered around what's it all about?"

Ken grabbed himself a small bowl of chowder and stood next to Mike gazing out the window.

"Every year before going into the hundred-mile wilderness the backpackers hold a spiritual gathering to honor the LADY OF WOODS. Some say they see her spirit while in the woods. Others say they see her all around here. You can talk to any of those young folks out there they all have their different beliefs of who the spirit is. There was a time years ago that a few loggers went missing in these parts. Some say it was the creatures come to be known as THE HIDE BEHIND. It was a thin dark thing that hid behind trees that you never seen coming. It was said that it would snatch you up and take you away."

Mike finished the soup licking his lips. "And, what do you think?"

Ken grabbed the empty bowl from Mike placing it in the sink.

"Me, I think those loggers ran into bears but that's a lot of wilderness out there so who knows what's out there."

Ken took a seat next to Mike.

"There was a woman back in 1955 that walked the Appalachian Trail on her own. She was 67 years old when she started the two thousand fifty-mile walk. Her name was Grandma Gatewood. She's sort of known as the patron saint of the trail for bringing attention to is poor condition back then. Many of the people around here feel that the Lady of the Woods is her.

You know that lady whose cabin you're looking for she believed it. Margaret Kahill would bring food and drink for the backpackers. She would tell all kinds of stories around the bonfire late into the evening. The backpackers believe she was in tune with the spirits and you know something, so do I. She had what you might call second sight. A lot of the backpackers felt she was a white witch. Bring up her name to the backpackers and they will tell you how she helped them with their karma." Ken threw his arms in the air. "Whatever the hell that means."

"Sounds like your jury is still on the fence." Mike said.

"I've seen a lot of things around here over the years and I'll never forget the day I saw her. It was very early in the morning in May some ten odd years ago. The sun was just coming up a light mist hung low to the ground. Cup of coffee in my hand when I stood on those very steps."Ken pointed to the front entrance. "There I stood like I do every morning sipping coffee and welcoming the day when all of a sudden, I see a woman all in white not walking with a stride in her step more like she floated there going through the woods. I called out hello, but she paid me no mind. There was not a sound and as hard as it is to believe, I could see straight through her. Maybe it was my old eyes playing tricks on me or maybe not. But the one thing I'm sure of is, those people out there, they sure as hell believe it."

"Well I'm sure to keep my eyes open and if I see anything out of the ordinary I'll let you know."

Ken refilled Mike's coffee cup and went back to stirring the pot of chowder. "Don't pay too much attention to those backpackers out there they look odd, smell funny and might do some crazy things, but they are harmless. They are here for one thing and it's that big mountain a hundred miles north. They will blow off steam here before they have to focus all their concentration on hiking through one hundred miles of unknown wilderness with nothing more than what they can carry on their backs."

Mike took off the ice wrap handing it back to Ken. "Thanks." He said. "I need to check in with my office is there a phone I could pay you for?"

"No need, I'll show you where the phone is help yourself." Mike followed him down a hallway. "Phone in my office here take your time I got to go check on a few things. Just close the door when you're done."

CHAPTER 21

ROAD TO HELL

Jack sat behind the wheel and wiped away the crud from the corner of his eyes. He truly believed he would never drive a car again. He wanted to put the demons behind him and try to focus on the positive of what lie ahead. The moment he touched the steering wheel it all flooded in on a wave. The beating of his heart clicked off image after image in his mind like a clock broken and stuck in time. He heard it ...tick, Blood...tick, Death, tick, Run. It was like reliving a constant nightmare with no control of what evil image would work its way through the abyss and birth all its nastiness for the victim to chew on over and over again. He hoped that somehow, he could overcome it so that it wouldn't chew him up inside and leave him emotionally dead. How does one live with the constant self torment? If only he could some way turn his brain off. He wished he could make it stop.

Sara sat in the passenger seat. "Jack you'll be find." She assured him. "Just take it easy, I've really got to get some rest. If we could afford to take the time to stop we would but, you know that we need to keep moving. She squeezed Jacks hand. Wake me up for dinner when we get to Monson."

Jack turned the ignition and put the car in drive. Slowly he drove out onto the road heading north on Rout 6. He bit the inside of his cheek and wished Sara pleasant dreams. How he wished for pleasant dreams instead of having to deal with the constant daytime nightmares.

The road climbed, and he could no longer see the river as the road gave way to the ever-thickening forest. The sun hung high in the sky peaking in and out of growing cloud cover. He tried to clear his mind and think of the beautiful sight of the mountain range and river he saw. He had a two-hour drive before he and Sara would arrive in Monson and he planned to let her rest until they reached there. Ahead the sky darkened and soon Jack found himself driving headlong into an approaching storm. Day turned to night. The air smelled of ozone. Thunder cracked, and a lightning flash lit up the interior of the car. Jack was glad to see that the windshield wipers worked when he turned the knob. Another lightning flash and the sky opened in all hell's fury, rain poured down sideways in a torrent of accompanying wind. Jack felt the tiny car rock and he tightened his grip trying to anticipate fighting the wind as he drove on. It was clear that he would need to find a safe place to pull into and out of the elements until the storm passed. He slowed the car to a crawl unable to clearly see the road ahead. Jack strained to see in the darkness and he knew he could go no further risking driving off the road into a ditch. There was nowhere to pull off to and he feared being hit from behind by one of the big rigs they had seen hauling lumber. He looked down at the speedometer and slowed the car to under twenty miles per hour. Jack wasn't sure if he heard the thunder first or saw the lightning flash first. All of it seemed to happen at the same time. He slammed on the breaks as the big tree falling in the road came to life within the fading flash of light.

The sudden jolt awakened Sara. "What's wrong?" She asked rubbing her eyes but another flash showed her a tree branch now blocking their way.

Jack saw the tree branch now reflecting in the cars head lights blocking their way. "God dam it." He shouted.

There was no turning back. They couldn't retrace a hundred miles of bad road to find a way around it. It was time to get out and see if they could navigate around it. He knew he had to move fast, there was no telling what might be coming down the road. He put the car in park and they both jumped out of the car. The rain came down heavy and the wind-swept droplets stung his face. Sara could barely see Jack on the darkened road. She followed his voice and came to stand next to him before she knew what was happening. Standing in the illumination of the headlights Jack could see that most to the massive tree had fallen on the roadside and that only a broken branch was laying across the road blocking their way. He got to the end of it closest to the road and found it was about ten inches wide.

Sara came up alongside him. "Come on we got to try to move this off the road." Sara bent down next to him holding the log in her arms the way one would hold a new born. Jack did the same. And as they pushed together, Sara slipped on the wet ground and fell forward scrapping her hands on the pavement.

"Are you okay?" He asked?

"I'll be fine." She lied. Her hands stung, and she stood there motionless trying to blow cool air on them.

Jack tried to push again but this time felt the twinge in his leg and a pain shoot its way up his back. For all their efforts they had only managed to move it a foot. Jack could he she was spent and quickly realized it would be too heavy for them to move alone.

"How are we going to get around this?" Sara asked standing there in the head light her body soaked with rain.

"Do you have any tools in the trunk of the car?"

"Like what?"Sara frowned.

"Well, I'm hoping for a saw or an axe."

Sara popped the trunk and came up holding a tire iron in her hand. She dropped it when she heard the long sigh coming from Jack's mouth.

"I heard you the first time." She yelled at Jack in frustration. "You don't have to be making that grumbling sound."

Jack's felt the hair stand on the back of his neck. "That's not me!" He shouted over the crack of thunder. He slammed the trunk shut. "Get in the car... get in the car!" He shouted.

Sara saw Jacks eyes widen with fear. She could hear the panic in his voice and began to run to the side of the car. Jack closed his door and fired up the car. "Hold on." He shouted.

"What are you going to do?" She asked.

247

"Get us the hell out of here. That grumbling you heard, I'm afraid is a semi truck down shifting coming this way fast. If we not do something now, when it gets here, it's going to be hell to pay."

Jack edged the car up against the log and pushed down on the accelerator but, the car's tires slipped on the wet pavement making no progress. The rumbling grew louder and they knew that it wasn't the thunder. Jack backed the car a few feet. He turned toward Sara shifting it into drive. "I'm sorry." He said.

"Do it!" She shouted as Jack floored the pedal sending the car headlong like a raging bull into the log. The force of the car hitting the log sent them back in their seats. The sound of glass shattering was instantaneous as metal hit wood. One head light went out as it hit and darken the lift side of the road. This time the log moved and slid along scraping the quarter panel of the driver's side. Fifteen feet past the log lightning flashed and out of the darkness appeared a massive wall of movement taking up the full view of the car's windshield. A deafening blaring of a fog horn screamed in their ears. The tractor trailer roared past them hitting the log and shattering it sending wooden spears into the air like a box of toothpicks. Jack split the image in his mind seeing the wood flying toward their car and in the rear-view mirror he saw the cab of the tractor erupt in a fiery ball of flames as it careened out of control past them.

"DUCK." He shouted, pulling Sara under him and placing his body above her, waiting for the impact.

With one eye he watched as the pile of timbers flew over the car landing twenty feet behind them. In the rear-view mirror, he saw the exploding mushroom gas cloud erupt into the air and he saw the rippling of the shock wave as it rapidly approached their car. The wave engulfed the car and the force of the explosion shattered the rear window sending glass flying around them.

Jack found himself covered with small square blocks of glass and let Sara up. "You okay?" He asked.

Sara looked at him she could see his lips moving but she couldn't hear what he was saying. She felt a pain and heard a ringing in her ears. "I can't hear you." She said. "I've got ringing in my ears."

"Yeah me too, it will pass." He assured her.

Jack stopped the car and put it in park. "We got to go check." He said. He felt his hands shaking as he reached for the door handle.

Sara burst out crying. Immediately she could sense it. "There's nothing there to check." She said.

"Stay here; I'll only be a minute."

Jack walked thirty feet down the road toward the wreckage when a second explosion knocked him back and off his feet.

Sara sat their wiping tears from her eyes when she heard the second explosion. She knew Jack had told her to stay put but, she decided to open the door to go check on him.

Outside the car in the dim illumination of the one head light she saw a figure standing there, flames all around. The ringing in her ears had subsided and she could now hear the rain hitting the roof of the car.

The image appeared now in front of her as a woman yet still made no sound. In front of her was no devil, no phantom from the woods and no odd spirits. What stood in front of her she realized now as the driver of the wrecked tractor now engulfed in flames on the side of the road. Sara stood staring at the woman in the flames. Sara spread her arms out in front of her as if waiting to receive a hug from a lost child.

"COME ON... She urged. It's time for you to go. It's okay, you are safe now it's time to rest ...go."

The woman slowly moved toward her as if floating in the air. Sara could see the flames growing larger as the woman moved toward her until she was completely surrounded by them. She felt nothing as the woman passed through her and disappeared. Suddenly she felt at peace and calmness overcame her. She smiled knowing that she helped the woman crossed over to where she needed to be and not left there on the side of the road wondering aimlessly for eternity.

Sara turned hearing Jack approach the car. He shook his head. "There's nothing left. Why are you out of the car?"

"I had to help." She answered.

"There's no helping." He said.

Sara's voice choked up. "The driver was a woman." She said. "I crossed her over not more than a few moments ago."

"Wow...It seems I cause death and you fix death."

"It's not like that at all." She said. "Things happen for a reason that neither you nor I can do anything about. Call it what you want, fate, karma or the ultimate hand of GOD that keeps the wheels of everything spinning. Good or bad, it's up to us to play the hand we are dealt and to do our best to make things right. You're not the cause of anything that happened, because they happen with or without you is all. There is nothing you or anyone can do about it. Once you put that in your head your soul will come along for the ride and you can start to move on into a better life. First, I thought my being able to see dead people was a curse. But, I realize now that it is a mission given to me for a purpose. And that purpose I feel is to help those that would otherwise stay lost forever if not crossed over."

Jack put his arms around her and hugged her tight. He wasn't sure what his purpose was at the moment but hoped he could recognize it when it happened. "Let's get out of here." He said. "When we get to Monson we can call it in to the authorities."

Wind pushed through the open widow letting rain swirl around the inside of the car. Everything was wet, and Sara shivered in her seat. She turned the heat up to high in the car in an effort to dry her clothing. The car was a wreck and if anyone was looking for them, they stood out like a sore thumb.

It was late afternoon when they arrived in Monson and pulled into a gas station to fill the car.

"Fill it up." She told the approaching attendant.

Jack was out of the car and heading toward the small store attached to the station. He turned to Sara. "You want something hot?"

Sara got out of the car stiff. Her clothing stuck to her like Velcro and made a scraping sound as she walked.

"Sorry sir." The attendant called out after him. "Miss Betty's closed. No one coming by. Their all up at Ken's place."

The attendant finished filling the tank and Sara paid the twenty-four dollars. "Can you tell me where we might be able to get a bite to eat this late in the afternoon?"

The attendant didn't pay much attention to their car. "Are you guys here for the festival?" He asked. Sara looked at Jack. "No." She answered.

"Festival, what's that all about?" Jack interrupted.

"It's a festival put on by the backpackers. They seek the blessing from the Lady of the Woods for a safe journey before they enter the hundred-mile wilderness. They been doing it now let me see... ten years now."

Sara turned to Jack. "You spent time here you ever hear of that?"

Jack was standing in front of a soda machine feeding it change and came back to the car handing Sara a coke. "No." He answered. "But, I could use something more than this cold soda."

"Wally can fix your busted window, but he won't be here till morning."

"Yeah." Jack had a smirk look on his face. "But what I'm interested in at the present moment is food and them some place to shower and spend the night."

The attendant stood there rubbing his hand with a shop towel. Jack could see the look on the man's face he might as well been a hundred miles away.

"Might take a day to order that window though, I don't think Wally got a replacement in his shop."

Sara could see the color change in Jack's face and she knew he was becoming frustrated with the attendant. She walked over to the side of the man shaking him on the shoulder. "Excuse me sir about a place to eat?"

"Oh, yeah."The man said. "It's little late but the Green Lantern might still be open. Or you could try Ken's place but I'm sure there a lot of people there so" ... he stopped raising his hands in the air.

The attendant went and sat down on a milk crate near the front entrance. Sara sipped at her soda looking at Jack for a direction.

Jack waved her back to the car. "I think I remember where that place is and besides this town is only a mile square I'm sure we can find it. As they pulled away they heard the attendant yell out. "Just down the road."

A mile further Jack saw the glowing neon sign in the dim light of the late afternoon. He pulled the car into the parking lot adjacent to an old phone booth. Outside the car he started walking toward the booth leaving Sara behind.

"Sara." He called back to her. "You go in and order whatever you're having, get two I'll eat anything. I've got to make a phone call."

"Who do you need to call? You can use my cell phone. It's in my purse in the car. Don't know if it's able to get a signal way out here in the boonies."

"No, that might have a trace on it. I've been wanting to check on my… He stopped himself and smiled back to Sara… Our grandmother." He said. "Since leaving Elizabeth three days ago it's almost all I can think of."

"You haven't spoken to her since you went to see her in the hospital?"

"No, I never got to see her she was asleep when I went to the hospital all I got was the letter."

Sara laughed. "Yeah it's amazing what a mystery letter might make a person do." She waved her letter in the air over her head walking toward the cafe.

Jack turn and walked toward the phone booth. He pushed open the folding glass door and slipped inside. Once inside he found himself spinning in a circle. And, when he came full circle he realized that there was no phone only a small metal shelf and empty black box where the phone had once been. "Son of a bitch." He said. He slammed a fist on the shelf.

When he tried to open the folding door, it was stuck, and he had to kick at the bottom in an attempt to open it. On his third kick, it finally freed and snapped open but not before he broke the glass with his boot.

Outside the booth he could see Sara just standing still in the driveway half way between the car and the cafe in some sort of a trance. "Now what?" He said as walked toward her.

He came up alongside her putting his hand on her shoulder. She jumped. He could fell her shaking. "What's wrong is the place closed?" Sara shook her head.

"I don't know." She said.

"Well then what is it?"

"I can't go inside." She answered with a look of terror on her face.

"Why you look, pardon my expression, like you just saw a ghost."Jack's eyes widened when he realized just how bad she looked.

Sara started to cry. "Don't you see it? The place is packed."

Jack looked around in the parking lot there was only one other car and when he looked up through the window of the cafe he saw only one person sitting at the counter.

Jack turned and held her shaking hands. Her face turn flush and he could hear in her voice that she was genuinely scared.

"You don't see them?" She asked. Suddenly Jack felt her stop shaking and her body stiffened as if she was being taken over by rigor mortis. She stood there staring wide eyed straight ahead. "No... no...no."

Jack was about to say who when he realized what it was he was unable to see.

Sara nodded. "It's too many. It's too overwhelming. I can't answer them all."

Letting go of her hand Jack turned toward the window. "But why? Who are they all and why would they all be in that cafe? How many?" He asked.

"Something is wrong here Jack, something is very wrong here this shouldn't be happening. The place is full, maybe a hundred or more young, old, and children they are just sitting there. Sara couldn't hold it in any longer and broke out crying when she saw a woman dressed in a wedding gown. She wiped her face and shut her eyes tightly.

"I wish I could help. I don't know why but the feeling I get is that they are recently lost. For some reason they followed each other until they all wound up here. They usually go to something or someone they were familiar with. And, there are a few wondering near the door outside trying to get in."

Jack swallowed hard. "God I'm glad I can't see what you see."

Sara could see that he now had a determined look on his face.

"Well, I hope they don't mind some company." He said. "Because I'm still hungry and since I can't see them or help them they are going to pay no attention to me. So, I'll go in and get the food you go back to the car and stay out of sight, so they don't come flooding out of there like a tidal wave to get to you."

"Jack you need to be careful. There is something I haven't told you. If the situation is right they can attach to you."

Jack bit the inside of his cheek. "Oh, just great and how the hell does that work? If my life wasn't a complete mess already, the last thing I need right now is a haunting."

"Jack your life is not a mess, just think about how brave it is to take the journey we are on together. And, all the obstacles you've overcome to get this far trying to seek the truth about who you are. Think about whom we are and what this all means. We need to keep going."

Jack took in a deep breath and let it out slowly. He felt his hand beginning to shake. The air around him changed becoming heavy with a smell of ozone. He felt the hair on his arms tingle as if he was in an electric storm. He checked the sky, but the storm was well past them and only a warm breeze blew for the south.

"Just remember." She said. "If you go in there and acknowledge their presents in the slightest, any one of them might feel that they know and are familiar with you. They will feel comfortable with you and attach themselves to you. You got to go in there feeling nothing. Get what you need to get, don't think of them and quickly get out."

Jack walked slowly toward the café. "Don't worry I have a plan."

He started singing: "Before too long I'm humming along some. When I get some cash, I'll buy your past from the boy who made it all wrong. Before too long I'm humming along some. When I get some cash, I'll buy your past from the boy who made it all wrong..."

Inside the cafe Jack sat at the first stool he came to. He remembered being in the cafe as a child with his grandmother. He always ordered the same thing a grilled cheese sandwich and a chocolate milk shake.

He seated himself on a stool at the center of the counter. He felt nothing and kept singing in his mind. He split the image in his mind with one eye on the cook and the other on the middle age man sitting at the end of the counter stuffing his face with meatloaf. As far as he could tell, there were only three people there.

"Sorry were all out of meatloaf that was the last" The cook pointed to the man at the end of counter.

Jack stopped singing to himself and focused his attention on the man in front of him. The cook was wearing a giant paper hat with part of the top burned off. Jack chuckled to himself, but he was glad to see it as it helped take is mind of the entities around him.

"We drove a long way." Jack answered. "At this point anything you got would be fine."

"I'm just about to close up for the night but I can make you a couple of ham sandwiches and the coffee is still fresh."

"That will be fine just make enough for me and the little lady out there."

"You guys in town for the festival?" The cook asked as he disappeared into the kitchen.

"No, not at all." Jack answered.

"Well not too many people come through town this time of year especially when the no-se-um season is about to take hold. Just thought."

Jack shook his head as the cook finished placing the sandwiches into a bag. "I remember them as a kid." He said.

"Those tiny creatures are born of hell they show up this time of year. If enough of them are able to get together they will carry you off, suck your blood and drain your body, stripping it clean until nothing is left except dried brittle decaying bones begging to turn to dust."

Jack heard a laugh come from the man at the end of the counter and he added to the conversation. "You need to cover yourself in about five gallons of DEET to do battle with them."

"Thanks." Jack said. I'll keep an eye out for them."

"No, you won't, son you'll never see them, but you sure as hell will feel them."

"Oh yeah." Jack answered.

Jack paid the bill and started walking out when he remembered the other phone call he needed to make. He turned back to the cook. "I noticed your phone out-side is missing."

"Yeah the phone company took it out three years ago and never came back. Is there something I can help you with?" Jack was hoping to make the call anonymously, but this was the best he was going to do. And besides the old cook didn't know him or where he was going.

"Yea, if you don't mind about ten miles south on route six I came upon a wreckage of a tractor off the road and into the woods." It was another lie, thought Jack.

"Was anyone hurt?"

"I stopped to check but it was too late. The wreckage was totally burned out."

"You don't have to call in anything. You can tell old Roy here down at end of the counter he's the Deputy Sheriff around here. Jack wanted nothing more than to have to explain anything to the local cops and started to walk out. When he heard the cook call out behind him.

"Hey Roy, I got a young fella here says he passed a wreck off in the woods down around Turners Point. You better check it out."

Roy finished his coffee and came up behind Jack and took the seat Jack had just occupied.

"So, son tell me just what happened."

Jack spun on his heels. "Like I said it looked like a wrecked trailer in the woods."

"What's you name son?"

"Jack Kahill." Dam, he thought as it spilled out from his lips before he had the wherewithal to lie.

Roy grabbed his coat and headed out the door. "I'll check it out." He said. "Call it in Pete will ya? I'll come back later and settle my bill."

Jack followed behind Roy and was just about at the door when he heard Pete call out to him. "Excuse me son, did you say your name is Jack Kahill?"

Jack turned slowly around. He knew there was no use in lying now the man obviously heard him announce his name.

"Yes, sir I'm Jack."

"You know I thought you looked familiar."

And how can that be? Jack wondered but said nothing.

Well, just thought you'd like to know. There was a man here early this morning looking for you. Suddenly Jack's eyes widened and he felt the hairs on the back of his neck stand on edge.

"Oh, can you describe what this fellow looked like?"

"You know I should have known it just buy your accent I'm pretty good with accents ya know. He had this thick New York kind of accent like you, but what stood out the most about him was the military hair cut he had."

Jack stood there squirming he wanted nothing more than to get the hell out of there. "Did he say where he was going?"

"He mentioned something about The Barry Funeral home. And he was looking for a place to stay I sent him to the only game in town, Ken's Place. He didn't look much like a one of those hippies up there and I can't imagine him staying there."

Jack thanked the man for his time gathered up his bag and coffee cups and walked quickly back to the car. When he arrived at the car he found Sara sound asleep in the passenger seat. He wished he could let her sleep. But, he needed her help that nothing from the cafe had attached itself to him.

"Sara." He shook her arm. She opened one eye and looked him over. "You're okay." She said.

"No, get up I got coffee and food. And we got bigger problems to deal with."

Sara rubbed her eyes. "I told you nothing followed you."

Jack took a bite of the ham sandwich swallowing half in one gulp. "It's not the dead I'm worried about it's the living we need to worry about."

Sara took the bag from Jack and sipped at the coffee. "What are you talking about?"

"First there were two living souls in there the cook and the other a Deputy Sheriff who at this very moment is headed south to check out that nightmare we just came through. And second and possible worse is that Mike Shannon is here looking for yours truly."

"How do you know all of this?" How long have I been asleep?"

265

"I don't know. I fucked up trying to concentrate on anything other than the Velcro zombie festival inside there. The fucken phones don't work around here. I had to tell them about the wreck. And, when the Deputy Sheriff started asking questions I slipped out my name."

"How did you find out that old crew cut is here?"

"When I spilled my name, he started blabbing about a guy from New York..."

Through a mouth full of food Sara finished... "Looking for you."

"I got an idea."Sara winked. "You said it before, hide in plain sight."

CHAPTER 22

BUMPS IN THE NIGHT

Mike Shannon stood in the large hall as more doors were being laid out between folding chairs. He watched through the front door as two things around him started to grow larger. He watched as the wood pile for the bonfire now reached ten feet tall. More people were arriving, and the place was quickly getting over crowded for his liking. In two hours the bonfire would be lit, and the beginning of an all-night ruckus would take life. The noise and commotion out -side was getting louder by the moment. Near the bottom of the steps a group of twenty backpackers now sat in a circle around one guy banging on bongos and another guy strumming on a ukulele. Mike shook his head there was no way he was going to stay here and put up with all the shenanigans without shooting them all, so he could sleep in peace and quiet.

Ken was setting out bowls on a table when Mike came in. "Ken I'm not going to stay the evening. There would be no way I could get any rest with all that happening out side."

"Yep." Ken laughed. "I'm surprised you lasted this long. I completely understand. But where you going to go? The closest town with a good hotel is sixty miles away in Bangor."

"I know it's late, but I think I got about three hours before it gets dark I'm going to check out that orphanage on the other side of Monson pond and see if I can talk to the caretaker there. It's a long shot, but no offence, it beats staying here. I'll sleep in my car near the farm hopefully I won't have to shoot one of the cows for making too much noise. I'll pick you up in the morning."

Ken handed him a brown paper bag. "Here take this cha...dder. I'll be ready." He shook Mike's hand.

Tents took up most of the both sides of the drive and Mike had to enlist the help of moving his car from one of the campers there for fear of running one of them over. Mike didn't look back and he breathed a sigh of relief when he hit the main road, glad to be away from all the noise. He hit the accelerator and the car roared down the road. This time he was on good paved road with a freshly drawn map.

Down the road Jack found an old farm stand with a drive and a patch of stones behind it that dead ended into a thicket of overgrowth. It would be a perfect place to ditch the car out of sight.

Jack grabbed his pack from the trunk and slung it over his shoulders and then went about helping Sara with hers.

Sara adjusted her straps. "We are going to march right in there and pretend we are fellow backpackers."

Jack kicked at a rock in the driveway. "That's your plan?"

Jack went over to a small birch tree and snapped off a small sapling and placed it between his teeth sucking the birch sap. He picked up a stick and leaned on it. "How's this look?"

Sara looked him up and down. "It will be dark soon and I'm sure we will blend right in. We certainly smell like backpackers. I could really use a shower and to get out of these cloths. Do you think they have a place to sleep?"

The walk was about a mile and the sounds of the crowd of people ahead got louder with each step. The sun was almost gone and over head the first twinkling of the North Star could be seen in the sky.

Jack stopped. "Listen to that, I don't think you're going to get much sleep."

"Just watch me I'm so tired I could just about sleep standing up."

They stopped at the beginning of the drive near the street. The driveway took a bend to the right some two hundred feet ending at a large oak tree. Jack could see a person dressed like an Indian warrior standing on a platform fifty feet up the tree teetering on the edge of a branch.

A cable wire was strung from the tree ending at the wood pile in the center of the stone circle. One of the people around the circle stood up and blew a horn and at that moment the warrior in the tree lit the tip of the spear on fire. He jumped up grabbing hold of a pulley on the cable with one arm and with the other arm holding the flaming spear. He slid down the cable flinging the burning spear into the wood pile ten feet above it. When he hit the ground, he rolled into a ball coming to his feet next to the circle. The flaming spear hit its target and lit the darkened sky alive with color. The crowd around erupted with cheer.

On the ground he went about dancing and shaking a rattle on a long pole in an Indian war dance. He drank from a clear bottle and would spit out fire while spinning in a circle.

The bonfire roared to life and the group of people all got up together walking in a circle and started chanting.

"Lady of the Woods our journey's long we seek your blessing to keep us strong."

Jack and Sara made their way close to the fire the warmth was inviting and felt good against their soggy clothing. Jack felt a tap on his shoulder and when he turned a young girl with flowers in her hair flashed him a peace sigh and held out a joint for him. Jack waved her off the last thing he need was to be stoned when he need to be sharp and alert. He was already fighting the dreariness from the long drive.

Jack and Sara made the climb up the steps of the church and once inside they asked some people where they could find the owner. The person pointed to a man standing next to a long table across the hall. A line of people were forming, and they could see the old man preparing bowls of soup and handing it to the people that came up to the table.

Jack got on line he was hungry but what he really wanted to inquire about was logging and shower facilities first.

When Jack got to the front of the line he asked for two bowls not realizing what was presented was clam chowder. Sara was standing next to him and he handed it off to her. He paid the four dollars to the man.

"Excuse me sir."He said. "I know how busy you are, but we just arrived." He pointed to Sara. "We were wondering if you had any room for the two of us and we also would like to inquire about the possibility of a shower."

"Shower is no problem it's a dollar fifty each but as far as room there is no bunks available and I'm not sure if any space for tents are still available."

Ken finished filling bowls of soup from the pot he had. "Son." He said. "Give me a hand here in the kitchen. I got to get another pot if you don't mind?"

Jack and Sara followed him into the kitchen. Ken went over to the stove grabbed a spoon and stirred the pot. "It's going to be a very busy night." He said.

Jack and Sara stood there waiting for Ken to tell them how they could help. Ken turned off the pot of chowder and asked Jack to take it into the hall. Handing it off to Jack, he froze and just stood there looking at Jack as if he had seen a ghost.

Mike Shannon drove slowly along the far side of Monson pond the road took a sudden turn into the woods and the forest thickened. He stopped to check the map a quarter of a mile ahead he turned off the road and onto a private road, a sign on a wooden gate read no trespassing , property of Greenwood Orphanage. Mike pull up to the entrance gate finding it completely covered with vines. It appeared no one had come down this road in a very long time.

He reached over to the passenger seat opening the bag Ken gave him. By now he figured the soup was cold, but he didn't care there wasn't going to be any luxuries ahead of him. He popped the lid off and pressing his lips against the container found the soup to be still warm downing it in one gulp.

Mike left the car and came around the gate walking along a small path. In the distance he could see a large building surrounded by open fields. As he approached the building it looked nothing like what he had imagined.

It was immaculate clean and well maintained with a flower garden in front of a surround open porch. He stood there for a moment taking it all in when a man came from around the side of the building.

"You are trespassing mister ain't nothing here for you." The old black man said.

Mike noticed the old man spoke with a southern drawl even though they were well into the north woods of Maine.

He was wearing thick glasses that made his eyes like two small beads. His face had a grim look and his jaw kept moving like he was chewing on something strong. Mike guessed it to be chewing tobacco, but he never saw the man spit.

"My name is Mike Shannon and you must be Mr. Sampson the caretaker."

"Yes sir. But like I say there ain't nothing here for you. You should go back to where you came. It ain't safe here."

Mike thought about how to get through to the old man and gain his confidence.

Mike couldn't figure out what the old man was talking about. What was not safe? The building looked in immaculate condition as if it was ready to receive new guests.

"Why do you say it's not safe your property and building looks beautiful and well kept?" Mike pointed in the directions of the buildings.

"Yes sir." The old man paused for a moment cocking his head as if listening to someone whispering into his ear. "No, the woods, the woods are not for you there is danger there. You a city boy best not go in them woods."The old man chewed on his lip.

Mike though that the old man must be crazy it didn't seem like he was making much since. And he thought he would never get any answers out of the old caretaker speaking gibberish. "Let me ask you just how old are you?"

"Me I'm old as dirt I've been here forever." He said spitting at the ground.

The old man came close, walked up the steps and took a seat on a rattan rocker on the porch. "I know who you is... she told me you don't need to say anything more."

"She, she who?"Mike asked with a confused look on his face.

"Oh, yeah I sees her last night she come and tell me something wrong here and a new man come only he best not go into the woods it not safe for him. I know you is him."

"What lady you are talking about old man?" Mike was getting frustrated with the old man and the nonsense he was spewing.

"Oh, the Lady of the Woods. She come and tell me tings. Tell me something wrong big time, only she don't tell me what . But, last night I see more of them they all around, never see them before. They ain't supposed to be here only her supposed to be here. They shouldn't be out they should be deep, deep in." The old man pounded his shoe against the ground.

Mike remembered this was the same thing Ken was talking about, the Lady of the Woods.

Holy Christ- thought Mike. Could there be a connection or has the old coot got them hippy backpackers confused with goblins in the night.

Mike came up on the porch and bent down so he was eye level with the old man. He took out his cigar case placed a cigar between his teeth offering one to the old man.

"Oh boy, I ain't seen one of those since my time back in the islands." The old man licked his lips. "Now I don't mind if I do's."

He pinched the cigar between two fingers placing the cigar between pursed lips.

Mike took note of the man's hands. They had no wrinkles and looked velvety soft like that of a young boy. They were certainly not that of a man of advanced age and hard caretaking that he presented himself to be.

Mike lit the old man's cigar and watched as the old man puffed out plumes of smoke.

"I need to ask you something important."

"Ok young fellow ask your question." The old man seemed to lighten his attitude some. And he sat back in the rocker raising his chin with a smile on his face blowing rings of smoke into the air.

"I came here to ask you what you remember of a boy lived here a long time ago by the name of Jack Kahill."

The old man pursed his lips looking off into the distance giving thought but quickly said. "Second sight that boy got, he got, oh yeah second sight. Given a raw deal."

Lost again thought Mike- not again.

"Yeah he live here, in and out long time. Got him a sister too only he don't know it. She special too, she got the gift. She see

276

better than me and then some. She's a helper too, she help them lost souls, help then to get to where they need be."

Mike was finally catching on.

"You mean she can see the dead?"

The old man shook his head up and down.

"His grandmother special too, some think she the Lady of the Woods but ...no, not her. She don't come here they had a place back in them woods near Monson."

"Yeah, I know but I couldn't find it."

"Ha." The old man laughed. "You not supposed to. Like I say, you city folk."

"Do you think he could fine that cabin?"

"He find that cabin blind folded I'm sure as I'm sitting here. But, I don't know why he want to, it be abandoned a long time. Like this orphanage be abandoned a long time, but I keep it up give it life, give it what it needs. It give me life, purpose something to do. All those souls that were here long ago they come back need some place to go. You stick around you see she come to you in the night let you see."

"You know, I just might take you up on that."

"Yeah, you no good down there at that festival too much noise, no rest for you there. Well come on we'll find you a place so quiet only the dead will visit you."The old man laughed.

The old man got up and motioned for Mike to follow him inside the house. "Come on she told me to let you stay let you see."

At the end of a dark hallway the old man stopped before entering the room he extended an arm above him and gently touched a cross fixed to the wall atop the door. He opened a door on the right and stepped inside touching a light switch. Mike followed him inside. The room was large well-lit with a beautiful high post bed in the middle of the room. It held on each side of the bed a night table. On the far end of the room he saw a sitting area with a desk and chair.

"You be comfortable here. Go past that door you find a bath and toilet. Water sometimes not too hot but you be fine. I bring you some stew shortly."

The old man left him and walked out the room stopping at the doorway and turned back. "Thanks for the cigar. They might come tonight don't leave the house." He closed the door behind him and Mike found himself alone.

Mike took off his holster and laid the gun on the bed. He found a fresh towel hanging on a rack in the bathroom and went about washing his face when he heard a knock on the front door. When he opened the door, he found the old caretaker standing there with a tray of food and hot coffee. If Mike didn't know better, he could imagine he was at a luxury hotel.

"Yes sir. This be my specialty hot beef stew, got a secret got a secret. You try it best ever and the coffee ain't bad too." The old man laughed through cigar smoke.

Mike took the tray and placed it on the table. He went for his wallet. "Mr. Sampson, let me pay you for all this hospitality."

"No, no Lady say take care you. Take no money. You here for a reason."

Mike was still not sure what the old man was getting at and every time he tried to ask something the old man just talked in riddles. The old man smiled at him and wished him a good night closing the door leaving Mike alone.

The soup was wonderful, the coffee hot and delicious. On the third bite of the stew Mike finally recognized what he thought the secret ingredient was in the soup, anchovies. He wasn't a big fan, but beggars can be choosers and besides when he was in Vietnam he was sure he ate rat once, although his buddies tried to assure him it was beef.

When Mike finished the soup, he wished he had a television to watch or even a radio to listen to but there was nothing in the room. There's got to be something to read in here he thought and walked around the room in search.

 On his second time around the room he came to a table next to the bed and found a bible face down opened to a page. He wondered how it was possible that he over looked it the first time he walked around the room. He picked it up and read:

John1:5, THE LIGHT SHINES IN THE DARKNESS, AND THE DARKNESS DID NOT COMPREHEND IT.

He put the bible back on the night stand he checked the chambers in his revolver and waited for the night.

"Stand still boy let an old man look at you."

Jack stood there as Sara came up next to him.

"Yeah that's it." Ken said pulling at his beard. "I know you're that guy the bounty hunter from New York is looking for. He's been flashing around a pretty good photo of you around here. Best you keep letting that stubble on your face come in full, so you don't look too much like that photo he's got. I haven't seen you since you were a little boy coming around town with that lovely lady Mrs. Kahill."

Jack felt his chest pounding and he turned white as a ghost. He thought about running. Sara grabbed his hand. She was stunned, saying nothing.

Ken saw the look of panic overcome Jacks face. "Calm down boy you're in good hands here. I got something to show you here in the hall."

Ken walled out of the kitchen waving a hand for Sara and Jack to follow. In the vestibule of the old church near where once the tabernacle stood was a painting of an elderly woman offering a wicker basket of vegetables up to the heavens.

"Come look close." Urged Ken pointing at the painting.

Jack didn't need any coaxing he recognized the woman right away. "That's my grandmother." He said. "I don't understand."

Ken came and stood on the top marble step next to the painting. "She was a wonderful woman. This, he pointed out is all because of your grandmother all of it, the festival, everything. They are all here because of her." Ken was about to go on when Jack cut him off.

"Was? What do you mean was?" Jack stood there with a confused look on his face and looked at Sara for answers. But, he knew what the answer was, even as Ken was explaining it.

"Oh, I'm sorry Jack I got word from some friends back in Elizabeth that she had passed away three days ago. I take it you didn't know?"

Jack shook his head. He had the look of shock on his face. Now he would never get to say he was sorry to her. He felt like he just got hit with a ton of bricks.

Sara stood next to him holding his hand. She felt his life force leave him as his hand went limp and he became stiff with a heart broken emotion on his face about to burst like a tidal wave.

Jack choked back tears. "Why is there a portrait of her here? I don't remember her ever mentioning any of this."

"Fist you have to understand I loved your grandmother but other than being a very close friend of mine she never had the same feeling for me. She was special to everyone around here. Her love of nature and the knowledge of all the medicinal plants and her willingness to help the hikers before they entered the hundred-mile wilderness made her a legend. She was in tune with the Lady of the Woods and if I could be perfectly honest with you, I and all the backpackers thought she was a white witch."

Jack looked over to Sara. "That would explain a lot."

Sara nodded.

Ken offered his hand to Sara. "I'm sorry, but do I know you?"

Sara shook his hand "You're talking about my grandmother too." She pointed at Jack. "I'm his step sister Sara." She said.

"Oh my god yes. I remember you went to live with your father in New York."

The music outside got louder. "Well come to the kitchen you kids have got to be hungry and you can tell me why you're here and why this fellow is looking for you, Jack."

Jack didn't want to rehash the past, but the offer of free food sounded like something he couldn't pass up.

In the kitchen Ken laid out fresh cold cuts, freshly baked bread and more of the hot clam chowder. He walked over to a large cupboard and carried back two pies placing them in front of them. Sara and Jack took up the two seats Ken placed at the table.

"That cha...dder is your grandmother's recipe. You two kids help yourselves." He pointed down a hallway. "There are a couple showers out back and some fresh towels when you get freshened up come back to the kitchen I'll make some fresh coffee and we can finish our talk."

Jack tasted the chowder it was close maybe even exactly the same recipe his grandmother would make penned by her very hand and given to Ken lovingly. But, it just as well have been mud and rock soup. He felt it would never be the same because she wasn't there to enjoy it with.

CHAPTER 23

THE DARKNESS SPEAKS

Darkness stuck to everything deep and stuck to whatever it touched surrounding everything and absorbed by everything until it became part of it, not allowing anything to be seen.

Mike awoke to a silence he never experienced before. He wondered what is the noise you hear when it is silent. He coughed clearing his throat. There was no echo; the sound traveled nowhere dying right where it had been born. He got up out of bed tapping at his wrist watch to see the time, but nothing happened. It would not illuminate.

He felt his way along the wall until he came to the wall switch and tapped it. The light failed to come on. He didn't think too much of it as being this far out in the woods it was possible that everything ran on a generator. It was reasonable that the old caretaker could have the power turned off for the evening.

Slowly he felt his way along the wall having to find the toilet. As he stood there a light flashed from outside through the window illuminating the room in an eerie glow. He welcomed the light and glad to see he wasn't urinating on the floor.

The light faded slowly, and he suddenly realized that all his movements made no sound. If it wasn't for the feeling he felt when he pinched his forearm he could have just as well been dreaming. He crept along until he came to the nightstand next to the bed wrapping his fingers tightly around the handle of the revolver.

A flash of light from outside brightened the room long enough for him to get to the door. Well let's see who's playing games out here in the dark he thought. Some jackass backpacker is about to get an ass kicking.

He held the gun steady in front of him. He didn't want it to come to the point of having to shoot someone but if threatened he wouldn't think twice about pulling the trigger. If he had thought twice about the approaching noise in the jungles of Vietnam and not shooting at it, he would have been dead. But this was not Vietnam and there were no sounds to aim at. And, if he had just randomly shot at some person carrying a flash light at night in the woods it wasn't going to end well. He opened the door and stepped out onto the porch.

The air was worm and still. A light hint of what he recognized as lavender floated past him. There were no sounds, no crickets, and no owls screeching. The creatures of the night were absent.

He held his arm up and couldn't see the gun in his hand. Suddenly in the distance a glowing figure appeared off in the woods walking from his left to right.

"Hey." He called out. "You there in the woods I can see you there. This is a dangerous game you're playing someone is going to get hurt."

He heard no reply and oddly not an echo of his own voice returned. What he could see of the person walking was just a glow. There was no sweeping flashlight movement that a person walking in the dark in the woods would need to make in order to see where they were going. He called out louder this time. Nothing returned.

The air surrounding him turned cold. He reached into his pocket and found his cigar lighter. Flicking it sent sparks into the air and he saw his breath. He tried it again but this time nothing happened.

He wanted to take off after the person walking and put an end to the game these backpackers were playing but remembered what the old caretaker had warned him about not entering the woods. He reached around himself with his other hand as if trying to grab the air. He could put his hand through it feeling cold about a foot surrounding him and just past that the air felt warm. It was as if placing his arm through an invisible barrier. Why the hell is it so cold just around me? He thought.

He remembered how the soldiers in is unit would often talk about phantom spirits walking the jungles at night and how the local village people would tell them of the Batutut a creature similar to Sasquatch they feared living in the jungles. Although once possible he couldn't imagine how it could survive the fallout of Agent Orange and constant bombings.

Suddenly everything around him lit up and he had to shield his eyes with his hand. After a few moments his eyes adjusted and there on the ground and in the woods appeared people walking all around. He lowered his fire arm; it would be of little use shooting something he could see straight through and into the woods. Turning toward a noise he heard coming from his left, he saw in the glow old Mr. Sampson walking toward him on the porch.

"Now you see." The old man said. "They don't belong here."

"I don't understand it." Mike answered. "I've never seen anything like it before. Still not sure I even believe it. What do you think it all means?"

"Something is very wrong here. I've been here in these woods for near seventy years the only person that would come is the Lady of the Woods. But now all these people wondering around like they lost."

Jack knew he had taken too long in the shower when the water turned cold. It was relaxing, and he just wanted the time to think. So much had happened since leaving the Maine state prison a little more than three years ago. He felt bruised and beaten his body ached all the time and the constant mental torture left him with a feeling of just giving up. But there were too many questions that still needed to be answered and promises to be kept.

"You done over there? Sara called out from the next shower stall. "Let's check in with Ken and see if he can put us up for the night."

"Yeah." Jack answered. "We still need to plan our next move."

Jack was dressed in fresh clothing and standing outside the shower stall waiting for Sara when she came out holding a necklace handing it to him.

"Here I want you to have this. I should have given it to you before, but I didn't think about it until now."

Jack held the necklace in his hand. "What is it?" He asked.

"I didn't say anything at first but ever since we got here I've been getting this feeling that something is very wrong here just like the feeling I got back at that cafe only stronger. I haven't seen anything yet. It's just a feeling."

Jack nodded, he knew that if she said something he could trust her and the feeling she would get to be an early warning system. Jack felt that he couldn't agree with her more. It seemed that the further along they got the more bizarre things became.

"It's a Celtic Shield. It will help ward off evil and help to protect you."

Jack put on the necklace. It was the second time in his life that he had been given a gift of protection. The Saint Christopher medal his grandmother had given him he wasn't sure helped. The accidents, his time in prison and the near-death experiences of the train and tractor left him wondering.

For better or worse, other than the physical and mental scars he always landed on his feet like an alley cat checking off one of its nine lives. Just how many more he had left in his bag to scratch off he wasn't sure.

Jack could smell the fresh coffee as he and Sara walked back into the kitchen. Ken was cutting an apple pie and setting plates.

"Well now don't you two look refreshed. I don't have much here, but the little comforts go a long way." He placed two plates of pie and a pot of coffee in front of them.

Sara took a bite of pie. "This is delicious." She said.

"Well you got your grandmother to thank for that, again her recipe."

Sara took note it was the first time someone had said your grandmother. She smiled finishing off the piece of pie.

Ken grabbed himself a coffee cup and came to sit across the table. "I think you kids need to know that your grandmother had prearranged to have her remains shipped here to Monson and that by now she should have been cremated. That's what she wanted. I would think that she is at the Barry funeral home by now. After the cremation we are going to take her remains and spread it in the woods and some of the backpackers want to spread her ashes on top of Mount Katahdin. We didn't know about the two of you, so we hope you have no objections."

Jack and Sara both shook their heads no at the same time saying. "Do what she wanted."

"I need to ask you kids why are you here? You are obviously not here for the festival and I'm sure you were not aware of her passing. Please don't take this the wrong way but why are you here? If I had to guess I'm sure it's got something to do with old flat top from New York City."

Sara urged Jack on. "Go ahead Jack you can tell him I believe what he is saying is true that he loved her. Just take a look around at all the people gathered here because of her."

Under the table Jack squeezed Sara's hand. "I lost contact with her some time ago. I got word of her being in the hospital and went to see her three days ago. When I arrived, I found she was heavily medicated and asleep, so I never got to see her or had the chance to make thing right and for that I will forever be regretful. While at the hospital I was given a letter, she wrote to me saying that I should go to her old cabin in Maine that there was something there she wanted me to have. Along the way here I found Sara and here we are. Jack purposely left out the part about the accidents and being followed to Maine by Mike Shannon. He felt that he shouldn't go into too much detail and to keep some things hidden until it became necessary to bring that scary past back to life.

Ken gathered up the empty dishes placing them into the sink. He came back fishing a set of keys from his pant pocket handing them to Sara.

"Here you go this is the key to the spare room upstairs it's the one closest to the bathroom. There are two small beds. You might not get much sleep because of all the noise, but you will be safe there."

Ken knew there was more to their story. Two kids that haven't been in Maine in more than three years suddenly show up being looked for by a bounty hunter from New York. Just at the time that their grandmother is being cremated and celebrated and claiming not to know about it just didn't sit right.

"Well." Ken said. "About that fellow from New York don't you worry about him he's not here and he won't be back until the morning. He and I are going to get together and check out something strange he found out on old Blanchard road. This festival will be over by the morning and the backpackers will be heading off into the hundred-mile wilderness."

Upstairs Sara unlocked the door. The room had a smell of mold and mildew with two beds jut up against opposite walls and a common chest of draws between them. She stepped inside and found a light switch on the wall that worked a small lamp on a night stand near the far bed and worked a small ceiling fan overhead. She set the dead bolt lock behind her and went over to open the window but found the noise from outside too much and closed it. She unpacked her bag laying her belongings on the bed choosing not to put anything in the dresser for fear of picking up insects. Sara sat at the edge of the bed arranging and folding her clothing.

"Did you catch what Ken was saying?" She asked.

"About what?" Jack tossed his pack on the floor near the bed and fluffed the pillow. All he wanted now was a few hours sleep. The bed was lumpy, but he didn't care it was better than sleeping in a subway station on a wooden bench. He hoped that nothing would attack him in the middle of the night especially the no-see-ums he'd been warned about.

"I just can't help thinking what Ken said about Mike finding something strange out on old Blanchard road. It must be something big to make them want to go back out there in the morning to find out what it is. Do you suppose it has something to do with what is going on around here? Maybe we should follow them in the morning to see what it is."

" No."Jack answered. "What we need to do is go to that funeral home and find out about where the baby is buried and where our grandmother's remains are. Then ..."

Sara cut him off. "I know... don't say it."

"I'm going to the rest room do you have any tooth paste?"

Sara fished in her bag and came up with a small tube. "Here you go, but no brush."

"I'll make due. Just keep this door locked while I'm gone."

Sara lay on the bed her eyes were heavy and her body wanted to sleep but she felt the phantoms of the night calling out to be heard. How many were there and what set this all-in motion that there would be so many lost souls. She was glad to be on the second floor as the distance from the outside gave her a bit of insulation and the feeling wasn't so strong. Shut it off she told herself. And she closed her eyes.

The water from the faucet in the restroom wasn't too hot. Jack found a wash cloth in the closet wet it and dabbed it with some tooth paste and went about brushing his teeth. He wondered just how much he could trust the old man Ken. He didn't want to give the old man any information that the old man could accidentally pass along to Mike. He didn't remember ever seeing him around when he was in Maine or if his grandmother ever mentioned him. The one fact that he was certain of was the fact that Ken cared for her deeply.

Sara heard the nock at the door but she didn't want to get up. Her eyes were heavy and the muscles of her body heavier. A second knock at the door was a little louder and Sara forced herself up. "Alright Jack hold on." She called out unlatching the door and walking back to lie on the bed. Sara had her eyes shut and only heard the approaching footsteps.

Jack finished in the bathroom leaving the wet towel hanging on the door knob as he walked back out into the hall. He saw a light coming from the doorway of where he had told Sara to keep the door locked. Slowly he approached the room clenching his fists and tensing his body for a fight. At the door Jack found Ken seated on the bed next to Sara holding a small gray duffel bag in his hands.

"What's going on?" He asked.

Ken got up leaving the sack on the bed he slowly untied the string at the top and fished out two decorative wooden boxes. He removed the lid of one revealing a dusty old bottle. "This is a bottle of 100-year-old scotch you grandmother gave me a long time ago. I've had this bottle for seventy-five years and I can't think of a better time than now to drink a toast to a great friend, a beautiful woman and to you who I'm sure she loved so much. Ken placed three shot glasses on top the dresser and handed the bottle to Jack. "I think it's only fitting if you would do the honors."

Jack popped the cork out of the bottle and poured the three shots. It had been more than three years since he had a drink, but he couldn't refuse such an honorable expression of love for his grandmother.

"Cheers." Ken held his drink up in front of him. "To a lovely woman may she rest in peace. And to her grandchildren I hope you fine all you're looking for."

Sara coughed and choked when she sipped at the drink. Ken laughed patting her on the back.

Jack poured the whole shot in his mouth at once letting it linger there for a moment before he swallowed. It was smooth the way he remembered fine liquor to be. It was rare that he would ever enjoy something as fine. When he was drinking heavily it was usually cheap beer and cheap whiskey until he fell down drunk not remembering the details of the evening. He recorked the bottle handing it to Ken.

"I can leave this bottle with you guys I'm sure a couple of belts will get you to sleep just fine."

Jack looked over to Sara she shook her head no. "I think you should keep it. She gave it to you, I'm sure she wanted you to enjoy it. I'm not much of a drinker anyhow."

Ken took back the bottle pulled the cork and poured himself another drink. This one is for her and he pick up the shot glass pouring off a small amount onto the floor. "For the souls of the departed, bless you." He said finishing off the rest with a smack of his lips.

Ken placed the second box on the bed. "This young lady I'm sure she would want you to have."

Sara held it in her hands, it was a beautifully decorative wooden box carved in the shape of a serpent. She heard a rattle from the inside when she moved it.

"Open it encouraged Ken. "It's all hand carved by your grandmother. There is a little secret to opening it you have to pull off the serpents head." Ken laughed. "I loved her sense of humor."

Sara followed the directions and spilled the contents onto the bed. There were six hand carved figurines she recognized as Native American spiritual totem symbols. She picked them up one at a time studying its intricate detail and placing it back into the box. The last one was a cactus and she knew its significance to the Native Americans of enduring tough situations. She was just about to pick it up and place it back in the box when she noticed something shinny peeking out from underneath. She reached down and pulled out a key.

Ken came up next to her and Sara placed the key onto his out stretched palm. "I believe that is the key to the cabin. You remember how to get to that cabin Jack?"

"I'm sure I can find it."Jack answered.

Ken moved off toward the doorway. "It's been a long while since I've been down that road. I'm sure that the entrance to the cabin is well overgrown. There is a tool shed across from where you took your shower you can help yourself to any of the tools there. I'm heading down that road early in the morning with old flat top to see why he couldn't find the old cemetery."

Ken reached into his pocket and flipped Jack a key. "That's the key to my old pickup truck it's parked next to the shed. It will take you anywhere you want to go, and no one will give it a second look, if you know what I mean?"

Jack shook his hand and thanked the man and as he turned back to the room Sara moved past him in a flash and hugged Ken.

"You kids be careful. There is something strange going on around here. Let me know how you made out." Ken waved, closing the door behind him and walked down the stairs.

"You know Jack I'm convinced something odd is going on around here from the time we were back in my shop in New York. Reading in the newspaper about the shenanigans going on with the Barry funeral home and then seeing all the spirits in the cafe makes me wonder. Then Ken telling us that your parole officer thinks he found something strange out on old Blanchard road which just happens to be the road we need to take to get to the cabin is odd. And, then Ken telling us that he thinks something odd is going on around here. Something drew me here maybe it's her or maybe it's the Lady of the Woods. I'm not sure but whatever it is, it must be a strong force to make me drive all this way. And of course, the weird feelings I'm getting. Should I go on?"

"No, you said it all."Jack locked the door and went to lie on the bed. "Do you suppose that it has anything to do with the festival? I don't know anything about the spirit word that's your department maybe they stirred something up."

"You know that those people out there believed our grandmother to be a white witch."

"Thought white witches only do good?" Jack asked.

"They should." Sara answered playing with the wood carvings.

Well maybe she was doing a little more. And I'm still trying to wrap my head around that whole Lady of the Woods thing. For now, I'm going to concentrate on finding the baby's gravesite and the cabin." Jack shut his eyes. "Best we try to get some sleep."

Mike felt the air around him cold and when he exhaled he saw his breath. Yet, he knew that when he arrived earlier that the day had been warm. Big temperature swings were common for the back woods of Maine, so he didn't think it too much out of the ordinary. But just to have a cold spot near him was something out of the ordinary and it gave him pause.

When he looked out toward the darken woods it was as if he was looking out at a time he spent as a child on a gentle late spring evening camping trip with his parents in Vermont. They would sit around a cabin playing games waiting in anticipation for the cool evening.

Mother would be busy in the kitchen washing out old glass mason jars, checking the rings and affixing lids with the proper fit. Dad would be rummaging through a tool box looking for the right size screwdriver punching holes in the lids. And when they had everything set they would gather up the cattail punks they had cut from the bog earlier that day that were hung along the rafters drying. When darkness fell the fun would begin. Everyone was given their own jar and dad would light a cattail blowing on the end until it glowed red hot stinking up everything around it with a putrid smell the mosquitoes hated.

Deep into the darken night on a high of simple childhood dreams the jars would be opened and closed repeatedly. Each time a tiny little life force would be deposited inside glowing with a rhythmic cosmic dance who wanted nothing more than searching for love.

But the dark woods suddenly flashing around him now were no summer lighting bugs. These were once people flashing in and out of existence walking now in an empty darkness of night. What a shame he thought that these people could be aimlessly looking for a loved one.

Mike pulled out his cigar holder and placed a cigar between his teeth. He offered one to the old care taker. "Don't mind if I do." He said grinning ear to ear.

Mike tried to light the cigar but again the lighter wouldn't work.

"Can't understand why this lighter won't work I just got it."

The old caretaker came over holding a small box of wooden matches lighting Mike's cigar.

"Oh, I know why. Ever since they showed up everything around here went screwy."

Mike took a long draw of the cigar and puffed out the smoke, but it didn't dissipate. It seemed to swirl there in the air as if it was attached to something. "Watch this." He said to the old man puffing out smoke again.

"Oh, yeah there is someone right front you."The old caretaker said.

Mike could see nothing there but when he stuck out his arm the area was freezing cold. "How long did you say this was going on?"

The old care taker struck a match lighting his cigar. "Bout four or five days now I figure."

Well they don't seem to be trying to bother us any. It will be light in a few hours so I'm going to go back to sleep. He bid the old man a good night and watched as he walked away in to the darkness surrounded by an occasional flash of spirit energy.

Mike stood there for a moment trying to take it all in. He had never seen anything like it before and he shook his head wondering how the hell someone can explain what he had seen.

Finishing his cigar, he turned and walked back to the room. He reached for the light switch along the wall and this time the light came on momentarily blinding him. This was something new he thought and when he tried the lighter it came on the first try. That's got to mean one thing he thought, and he went to check. Opening the door, he heard the sound of crickets and he saw no flashing only the darkness of the woods. Turning back to the room he took off his holster tossing it on the bed landing on top of the bible. He was sure that he had placed the bible on the night stand before he left the room. Reaching down to move it he noticing that it had three book marks in it that he was positive was not there before. "Okay whatever game this is I'll play." He said.

He picked up the gun placing it on the night stand. He kicked off his shoes and lie on the bed. Thumbing through the bible stopping at the first book mark, he read aloud:

ISAIAH 5.20 *Woe to them that call evil good, and good evil; that put darkness for light, and light for darkness; that put bitter for sweet, and sweet for bitter. Pulling out the second book mark he read:*

ISAIAH 26.19 Your dead shall live; their bodies shall rise. You who dwell in the dust, awake and sing for joy for your dew is the dew of light and the earth will give BIRTH TO THE DEAD.

Mike rubbed at his tired eyes and he was fighting them to stay awake. He pulled the third card and read:

PSALM 91.5 You will not fear the terror of the night, nor the arrow that flies by day.

Mike closed the book and placed it alongside the gun on the nightstand. If someone was trying to tell him something this was an odd way of doing it. Could one of the backpackers gotten past him and snuck into the room?

Although it was difficult to see outside in the darkness he was sure that the only living begins around was the old caretaker and himself. He was sure that if the old caretaker wanted to tell him something he would spell it out bluntly right to his face. He remembered what the old caretaker had told him about the Lady of the Woods and how she would show him the strange circumstances going on around here. Mike shut off the light. Closing his eyes, he hoped that the morning would arrive fresh and that the night's festivities were over.

CHAPTER 24

INTO THE TANGLED WEB

BANG... Mike opened one eye. Bang again. This time he sat up and reached for the revolver. This can't be for real he thought. Why would someone be banging on the door in the middle of the night? "Keep banging and I'm going to shoot your ass." He yelled out.

From the other side of the door the old caretaker kicked at the door with his shoe. "Do that and you ain't gona be having no coffee and these fresh baked muffins will be no good with blood all over them."

Mike opened the door finding the caretaker standing there holding a try with a coffee pot on it and what smelled like blueberry muffins wrapped in a towel. He could see steam rising from it. "Come in. What time is it?"

"No -no. It be 6 am. Take the tray. The Lady say time for you to go. Drink you coffee you got places to be."

Mike took the tray and placed it on the table. He unfolded the towel and took a bite of the warm muffin and washed it down with a gulp of black coffee.

"Your right." He said. "And I've been thinking where the best place to get answers about the dead is? From an undertaker."

The old man smiled offering his hand. Mike shook it and thanked the man for his hospitality.

Walking away the old man looked back pointing at the gate. "Hey, old military man." He yelled out. "Remember what was said a long time ago. When you're going through hell you better keep going. Be careful. You think it crazy in here wait till you see what out there."

"I find anything I'll let you know." Mike closed the door and quickly washed up in the bathroom. He put on his shoes and holstered the gun on his belt. He found a paper cup on the tray poured another cup of coffee stuffing the remaining muffins in his jacket pocket and started the walk back to his car.

A layer of fog hung close to the ground and Mike felt the morning coolness deep into his bones. He had always wanted to start working out and taking better care of his health. He knew that his daily ritual of smoking two cigars was probably going to kill him. His firm belief was that the heart only had so many beats to it so why speed it up unnecessarily. The walk was short to the car and didn't give him much time to go over in his mind the events of last night. He told himself it was something he would go over later with Ken. For now, he would have to concentrate on picking up Ken and finding the right road to the cabin.

Twenty minutes later Mike was pulling up the drive of Ken's place. The last of the backpackers were packing up and heading out. The smell of smoke lay heavy in the air and he could see ambers still glowing in the fire ring. Mike was about to get out of the car when he saw Ken coming down the steps holding a large paper bag.

Mike came around the passenger side of the car unlocking the door and helping Ken inside.

"Hope you like and egg sandwich on a roll."

Mike could already smell the bacon through the bag and his mouth was salivating. When he bit into the sandwich he was delighted to find that the egg was not over cooked and the bacon extra thick and smoky. He put his hand in his pocket pulling out the crushed muffins and tossed them out the window over the car.

Ken sat in the passenger seat with the large bag on his lap and opened a sandwich for himself, wrapped in tin foil.

"I'm hoping you got some Mississippi mud in that bag."

Ken handed him a cup. "Yep dark with extra octane. Did you get any sleep out there?"

Mike sipped at his coffee. "Let's just say that not since Vietnam have I experienced anything so odd in the night. And I now truly believe what you say about the strange things going on around here."

"Yeah it used to be that you only see the Lady in the Woods on occasion but now it's gotten worse. I don't think that the backpackers of the festival have anything to do with it. We've been having that festival to some degree for as long as I can remember and nothing like that has occurred before."

Mike started the car and headed back toward the funeral home. "I'm going to drive back the way I remember, and you tell me where I went wrong."

"Just take it nice and slow I don't want a lap full of hot Joe. Like I said that road is in bad shape."

Mike saw the funeral home ahead and took a right turn. Ken quickly gulped down the remainder of his drink putting the empty cup in a cup holder. "There's a full thermos in the bag if you want more coffee."

"Maybe latter." Mike waved him off. I'm interested in finding that graveyard."

Mike felt the car rock as the road quickly went from black top to stone and then a mix of stone, dirt and potholes. Just past the funeral home he pulled to the side of the road looking through the windshield at a graveyard behind the funeral home.

"That's the newer graveyard." Ken said shaking his head up and down. "Now if you kept going down this road you can't miss the next graveyard and just past that is a small road off to the right that leads to the cabin."

Mike stepped easily on the accelerator. "Well we will see."

Slowly he drove along the road like a slithering snake navigating the car around pothole after pothole. A mile later he again pulled the car to the side this time getting out stretching his legs.

Ken opened his door and followed Mike standing at the front of the car.

Ken didn't see anything out of the ordinary pointing out to Mike the cows across the street that will follow you along the road as you walked.

Mike reached into his pocket and pulled out his cigar holder placing a cigar between his lips and Ken took the one offered.

"What say we do a little walking it's still cool out and the bugs haven't arrived yet."

"Lead on." Mike answered lighting his cigar.

"Doctor says that I shouldn't but the hell with that. You know I'm eighty-six years old and there are a lot of things I'm not supposed to do. But I got a theory there are only so many days and so many words in your book and once you go through them all and come to the end of the story its best you arrive there with no regrets. So, cause no harm try your best and eat that forbidden fruit every now and again. Most importantly love. Oh, and I don't mean hop in and out of every hen house you come to. No, a man should have a woman he cherishes as more than a lover, a mother, but a true soul to share life together with. I had her, I thought. Her name was Margaret Kahill."

Ken stopped walking and turned around to Mike smiling with a cigar hanging on his lip. "How about a light?"

Ken reached the beginning of the rock wall first and climbed the small incline. He called to Mike. "I want to show you something." When mike approached he bent down along the side of the hill and picked a small wild strawberry handing it to mike. "Trust me you have never experienced anything like this popping one into his mouth.

Mike took hold the offering in his palm. It was no larger than a thumbnail. He popped it into his mouth and was immediately rewarded with a flavor explosion that seemed impossible for something so tiny. "Wow." He said.

Ken was now about ten feet ahead of him with his baseball cap off filling it with the tiny morsels as he walk up the road along the rock wall. "Did you happen to notice the white markings painted on the wall?"

Mike stopped walking picking a strawberry Ken had missed. "I see it now that you mention it, but I didn't pay it any mind."

"They are trail markings for the Appalachian trail. It goes right through here. I found these small berries as a boy when I would hike the trail with my father. They are a nice little welcome for the hikers, but you got to get them before the rabbits or bears get them.

Ken had his head down still picking strawberries when Mike caught up to him. "Well this is it the end of the rock wall and the beginning of my nightmare."

Ken looked up and dropped the hat spilling the strawberries. He could see the row of trees separating the two properties. He climbed the small embankment and looked right. Across the street he could see the end of a fence line with cows gathered there looking back at him right where they should be. When he looked left again he saw an empty freshly plowed field.

Mike came up alongside Ken picking up the hat and placing his hand on his shoulder. "What's wrong?" He asked.

"EVERYTHING! We need to find a way down into that field."

"Wait here." Mike said handing Ken the empty hat.

Mike back tracked along the berm and found a deer path through the row of trees. When he came back he found Ken seated on a tree stump shaking his head.

"If you're up to it we can make it thru the tree line by way of a dear trail it's got some roots to watch out for, but I think we came make it."

Ken reached his arm out and Mike grabbed hold helping Ken to his feet. "Lead on young man we need to get down there."

Mike stepped down onto the field holding a hand out to ken helping him down. He paused for a moment allowing Ken to catch his breath. Mike was about to walk on when he felt a hand grab his arm stopping him. "Your armed, aren't you?" Ken asked taking Mike by surprise.

Mike patted at his waist. "If you're expecting something let me know now before we go any further."

"No." Just in case Ken pulled out a 38 special from his pocket its barrel flashed in the sun light. "It's always a good idea to pack a little heat you never know what you might run into."

Mike wiped his chin. "Well I'll be." He said. "Do you want to lead on?"

Ken put the gun back in his pocket and took the lead stopping in the middle of the field. He bent down scooping up a hand full of dirt and rubbed it between his fingers. "Freshly tilled still has moisture."

Mike stood there with a puzzled look on his face. "I'm no farmer but isn't that how it should be."

Ken stood there for a moment looking Mike dead in the eyes.

"NOT WHEN THIS IS SUPPOSED TO BE A CEMETARY." Ken's anguished voice cut the silence like a knife.

Mike started to walk away. "Wait a minute. What are you talking about?"

"You remember that second older graveyard you were supposed to see as you drove along the road well this is it." Ken kicked at the ground spinning a small dust devil into the air. "Or was it."

"Are you serious?" Mike bent grabbing some dirt allowing it to fall between his fingers.

Ken shook his head up and down pointing out to the field. "There had to have been a hundred or more graves here. Some dating back to the early seventeen hundred."

Mike looked out into the field taking in a deep breath and exhaled very slowly. He stood trying to take in all that Ken had said. Suddenly he could a see person a hundred feet away standing in the field. Mike drew his gun from his holster and called to Ken to take a look.

Ken caught up to Mike grabbing his wrist lowering his arm. Mike yelled out to the man in the field but the man paid no attention to him. "What you do that for?" Mike said with a surprised look on his face.

"You can't shoot the dead." Ken answered.

"What you are talking about?"

"Well you got to ask yourself why a man would be standing in an empty field with no shoes on while wearing a suit from the early eighteen hundreds and not worker clothing?"

Mike put his gun back in the holster. He could see now that the man was indeed dressed wrongly for a farmer.

"I don't know who that man once was but he's standing about where my father's grave would have been."

"I'm sorry." Mike offered.

Ken patted Mike on the back. "No need my boy."

The two men started walking closer to the man in the field when he suddenly vanished.

When they reached the spot where the man had been standing Ken tripped and fell into the dirt. He tried to right himself by pushing off the dirt with his hands. Mike hurried to his side picking him up and went about dusting him off. Ken came up holding something in his hand. And when he looked he was shocked to see that he was holding a femur bone in his hand.

Mike stood there his eyes looked like two dark saucer cups. "Holy shit." He said. "I've experienced a lot of things in Vietnam, but I've never seen anything like what I've experienced in the last few days here. I just pray that bone your holding is..."

Ken cut him off. "Let's just rebury it where we found it." He pulled a large pocket knife from his pocket and started digging in the dirt. Mike knelt next to him moving the dirt with his hands. A foot down Ken placed the bone into the hole and covered it. Mike got up and helped Ken up on his feet.

Ken turned to Mike. "I'm going to say a few words your welcome to stay if you like."

Mike nodded. "I'd like that."

Ken faced the sun and raised his hands in the air. "AS I WALK, AS I WALK. THE UNIVERSE IS WALKING WITH ME, IN BEAUTY IT WALKS BEFORE ME, IN BEAUTY IT WALKS BEHIND ME, IN BEAUTY IT WALKS BELOW ME, IN BEAUTY IT WALKS ABOVE ME. BEAUTY IS ON EVERY SIDE AS I WALK, I WALK WITH BEAUTY."

When he finished he grab some of the dirt, tossing it in the air.

"What was that?" Mike asked.

Ken brushed his hands on his trousers. "It's an old Native American blessing taught to me by Margaret Kahill. She was a very knowledgeable woman."

"No offence." Mike said shaking his head. "I think it's going to take more than a blessing to straighten this mess out."

"I think your right. Let's get to your car and when we get back I'll call an elder friend of mine and the local sheriff. Let them get to the bottom of this." Ken started walking away.

Mike stood there for a moment looking back to see if anything else would materialize. Seeing that nothing had, he turned and hurried catching up to Ken. "What's an elder? He asked.

Ken stopped and turned to face Mike. "The chief from the Maliseet people." They have been living on this land for hundreds of years and to them this land is sacred."

"Wait I've got an idea I still need to find my guy. Give me twenty-four hours before you do anything. Let me go to that funeral home and ask a few questions before we call in an air strike."

Back in the car Mike asked. "What the hell do you think happened here? How does someone wipe out a graveyard and what did they do with all the headstones?"

"I can't imagine other than no one comes down this road and it's sort of hidden from the road so if you weren't looking for it you would never know that it was there. Promise me that you'll get the bastard that did this. For Christ's sake my father was buried there."

Mike pulled the car close to the church entrance and went around the passenger side holding the door open for Ken. He shook Ken's hand. "Before I leave I need to ask, do you think the guy I'm looking for could be here?" Mike handed him the bag from the back. "Thanks again for breakfast."

"Hard to say." Ken answered. "There really isn't much there other than an old dilapidated cabin."

"Yeah." Mike said as he got in the car and rolled down the window. "A perfect place to hide. Remember twenty-four hours if I'm not back by then send in the troops." He waved out the window as he drove off heading toward the Barry funeral home.

CHAPTER 25

NO STONE UNTURNED

Sara was already awake and freshening up in the bathroom when Jack heard a knock at the door. He wanted to sleep more. The night was rough with the noise coming from the festival. He and Sara had been offered to join the festivities sometime in the night by the same hippy lady who offered Jack a hit on a joint earlier in the day.

A knock came again at the door. "What the hell time is it?" He called out. From behind the door he heard a muffled voice call back. "It's breakfast time that's what time it is. Open the door for an old man with his arms full."

Jack got up from the bed and went to open the door but as he got to the door knob the door suddenly flung open hitting him in the knee. Sara came in followed by Ken holding a tray with a coffee pot and two plates of hot cakes.

"Well I'm glad to see you kids lasted the night but any good adventure starts with a good breakfast." Ken laid the tray on the nightstand.

Jack said nothing rubbing at his knee. He pushed past them heading to the rest room.

Sara poured a cup of coffee and grabbed a plate of the hot cakes and sat on the bed. "Is old flat top still here?" She asked.

Ken was just about at the door when Jack came back to the room. He turned back to Sara. "He's gone for the next twenty-four hours. So, you kids are safe to mill around till then."

Jack grabbed a coffee. "Well I'm getting out of this room. I could use some fresh air." He turned looking at Sara. "What about you, how do you feel, anything strange?"

Sara got up and helped herself to another helping of hot cakes. She didn't know why she was so hungry. Had she been back in New York City she couldn't imagine herself, eating this much. Was it the Fresh air of being in Maine or not getting enough sleep the last few days, she wasn't sure, but Ken was a true blessing and she felt thankful for the meal. Sara stood looking out the window.

"Last night was odd. I was up sometime early morning I could feel them. When I looked out this window I saw flashings of people walking about in the woods. Maybe it was just the backpackers, I don't know."

Ken gathered up Sara's empty plate and cup. "What you saw little lady was what has been happening around here for the last week or so. It's got nothing to do with the backpackers. Early this morning while you were still sleeping I took a ride with Mike down Old Blanchard Road trying to figure out why he got lost on that road and couldn't find the old cemetery that is there. Only now when we got to the road there is no cemetery. It's a freshly plowed empty field. Only I don't think it's empty."

Jack put his empty cup and plate back on the tray. "What do you mean?"

"We drove down that road and everything looked normal until we got to the end of the rock wall. When we got to the top of the berm there we could see that the old cemetery was gone and the only thing that was there was a freshly plowed field."

Ken bowed his head and Sara could see tears welt up in his eyes. "What's wrong?" She asked.

Ken swallowed hard and choked out. "I found a bone."

Sara shuddered when she felt a cold chill run up her spine. "How can that be?"Sara asked.

"I wish I knew. It's something Mike is looking into now. But let me ask you something, a moment ago you said that you saw things in the night and that you didn't feel anything what did you mean by that?"

Sara looked at Jack for direction. He shook his head okay. "Go ahead tell him." He said.

Sara drew in a deep breath held it for a moment and let it out slowly. She sat on the bed and opened the wooden box picking out the carved figure of the Bear for strength.

"Ever since I was a young girl I've had the ability to see and feel the dead. Some people call it clairvoyance but mostly I help lost souls to cross over. Sometimes it's a gift, but most times it's a curse. Especially now."

Ken came over and sat on the bed next to Sara holding her hand.

"I Know." He said. "Your grandmother was the same. She would stop in mid stride and ask me if I saw what she was looking at and I would look out seeing nothing saying no. I would see her sometimes as if she was talking to the wind. Oh, child I'm sorry for you. It must be awful sometimes having such a burden of never being alone."

"Especially last night." Sara answered.

Sara got up and went to the window. "I had a hard time sleeping last night I could feel them calling to me and when I looked out this window I saw people walking in the woods. One moment they are there and then the next their gone."

"Kind of like a lightning bug." Ken added.

"Yes, I imagine so." Sara said. "But the question is why so many?"

"I'm sure it has to do with that cemetery that is no longer there."

Jack grabbed the set of keys Ken left on the dresser. He was already headed for the door.

"Let's go see for ourselves. Jack waved to Sara to follow. I'll take you up on the use of your truck. We find anything we'll let you know."

Jack was half way out the door when he called back to Sara. "Take your time I'm going to get some tools I'll meet you at the truck. We'll see if we can find out what is going on around here."

"Careful." Ken answered.

CHAPTER 26

INTO THE WEB

Mike Shannon eased his car up the driveway of the BARRY FUNERAL HOME and parked his car in an open space alongside a black hearse that was there.

The funeral home looked dark even though it was a bright day with the sun shining high in the sky. The windows were dark with heavy drapery pulled closed across them. Vines of ivy were growing up the walls and sticking out between the gutters. Mike had to push an overgrown hedge back away from the steps as he walked up to the door.

He looked for a doorbell but didn't see anything on the door other than a large rusted metal knocker in the shape of a gargoyle with its tongue sticking out. He grabbed it by the face and when trying to knock at the door found it to be rusted in place. Fuck this he thought and kicked at the door with the back of his heel. He could hear the sound of the knocking echo around inside the building as if it was a cave. After the third knock he could hear a sound behind the door of someone opening dead bolts and sliding latches that went on for what Mike though an unusual amount of time.

Once inside he told himself that he would have to take a look at that door to see how many locks were actually on it. He wondered why so many locks. Who the hell would try to break into a funeral home?

When the door opened he could see nothing. It was pitch dark inside. A voice floated there in the darkness. "Good morning how can I help you?" The voice was followed by the large stature of Montgomery Barry.

Mike couldn't see the man as the top of the doorway blocked him from being seen.

Montgomery ducked under the doorway and the huge mass of the man spilled into the light. He stood there for a moment squinting at the nastiness of the bright light.

"I'm so sorry for the delay. This is a service entrance and one not used too often. The main entrance is on the other side of the building."

"Oh, pardon me."Mike said. "I thought…"

Montgomery cut him off. "It's quite alright." He said blinking at the light.

Mike could now see the large man standing in the doorway. He guessed him to be about a foot taller than he.

Montgomery ducked as he walked back through the doorway and adjusted the lighting just enough to see.

"If you would be so kind to follow me." Montgomery led Mike to a front parlor. "Please have a seat and I will be with you shortly."

Mike took a seat on a soft leather high back seat and he couldn't help notice how the air was stale with a smell of formaldehyde. He watched Montgomery as he walked down a hallway ducking each time he passed a threshold.

Montgomery sat at his desk and from beyond the torments of death two hundred eyes stared blindly at him, unable to do anything to change the course of events. They watched from a cold emptiness the living transformation of evil. Some young, some old, some disfigured, some in agony stuck forever more in that moment in time.

"THAT'S HIM ...THAT'S HIM THEY SHOUTED. HE'S HERE TO HARM US."

"EASY MY FRIENDS.HE CAN DO US NO HARM." Montgomery whispered back.

They watched as he took out the tiny delivery system that would do evils bidding.

From her place of honor, Jenny Harrows watched as he put on rubber glove to protect himself of the destructive forces at work. She watched as he opened the bottle and poured off the necessary amount into a vile and filled the small holding cell of the ring. It's pin point gleaming in the dim light.

Montgomery finished taking off the gloves happy that he didn't spill a drop. He placed the bottle back in the desk draw. When he got up he stopped and smiled at his trophy wall.

"Soon my friends soon." He whispered back to all the voices from the wall and walked out to greet the man now sitting in the waiting parlor.

Mike stood to greet the man when he saw a shadow coming down the hall. Montgomery feigned a smile as he approached. Deep down inside his soul he despised touching people, but this was a special occasion that called for delicate handling.

Montgomery walked slowly toward Mike offering his hand. "I'm Montgomery Barry how can I help you?"

Mike nodded and smiled holding up in one hand his credentials. "My name is Mike Shannon." He said as he reached out to shake Montgomery's hand.

Montgomery wrapped his long fingers around Mikes hand and immediately Mike felt a pin prick to the palm of his hand. His eyes widened, and he felt his heart race. The room started to spin, and he saw the walls beginning to melt around him. Everything moved in slow motion. He dropped his credentials and watched as they floated gently to the floor.

"Motherfucker!" He yelled as he reached and pulled out his revolver.

Montgomery pivoted to the side as Mike brought his hand up trying to take aim as the room melted around him. He pulled the trigger as he slumped to the floor. Mike saw the flash of the muzzle as he fell, and everything went dark.

Montgomery's pivot move was fast, but his tall stature made for a good target and the bullet grazed him in his arm just above the elbow. It continued going clean through the wall behind him imbedding in the photo of Jenny Harrows removing the top of her head.

Once he was outside, Jack walked briskly toward Ken's pickup truck. Two tires in the front were bald and the right rear was low on air. It was an old beat up Ford F150 whose glory days were long in the past. Jack wasn't sure if rust was eating it alive or holding it together. The morning was cool with just a few clouds and a light breeze blowing from the west. When he lowered the tail gate the whole truck rattled like it was going to come apart. Turning the key, the old truck fired up on the first try. Jack decided to let it worm up while he went to the shed to find some tools.

Jack was fighting to open the lock on the shed when Sara approached. "Dam this thing." He said. He hit the lock with the side of a closed fist and on the third pull it finally opened.

Sara stood on a small ramp that led to the door. "What do you think we need to break into a casket?" She asked.

When Jack swung the door open, he was amazed to find the tool shed packed with tools and well organized.

"Don't know." He said. "Look around take anything you think we could use and put it in the bed of the truck.

Sara grabbed two pointed shovels and started out the door. "I know what these are, after that I'm lost so I'll take these to the truck and wait for you there."

"Okay." Jack agreed. Over a bench he found a rack of tools neatly arranged in separate holders. He picked out a large flat screwdriver, a hand-held sledge hammer and an axe. In a tool chest he picked out a few various sized chisels and a magnetic flashlight. Under the table he found an empty bucket and some rags. He placed the tools into the bucket locked the door behind him and placed the bucket next to the shovels closing the tail gate.

Inside the truck Jack found the steering wheel too low resting almost on his knees but he couldn't find any way to adjust it.

Sara sat on the passenger side of the bench seat and immediately sunk into the seat. She got up placing her hand on the seat finding a hole in the middle of the seat. Well this is going to be fun she thought. She looked under the seat and pulled out a small pillow. It fit perfectly in the hole.

Jack pressed down on the accelerator and the truck kicked-up gravel behind it. Jack was pleased that the old girl still had some life in her. He drove out onto the main road and headed for Old Blanchard road. It had been more than four years since he been down that road, but he was sure that once he got there he could easily find his grandmother's old cabin.

Making the right hand turn past the Barry funeral home the road quickly deteriorated into a nightmare of ever worsening potholes that the old truck had a hard time navigating. Jack tried to slow down seeing pavement fall away to gravel but it was too late when he applied the old brakes. The truck hit the pothole too fast. Jack grabbed the steering wheel his knuckles turning white. Sara left her seat hitting her head on the roof of the truck and came down hard falling into the hole in the seat when the cushion moved.

Jack burst out laughing when he looked over at Sara seeing her stuck in the seat. He slowed the truck to a crawl. "I'm sorry about that." He said.

Sara looked over with a frown on her face when she noticed a graveyard out the window. "Is that it?" She asked.

Jack looked. "No, that's the newer one. The one we are looking for is just past the rock wall. You won't be able to see it from the road we'll have to get out and go through a tree line to see it."

A mile further down the road Jack eased the truck over to the side of the road. He was first out of the truck. "This is bad." He said. "That's an empty field just like the way Ken said he saw it."

Sara took in a deep breath she felt a heaviness in the air around her. "That's not a farm?" She asked.

"No." Jack answered. "You shouldn't be able to see it from the road. This should all be covered with trees. The only way you would know that there was a graveyard here was to have lived here. It was really old, and I used to walk through here when I was a child." Jack scratched at his head. "How the hell can this be?"

He climbed the berm holding out a hand for Sara. "Come on let's take a closer look." Sara followed him up the berm.

"I don't think I can go too much further." She said.

"Are you feeling okay? Is it your head?"

Sara shook her head no.

Jack stopped walking. "Oh." He said when he realized what was bothering her.

"Yep." She said suddenly pointing to the field.

"Wait Jack there's someone there. Jack turned looking into the field but saw nothing.

"There is a man standing about a hundred feet ahead. He's dressed in a suit from maybe the eighteen hundreds, but the really odd thing is he has no shoes."

"Is he one of them?"

"Yes." She answered walking past Jack.

He tried stopping her by grabbing her arm, but she brushed past him. "I'll be alright." She assured him. She reached into her pocket and pulled out the carved figurine of a Badger for its power of healing and confidence. She held it in the palm of her hand wrapping her fingers tightly around it.

"I'm going to cross him over. You can come with me if you like this one won't bother you."

Jack thought about it for a moment and decided that he was of no help to her. "I'll go play with the cows for a moment. Be careful and make it fast."

Jack watched from the top of the berm. He could see her walk to the middle of the field and sand there as if she was talking to someone. The way she was moving about with odd arm

332

movements made her look like a crazy person trying to take flight.

Sara slowed her breathing and focused her concentration. "Don't be afraid." She said. "It is time for you to go. Rest; there is no more for you to do here. You are unburdened walk to the light."

Usually she would feel calmness as the person walked through her. But as the man came close she felt an uneasiness she had never felt before. For a moment she felt a great weight overcome her and a feeling of being lost. It was as if she was being swept away on a tide into a whirlpool sinking into a dark void. She felt it difficult to breath and everything became dark. Sara yelled out screaming before she fell.

Jack watched as Sara raised her arms into the air falling unconscious to the ground not moving. He heard her scream and ran to her side and knelt next to her holding her in his arms. She was breathing is short shallow breaths and looked pale as a ghost. Jack patted her face continually calling her name.

"Come back Sara you can't go with them."

He could see her eyes moving quickly from side to side behind closed lids.

"LET HER GO." He shouted!

Suddenly Sara opened her eyes gasping for breath. Jack got her up and, on her feet, half carrying her back to the truck having her sit on the tailgate.

Jack could see that she was still physically shaken from the experience. She had an odd look of being disconnected on her face. "Listen I think I should take you back to Ken's place, so you can rest."

Sara shook her head no. "I'll be fine we need to keep going. We didn't come this far to give up now. I'm not going to let it kill me, but I'll be god dammed that I'm going to turn and run with my tail between my legs when things go wrong. No sir and neither are you. I'm going to get to the bottom of this and fix it if it's the last thing I do." Sara pounded her fist on the tailgate.

Jack wasn't sure if it was pure adrenalin or stubbornness on her part or an inner strength that was now working overtime on her behalf. He knew she was strong and she would go the extra mile when needed without hesitation. But he was growing concerned for her safety of dealing with all the lost souls trying for her attention and to what effect it was having on her health.

"Okay." He said feeling helpless. He decided not to mention how concerned he was for her health. He kept it to himself and made a silent promise that he would do everything in his power to protect her. But how does one protect someone from something you can't see. He would have to pay more attention to her feeling and reactions and be quick to guide her away from danger.

"What happened back there?"

Sara stood brushing herself off. "At first I felt the normal things I feel when a person I'm trying to cross over is approaching me. I feel their experiences, their emotions at the time of their death and their life force. This time though it was all the same until he went to pass through me that things changed. He had a demon attached to him that I didn't recognize at first. I let my guard down and my emotions rule me and that's when it jumped me and tried to take me down. I fought it off until I removed it from the man allowing him to move on peacefully. The last I saw, it was a shadow headed for the woods. That's when I passed out."

Jack stood there with his mouth agape. "That's just great. How the hell do we protect ourselves from that?"

"You have the necklace I gave you?" Jack pulled it out of his shirt showing her.

"I need to be sure that I carry all the protection Margaret made." Suddenly Sara looked around the bed of the truck realizing that the figurine of the badger was not in her hand.

Jack saw the panic look on her face. "What's wrong?" He asked.

"I have to go back I dropped the figurine and it needs to be together with the others if it's going to offer any protection."

Jack put his hand on her shoulder. "Stay here." He said. "I'll find it. I'll follow your foot steps to where you were standing. It has to be there."

"Please find it." She said as Jack walked back to the field.

Montgomery felt instant pain as the bullet grazed his arm. He laughed as he walked to the body prep area. He felt the adrenalin pumping through his body and he never felt so alive. He took off his jacket and shirt going to a cabinet and grabbing some gauze and medical tape. He took out a suture kit cleaned the wound in the sink threaded the needle and watched himself it the mirror as he sewed the wound closed.

A sudden oddness filled the air and he wasn't sure what it was until he realized he was whistling. He hadn't whistled since he was a little boy long before his parent's divorce. It was a wonderful time when his mother would toil over him. She was the only one to comfort him when he fell off a wet jungle gym smashing his face on the hard ground. It was a gashing wound that left him with a scar just above his lip. She cleaned and set his wound and held him close singing softly to him until he forgot all about his pain. He smiled to himself in the mirror checking his face the scar long gone. But the scar from the one person who he came to blame it on, haunted the wounds deep clawing out from its buried vault. And when he came to live with the one person he despised the torture in him grew like watering a lily with acid.

Montgomery finished bandaging his arm and put is shirt and jacket back on. The stitching close of his wound gave him an idea. He rolled out a short gurney in front of him. It was time to see his new friend in the sitting parlor. As he walked out into the hallway he remembered the song his mother would sing to him and he started whistling.

ASHES! ASHES! WE ALL FALL DOWN.

Montgomery found Mike still lying where he fell. He pushed the gurney alongside him and kicked him hard. Mike didn't move Montgomery knew the amount of Chloral Hydrate delivered through the pin was enough to keep Mike asleep for more than an hour.

He stooped over picking up the gun stuffing it into his pocket. Pulling the gurney closer to Mike, he lowered it as far as it would go, set the break and lifted Mike on to the bed strapping him to it. "Well my friend let's see how you're going to like your make over and new home." He rolled the gurney to the cadaver prep area and raised the gurney to a working level.

Montgomery went to a cabinet and threaded a new needle setting it aside and grabbed a roll of duct tape cutting four strips two inches long and tacking them by an end to the table. Picking up the roll of tape he proceeded to fold Mike's hands together the way he would do for a corpse presented in a coffin at a wake. Except, Montgomery knew there were no crosses to hold Mike's soul and no prayers to be said on his behalf. He took the tape and wrapped the hands together, empty as death itself. He picked up the cut pieces of tape and placed them over the eyes of Mike in an x pattern.

The next step he wanted to be perfect. He put on a pair of tight latex gloves and held the needle with skilled perfection making the first injection into the philtrum and the lower lip of Mike's face. He pulled it tight continuing right to the corner of the mouth and then reversed the pattern tying it off at the other end with a surgeon's knot.

Admiring what he had done, he patted Mikes face.

"There my friend now you're going to tell no one anything."

He fished through Mike's pockets taking his wallet and car keys. He walked outside and moved Mike's car into a wooded area in the back of the house out of sight.

Montgomery walked to his office and was horrified to see the missing head of Jenny Harrows. He grabbed his camera making a mental note that he would print a new photo of the beauty when he finished prepping Mike.

Montgomery fired off two shots of Mike. He then pulled out a body drawer and rolled Mike's body onto the cold slab pushing him in and closing the door.

Back in his office he pulled off the wall the ruined photo of Jenny Harrows and replaced it with the photo of the new comer. "Everyone, say hello to our new friend but keep an eye on him...He can't be trusted."

"NO... NOT HIM THEY SHOUTED BACK IN UNISON."

Montgomery leaned back in his chair and laughed.

CHAPTER 27

DIGGING DEEP

When Jack returned to the truck he found Sara pacing around. She looked anxious and scared. He held his hand open showing her the Badger figurine. Sara ran up giving him a big hug.

"Are you okay you don't look well?"He asked.

"I'll be fine. It's just that knowing what happened here has got me upset."

Jack opened the truck door and helped Sara in placing the cushion over the hole. "It's mid- morning someone has got to be at that funeral home let's check in there and get the location on the baby's grave."

Sara sat in the truck quietly tying all the figurines together on a string, placing it around her neck.

Jack drove the pickup truck to the front of the funeral home. Outside the street was nearly empty except for two backpackers coming up the street heading north to Katahdin. It made him wonder about the ashes of his grandmother and if her urn was inside and if the funeral home would give it to him.

He came around the side of the truck helping Sara out. The color to her face was back and she looked better.

Jack and Sara walked up the kill stopping at the front gate near the sidewalk. The Victorian style home was huge high on the hill overlooking the small town. The building was dark and showing signs of neglect with over growing weeds consuming it alive.

"I wonder what this place must have looked like in its heyday." She asked.

"I'm sure it must have been spectacular." Jack answered. "But now it looks like a haunted house you'd find on a boardwalk. I got to tell you I always hated haunted houses. You never know what horrors have taken place inside and what is hidden ready to jump out at you."

Sara laughed. "I think you're watching too many TV shows. But by the looks of this place and what I've read about the shenanigans going on about this place in the NEW YORK TIMES, haunted doesn't even begin to describe it."

"Do you think they will give us the info we looking for?"

"We are only asking for the location of a grave and the cremated remains of a loved one. There is no reason to expect anything else."

The huge arched door surprisingly opened easily when Jack turned the knob and pushed on it. He and Sara walked inside finding the place dark and hard to see. A young woman standing behind a counter half hidden by an arrangement of flowers that were wilted paid them no attention.

Jack took a seat and let Sara take the lead. He felt he was getting a headache from the smell of formaldehyde heavy in the air.

Sara knocked on the counter top starling the woman. She pulled ear plugs from her ears as she acknowledged Sara. Sara could hear loud music as the woman approached.

"Oh, I'm sorry." She said turning down the music. "How can I help you?"

"The owner, MR. Barry is he in? My brother and I would like to find a grave and we were hoping he could tell us where it's located."

"I'm sorry MR. Barry just left and will be out of town. But I can help you."

Jack's ears perked up when the word brother registered in his mind and he smiled at Sara when she turned to him. It was the first time that he realized he still had a family who cared about him.

The young girl reached under the counter struggling to lift the heavy large leather covered book. She dropped it on the counter the sound echoed around the walls and dust hovered over it as if a magnet was at work trying to capture the dirt.

The young girl started turning pages. "What is the name of the loved one you wish to find?"

Jack came up and stood next to Sara. "That would be our baby brother." He said and then abruptly stopped realizing he didn't know the first name.

The young girl stood there with a questioning look on her face. It was the first time someone came in not knowing what they were looking for.

"I hope that works for you." She said pointing to the necklace Sara had around her neck. "Are you Maliseet?"

"No. Sara answered just careful.

"I hope it works for you. What did you say the name was?"

Sara could see the panicked look on Jacks face, she squeezed his arm. "The name is Kahill. She said tapping the book sending little puffs of dust into the air. "You have to excuse my brother here all of this is so emotional."

The young girl pushed a box of KLEENEX toward Jack. She flipped the pages of the book back to the beginning and stopped when she came to the section starting at the letter K. "There are a few Kahill's here, but they are much older from the late eighteen hundreds and two from the early nineteen hundreds. The one you're looking for is Francis Kahill lot number 39 section 52. It's in the baby section easy to find. I'll write down the directions for you."

Sara took the note and handed it to Jack. "There's one more thing you can help us with. It an urn with the ash remains of Mrs. Margaret Kahill. Can we pick that up?"

"I'll have to check if it is still here." The young girl struggled putting the book back under the counter and then disappeared into a back room. A moment later she returned.

Jack could already tell by the look on her face what she was going to say.

"I'm sorry that is no longer here. It was delivered today to Ken's Place Hostile as per request."

Nervously Sara was tapping her fingers on the counter. "Whose request was that?"

The young girl handed Sara a final disposition card. "Margaret Kahill." She said. "She filled it out herself."

Jack and Sara thanked the girl for her time. There was nothing more they could do they would have to wait until dark. There was no use going further to find the cabin now without the key they needed.

CHAPTER 28

ON THE HUNT

The midmorning was cool, and the air was bright and fresh with a scent of pine. The sun was just peaking over the tall trees at the edge of the property. Ken was standing on the front steps of the church enjoying a cup of coffee when he saw a patrol car coming up the driveway. He recognized the man getting out of the car wearing a full uniform with a Smokey the bear hat.

Deputy Sheriff Roy Halperin came up the steps and extended a hand to ken. Ken put his hand out to shake the man's hand when a flash came over the man's shoulder from the woods. Ken grabbed the man's arm and swung him around like a dance partner.

Roy let out a "WOW" as he was spun on his heels. "What the hell you doing?" He asked.

"Just look." Ken pointed toward the woods.

'What the hell is that?" Roy said seeing what Ken was pointing at.

"That my friend is the Lady of the Woods." They stood silently as the woman walked on and vanished a few moments later.

Roy took off his hat and wiped his face with a handkerchief. "I've heard of her, but I never imagined it to be true or seeing her for myself."

Ken laughed. "That's nothing only the tip of the iceberg. Come on in and you can tell me what brings you around this part."

"Sounds good." Roy said following Ken into the kitchen and taking a seat at the table. Ken poured them both a cup of coffee. Roy blew on the hot cup letting off a light mist of steam that reminded him of the mist he saw outside. "That's quite a show you got going on out there."

Ken sat down. "Believe it or not that is the first time I witnessed seeing her. The first time was maybe ten years ago right in the same spot. So, what bring you out this way?"

"Well I was wondering if you ran into two strangers showing up here from New York City."

"A lot of strangers come through here what makes them so special?" He answered.

"Well down on Turners Point a few days ago I checked out a tractor trailer wrecked into the woods completely burned out and I run into a guy from New York City area at the Green Lantern Cafe." Roy pulled out a small pad. "Let me see here. Goes by the name Jack Kahill. Here's the best part I found an abandoned car that looked like it had been in some kind of wreck hidden near Luke Watsons place. The car is registered to a woman from New York City. So, the question is have you seen them?"

Ken shook his head. "No, we are just getting over the festival a lot of people were here they could have been hiding in the crowd. The only thing odd around here is what's been going on in the woods. Maybe they're up trail with the other hikers."

Roy sipped at his coffee. "It's possible." He said. "Now what's the odd things going on around here other than the thing I'm not sure I just saw?"

"If you think that thing you just witnessed in the woods was strange try multiplying it by ten." Ken answered.

"You telling me that there's more than that one wondering around in the woods? Well I got to see that for myself. I'm going to take a look around." Roy finished his coffee handing the empty cup to Ken. "I got to check in with the station but if you see anything give me a call. And I'm talking about living things."

Ken thought about telling Roy more of the strange thing going on and finding the plowed over old graveyard, but he promised giving Mike twenty-four hours before he would call in the cavalry. What could it hurt to have to deal with the night?

He felt bad lying to Roy about Sara and Jack but his loyalty to Margaret went deeper. He felt them to be family and would go out of his way to protect them.

Outside Ken waved to Roy as he watched the man drive away toward Bangor.

CHAPTER 29

THE CABIN

When Sara and Jack pulled back up the driveway they found Ken outside pacing back and forth. He let Sara out of the truck and drove further on around the side of the church to put the truck back where he had found it.

Ken had a troubled look on his face and Sara had an odd feeling deep in her bones that something was gravely wrong.

"What's wrong?" She asked.

Ken stopped pacing and came up to Sara and took her hand in his. "I've been here a very long time and I've only seen the woman in the woods once but today I've seen her three times. Something has changed, and I fear for the worse."

Sara felt her stomach do a flop. "I feel it." She said. "The ground is alive. Everything seams heaver and tense like static trying to cling to me that I'm having a hard time shaking off."

Jack came around the corner and stood alongside Sara. He went to give the keys to the truck back to Ken, but Ken told him to hold on to them.

"I got a visit from the Deputy Sheriff today looking for the two of you." Ken said.

"Shit."Jack said.

"Don't worry I told him I didn't see you. And that I don't know where you could be. But I'm afraid he knows about an accident on Turners Point."

Jack shook his head. "Dam that's my fault. It couldn't be helped."

"That's okay." Sara patted Jack on the back.

Ken took a seat on the church steps. "I'm afraid it worse than that. He said he found your car abandoned near a farm down the road and now he's going to start looking around. I'm afraid it's not safe for you kids to stay here any longer. Mike Shannon should be back soon and the two of them are going to cross paths and I don't want to see that happen. I think you should take the truck find the cabin and stay there until this blows over."

Deep down inside Jack knew their situation was not going to just blow over. There were too many things that he and Sara had to fix. The law was getting close and they would not listen to reason. And Sara was too far into it to not be held accountable as an accomplice at this point He knew he would certainly go back to jail but if the time came he would do all he could do to claim Sara's innocence in it all.

He looked to Sara, but she was already heading up to the room to gather up her belonging. Over her shoulder she said. "We got to leave here."

Jack went back to the truck and drove it up to the front steps.

Ken got up and started to go inside at the top step he turned to Jack. "Hide the truck well down that road into the woods; bring it back when you can. Don't cut down the overgrowth at the cabin. I'll fetch some extra blankets and some food for you two and I'll meet you back here in thirty minutes."

When Sara returned thirty minutes later she found Ken at the back of the pick-up truck placing two large tote bags filled with blankets two sleeping bags and towels into the bed. She placed her bag on the tailgate.

Ken and Sara were just about to go into the church when Jack appeared in the doorway with his pack slung over his shoulder.

Ken stopped at the top to the steps letting Jack pass him in the doorway. "When you kids are done come into the kitchen I have a box of provisions you can take."

In the kitchen Ken was placing a wrapped package of dried meats into an old Ballentine beer box.

Sara felt overwhelmed and tired when she came into the kitchen she knew that she and Jack owed Ken a lot for his kindness and she hoped that some day she could return to thank him for all that he had done. She walked up to Ken and placed her hand on his chest. She felt the rhythmic beating or his heart.

"I will tell you something if you don't mind." Ken shook his head no. "You are not a troubled soul. I feel in you a gentile kindness and a love for life." She kissed him on the cheek. Ken stood there smiling with a tear in his eye.

Sara stood there thinking a moment about the long journey she had been on and how she had the strength to overcome the problems that had come along. But she wondered just how she was going to get past the next wave of obstacles. She wondered who would believe that she was about to dig up a coffin that might have a treasure hidden in it. Who would believe the fact that an undertaker was wiping away the past for profit. She felt too many things were being replaced for misplaced emotions.

History was birthing itself into existence every breathable moment yet there were people who want nothing more than to rewrite it for whatever misguided purpose. Destroying monuments and denying the existence of the past will always bring about confusion in the cosmos to repeat the tragedies of the past. All things were here for a purpose of teaching us not to make the same mistakes again. As a journalist she wondered how anyone could ban books. It's the same as banning thought which is the most dangerous of offences.

Jack carried out the box of food to the truck and stuffed towels into the hole in the passenger side seat trying to make it as comfortable as he could for Sara.

Sara hopped into the passenger side of the truck and Jack was just about to turn the ignition when Ken came up to the driver side window.

"Listen Jack I don't know who's going to show up here first. The Deputy Sheriff is out there somewhere looking around and he could be anywhere. The deal I have with old flat top is if I don't hear from him by tomorrow morning I'm suppose to call out the cavalry. One way or the other there is going to be a lot of police around here so you two kids need to be careful and stay out of sight. I hope that guy Mike is okay, given what's been happening around here."

"Don't worry." Jack said he's a big boy and I'm sure he can take care of himself. Jack shook Ken's hand fired up the truck and backed down the driveway out onto the main street.

Ten minutes later they were turning right onto Old Blanchard road passing the Barry funeral home when Jack notice something out of the corner of his eye. He thought he saw there a car parked semi- hidden around the back side of the house and he slowed just long enough to see that it had New York plates on it. Could it be that the car belonged to Mike Shannon and he was there looking for information?

Sara noticed the slow down. "What's wrong?"She asked.

"Nothing he answered." He kept what he had seen to himself; he didn't want to worry Sara and drove on. He knew they had a bigger concern ahead of them of hiding the truck and setting up the cabin as a living space.

Was the cabin in any kind of condition that they could use? It had been years since he was there last, and it was in immaculate condition then. But how many years was it that no one was there? He knew that it doesn't take long for Mother Nature to reclaim her land.

Jack saw the hidden entrance way to the cabin ahead and slowed the truck to a stop. He let Sara out before he forced the nose of the truck into the overgrown thicket near the walkway.

The cabin was a quarter of a mile down the path and Jack was pleased to see that it was well hidden in the back of the woods.

There was no reason for anyone to come down that trail. And if they did it was for only one reason. He and Sara would have plenty of time to react to anyone coming to choose between fight and flight.

Jack pushed back the thicket making a small entrance to the path. He and Sara wound have to make two trips to carry in all the provisions they had with them. There was no possibility of leaving anything at the truck. It would certainly not be there long with all the wildlife roaming around in the woods.

Jack came down the trail through a row of tall white birch trees. He remembered how small they were when his grandmother planted them. He could see the cabin ahead and was pleased at how well it had withstood the harsh Maine winters. The small porch felt sturdy when he stepped up on to it. The image of his grandmother sitting in a rocking chair there flashed in his mind. He put the two packages he was carrying on the porch next to the door. Sara came up alongside placing the box she was carrying next to his.

"How are we going to get inside" She asked. "The windows are all boarded up."

"You have that key Ken gave you." Jack said.

Sara tried the key but it didn't fit. "This must go to another lock."

The only thing that looked alive around the cabin was a patch of beautiful marigolds coming into bloom, through dead leafs, in a small garden next to the porch.

"We'll let's see if it's still there."

Jack reached up to a light fixture near the top of the door frame and popped of the top pulling out two keys on a small ring. The first key he tried opened the door the second key he wasn't sure what it went to. It had to be important though because of the way it was attached to the ring with a strip of lavender ribbon tied in a bow. He remembered that anything his grandmother loved, or thought was important had a lavender bow attached to it.

Sara grabbed a package from the porch and went inside to check the cabin. She really didn't remember it.

She found it a little more rustic then she had hoped. It had a small kitchen with a counter and two cabinets on the wall. There was no stove or refrigerator only a pot belly stove in a corner for cooking. There was a room off the side that had two bunks with a horse hair mattress on it for bedding. She had to battle cob webs in every room as she went along. The next room was a common area with a nice fire place that had a long couch there with a pile of wood ready to make a comfortable warm fire. The disappointed thing she realized was that there was no electricity or bath room. When she looked out the kitchen window she let out a deep breath realizing where the toilet was. It was an outhouse about forty yards into the woods. She went about trying to set up some kind of normal living arrangement as Jack made another trip back to the truck to gather up the rest of their belongings and further hide the truck.

In three hours it would be dark enough for them to drive the truck unseen to the cemetery and begin their search for the grave of the baby.

CHAPTER 30

SWALLOWED BY THE DARK

Mike Shannon awoke with a splitting headache. He could hear nothing other than the beating of his own heart in his ears. The darkness that surrounded him was endless deep with no beginning and no end. The confinement of the space he was in made it impossible for him to move. Through his nostrils he drew in a deep breath that was filled with the smell of formaldehyde. He tried to yell out but found his mouth unable to move and when he pressed his tongue against the back of his lips he was unable to move it and the pain to the surrounding area was excruciating. He wanted to kick out but found his legs unable to move. He could move his hands a few inches up hitting some kind of a ceiling and went about banging on it with his knuckles.

Montgomery Barry walked in to the cadaver prep area and immediately heard the commotion coming from the body slab area. He walked over to the chamber holding Mike.

"Hold it down motherfucker." He said pounding on the door. "Or I'll end it for you right here and now. You just be patient in there I've got good plans for you but first lest play a game. It's called who's looking for whom?"

Although muffled, Mike could hear every word. It left him frustrated but he knew that given the chance he swore he would kill Montgomery Barry.

Montgomery stood in his office admiring all the trophies he had collected hanging there on the walls. But the one he was most interested in was the one of the little baby Kahill. When he arrived his worker told him about the recent visit of two people looking to find the gravesite. He was excited that after so many years that the wheels of motion had started to move. He took down the photo and the key holding it in his hands facing the wall.

"If any of you know what this key is for I want you to tell me now. Come on speak up no need to be shy here among friends."

No one spoke; they only stared back at him in silenced from some distant realm. He pinned the photo back on the wall in its place of honor. "Have patients my friends soon, soon we will find out what this key is for."

Jack decided to leave the covering of the cabin windows intact. It would help protect against the no-see-ums. When he unpacked the box of provisions given to him and Sara he was happy to fine that Ken packed a good size bottle of deet. It would come in handy when they go to the cemetery.

Jack went about starting a fire in the fireplace as Sara prepared a meal in the kitchen. He wanted to start looking for any clues around the cabin that his grandmother might have placed, helping them find whatever she left for them. That would have to wait he told himself. He needed to focus on what he and Sara had to do first.

Jack checked the back of the pickup truck all the tools were still where he had placed them. Sara went about fixing the seat trying to make it as comfortable as she could. The evening was moonless, and a covering of clouds helped to make everything dark. The air was damp with the possibility of rain. Lighting flashes were far in the distance and a low rumble of thunder was faint in the hills. Sara hoped that the lightning was the only thing that would flash into existence this evening. Everything seemed quiet and she didn't feel any spirits around, but she knew that could change any moment especially when standing in the middle of a cemetery.

Jack parked the truck just past the cemetery near the beginning of the wall. They grabbed the tools and started the short walk to the cemetery. The road was dark and there were no street lights. Jack thought he had a good idea as to the location of the grave. It was in a section that was dedicated to children near the road.

At the top of the berm they stopped for a moment allowing their eyes to adjust to the darkness. In the distance Jack could see silhouettes of statues standing guard among the tombs. Lighting flashed in the distance sending a beam of light that raced its way winding and caressing the marble guards standing watch until it faded and died.

Walking a short distance Jack and Sara came to the grave. He suddenly had an overwhelming feeling of sadness knowing he had a baby brother buried there and he was about to dig him up. Jack used a small penlight to illuminate the marker. It was a small stone that read Francis Kahill. It was thirty years old, but it looked like it was new. Jack called to Sara to show her the marker, but she had a shovel in the ground and was busy digging. "How far down do you think it is?" She asked.

Jack grabbed a shovel and started digging near the stone. "I don't know." He answered. "Usually a grave is six feet down but how far do you burry a baby your guess is as good as mine. Who knows what this undertaker did thirty years ago? Keep digging until you hit something."

A light mist began to fall and thunder rumbled echoing around the tombstones. The lightning flashes were moving off to the north and Jack was glad to see that the bad weather was moving away from them. He had been digging for an hour and was down to what he thought was four and a half feet when his shovel hit something hard.

Sara heard the thud and dropped to her knees looking over the hole. She shown the penlight down and they could see the top of the casket. It looked to be a simple pine casket. Jack took a few more shovels of dirt around the edges making it easier to grab. He handed up the shovel to Sara.

"This doesn't look to be too heavy and it's still in good shape. I'll tie some rope to the handles and we can pull it up." Jack climbed up out of the hole and sat on the edge. "How do you feel? Is there anything around that we should be worried about?"

Sara shook her head. "No, everything seems eerily quiet. Believe me I can't figure it what with all that is going on around here."

"Let's hope it stays that way." Jack hoisted up the tiny casket placing it at Sara's feet.

It was late in the evening when Deputy Sheriff Roy Halperin pulled up to Ken's place. The lights were still on and a few backpackers were busy setting up a tent in the grassy area in front of the church. He walked pass the backpacker who gave him an odd look. Inside the church he found Ken setting up folding chairs with a door spread across them.

"Ken."He said. "I'm glad to find you still up at this hour."

"Work around here is never done. What brings you out? Must be something important to bring you out at this hour."

"Well yeah, it's about what I found out about the people involved in the accident out on Turners Point. Seems a guy buy the name of Jack Kahill and his sister Sara both from the New York area have been seen around here."

"Hold on."Ken said. "Let's get some coffee in the kitchen you can sit and tell me all about it."

Roy followed Ken into the kitchen taking a seat at the table. Ken poured coffee and took a seat across from him. "So, what's going on?"

I've seen him back at the Green lantern a few days ago. He's got a rap sheet and he's got a parole officer on his tail also seen in this area. Guess where?"

"The GREEN LATERN." Ken answered.

Roy touched the tip of his nose with his index finger. "Bingo." He said.

Ken sipped at his coffee. He suddenly felt hot. What more did Roy know, and did he know that they were all at his place over the last few days?

Roy stood and leaned in closer to Ken from across the table. "Ken, I've known you a long time and I need you to be straight with me. Other than that trail you're the only game in town for a place to stay. These two kids and that parole officer could be in trouble and needing our help right now."

The wheels were turning in Ken's mind. He sincerely didn't want anyone to come to harm's way especially because of what he and Mike had found at the old cemetery. He knew what was going to be asked next.

Roy continued. "So I need your help in being straight with me. Did you see any of them?"

Ken swallowed hard and took another sip of coffee to clear his throat. "Yes." He said. "The parole officer his name is Mike Shannon and he was here for the last two days. But he didn't stay here. I think he stayed at the old orphanage."

Roy tapped his fingers on the table. "What about the two kids?"

Ken shook his head and shrugged his shoulders. "Roy, do you remember seeing the strange flashing in the woods the other night?"

Roy felt Ken was avoiding the question about the kids, but he couldn't figure out why. He decided to let it drop for the moment and hear out what information the old man did have.

"Yeah, damnedest thing I've ever seen."

"Well what if I told you it's been happening all over the place for the last week or so. Looks like an invasion of human lightning bugs out there in the woods. Just this morning that parole officer and I went out to investigate something he found along old Blanchard road.

"What was that?" Asked Roy?

"We found the old cemetery at the end of the wall plowed over."

Roy sat there scratching his head. "That's been there for hundreds of years."

"That's what Mike Shannon went to investigate. We think something strange is going on and it all has to do with the Barry Funeral Home. We had a deal that I would give him twenty-four hours to check things out and if I didn't hear from him I was to call out the cavalry. 7am will be the cut off time."

"Might be your deal, but not mine. I'll check things out and we'll straighten this mess out when I find them all."

Roy got up and put his hat on to leave. "Okay I'll be back when I got them. One last thing your boy is chasing a phantom. Turns out, Jack Kahill is not guilty. The second accident was not his fault. The old man ran the light and hit him. He is guilty however of leaving the scene."

Ken followed Roy out to his cruiser. "See ya in the morning." Ken said.

"Yeah, we'll go look at the old cemetery and trust me, I'll get to the bottom of this."

Jack pushed the end of the spade into the top side of the casket.

"You ready for this? This could be really ugly."

"I'll be fine."Sara answered her eyes as wide as saucers.

Jack popped the lid. Sara turned away choosing not to look. He fell to his knees removing the lid pushing it away to the side. Jack quickly rose to his feet grabbing the back of Sara's head and turning her to face the coffin.

"IT'S EMPTY." They said in unison.

Sara was first to ask the question. "How the hell can this be? Where is the baby?"

Jack was on his hands and knees feeling around the inside of the coffin. He came up holding a small canvas bag with a ribbon attached to it. He handed the bag to Sara. She turned on the pen light to get a better look. "Do you think it is...?"

Jack cut her off. He could see the lavender ribbon... "It has to be." He said.

Sara held her breath. The bag was heavy for its size. Who knows what their grandmother hid in the coffin so long ago. There could be anything in the bag, but she hoped it was the key they needed. Slowly she pulled on the ribbon bow and pulled apart the closure. Jack cupped his hands and Sara poured out the contents. Jack watched in anticipation as his hands filled with sand.

Jack opened his hands letting the sand fall into the coffin. "NOTING IT'S ALL NOTHING." He said choking back tears. "What does it all mean?"

"It means that motherfucker in that haunted house high up on that hill stole whatever was inside this casket." Sara kicked at the sand. She was now crying. "But what about the baby?"

"Well we are going to find out. I've got an idea." Jack placed the casket back in the grave.

"You don't even have to say, I think I know what it is and count me in." She said.

Montgomery heard the rumble of the thunder fading. He was disappointed that the storm was moving away. He felt the static in the air. The walk would have been more enjoyable with Mother Nature unleashing her scorn. It was dark and moonless. He enjoyed how it allowed him to relax and become part of the emptiness. He had a full bladder in anticipation of the task at hand. He whistled as he walked along in the darkness.

Jack and Sara crept their way up a set of steps that led to a back window. Although the window was covered by heavy shades he knelt at the window pushing his face against the glass and was able to peer in just where the shade came together near the bottom. He could make out a desk in the middle of the room. "This is it." He whispered back to Sara.

"Do you think it's alarmed?"

"No, just look at this place it's falling apart. You don't think this cheep bastard is going to spend money on an alarm system and besides it's the back woods of Maine not New York City. Hand me the small crow bar. I'll bet it's not even locked."

At the edge of the window Jack placed the edge of the pry bar between the window and the sill. The window rocked back and forth. He handed the pry bar back to Sara. "Would you care to do the honors?" He said.

Sara gently pushed the window up a few inches, finding Jack was right all along. It was never locked in the first place.

Jack opened the window slowly just enough for him to slip inside. Once inside he stayed on his knees helping Sara over the ledge. The first thing she noticed was how musty and old the room smelled. The room was dark and she could barely see her hand in front of her face.

Jack stood up feeling his way over to the desk he saw through the window. Sara came up and stood next to him. "This is obviously the office. Where do we look?"

Jack sat at the desk and took the pen light from Sara. He opened the draws hoping to find a file system but found only a camera, pins, tape and a stapler. He thought it odd that such a large desk had so few items in it.

Suddenly Sara felt dizzy. She had an odd feeling that she was being watched. She tried to shake it off but it was growing and then she heard the calling of many voices all jumbled together. She tried to listen for a brief moment for clarity but all the voices were on top of each other and she couldn't pin point or focus on just one. What were they saying?

Jack tried for her attention but she seemed to be miles away almost trance like. He grabbed her arm shaking her. "What's wrong?" He asked.

Sara could feel her heart racing. "I feel like I'm inside that cafe with a hundred voices trying to talk to me at the same time. I hear them but it's all jumbled."

"We got to get you out of here."Jack said moving toward the window.

"No. She said. "We need to keep going I can handle it." She touched the necklace tied around her neck hoping for its protection.

Jack held the pen light, pointing it onto her face. He wanted to be sure she was okay. He looked up at her face and saw the light reflecting on the wall behind her. He jumped back when out of the darkness two set of eyes were looking back at him. "What the hell is this?" He asked. He searched the wall with the pen light seeing photo after photo of people staring back at him.

"Sara." He called out. "You got to see this." He shown the light along the wall and face after face young, old and some grossly disfigured hung there staring back at him. "Holy shit." He said "What the hell is this."

Sara took a deep breath. "It's what's been trying to speak to me."

Where the wall ended a new one began with the same type of photos stapled to it. Jack could see that all the photos had something attached to. He walked closer to get a better look discovering that the photos had different objects attached to it. Some had crosses, some folded bits of paper and some money. One photo had a beer can pull tab attached to it. And suddenly it hit him.

"Do you know what this is? It's a trophy wall just think about it. All the things attached could be things people put in the coffin of a loved one that this motherfucker took out."

"Keep looking. You might find what we are looking for."

"You read my mind." Jack answered. He started scanning the third wall coming to the end near a door way the lead down a long hallway. He stopped. There pinned on the wall was the photo of the baby with a key pined to it. The next photo startled him. Shaking with fear, he dropped the pen light.

Picking up the light Sara shown it to where Jack was looking.

"OH SHIT." She said. "That's old flat top. Oh my God, what happened to him?"

Jack ripped the photo from the wall and placed it on the table. The photo of the baby he folded around the key placing it in his pocket. Sara held the light and together they examined the photo of Mike. "No one deserves this."He said.

Jack gave the photo to Sara. "Hold onto this we might need it later." Sara placed it in her pocket. "Mike Shannon is in serious trouble and we got to act now."

Sara thought for a moment. "We need to go to the police." She said.

"I don't think we have time for that. No, we got to search for him ourselves."

"He could be anywhere." She said. "This is a big place."

The hallway was dark and the small penlight only offered a small amount of illumination preventing them from crashing into a wall when the hallway made a sudden turn. Jack tensed his body for a fight if someone was to suddenly jump out at them. Sara held in her hand a long screwdriver hoping she didn't have to plunge it into someone.

When they turned the corner they entered the body prep area of the funeral home. Jack felt his breathing starting to become labored and the beginning of a panic attack coming alive deep within him.

"Wait, Jack. I feel something different in here." Sara said grabbing hold of his arm. "One person trying to reach out to me and a very strange feeling. It's a tension very heavy like someone over stretching a rubber band tearing the fabric of time ready to explode."

Sara walked around the room stopping at the body lockers.

"Jack come here." She called. "I could swear I hear movement over here."

"Back up." He said, rolling his fingers into fists.

Sara raised the screwdriver in front of her.

Jack went to the fist locker opening the door and pulling out the body. He flashed the pen light on the toe tag it read Lou Mancini. "Well this ain't our guy."

Suddenly Jack heard a bang come from the next locker. Sara held the light, her hands shaking. Jack slowly opened the door and saw socks and toe movement. He grabbed the slab and pulled it out along it's rollers until it could go no further, locking at the end. Sara held the light on the face of Mike Shannon.

Jack pulled out his penknife cutting the tape from Mike's hands and wrists. He left the tape covering his eyes and the stitching sewn into his mouth alone it was something better left to professionals to handle.

"Is he alive?"Sara asked.

Jack felt for a pulse on Mike's neck. "Yes. He just knocked out and in bad shape. I'm going to get him down and out of here."

Jack picked up Mike and slung him over his shoulders in a fireman's carry. Sara led the way with a screwdriver in one hand and a flash light in the other.

Sara found the back door, unlocking it and once outside Jack carried Mike to the pickup truck. He laid Mike on the bed of the truck. Sara went around and gathered up the pillows from the cab placing them around Mike for protection from rolling around.

"Sara, drive him to Ken's place, call the authorities and get him to a hospital."

"Wait what are you going to do?"She said her hands shaking.

Jack grabbed a shovel. "I got this and I'm going to see what I can hit with it."

"Jack, you don't know what this guy is capable of."

"Don't worry I'm not going to let that bastard get me. Hurry back with help."

Sara got behind the wheel of the pickup truck and took off down the road. Jack slung the shovel over his right shoulder and walked off into the darkness of the cemetery.

Shadows walked with him as he went along. Jack felt confident that he could handle himself against Montgomery as long as he was quick to react and not hit by surprise.

Jack came to a large flat marble crypt. He could make out an angel statue with large feathered wings hovering over him. He sat there listening to the darkness for any signs of movement. There was nothing, not even the sounds of crickets.

He was suddenly overcome with emotion. Everything that had happened to him flooded in. All the running, the lies and constantly looking over his shoulder trying to avoid what might be coming at him next was too much. He felt tired of running and wanted nothing more that to have it all stop.

He fell to his knees in front of the statue and started to recite the Lord's Prayer. Suddenly he saw a flash in the woods. He could see a woman walking there briefly move along some and then vanish as quickly as it began. He wanted to call out but realized there was nothing to call out to. He thought of Sara and how difficult it must be for her to have to deal with seeing the dead all the time. He felt miserable for her, knowing that she was never truly alone. He on the other hand had felt alone his entire life and was now grateful that he had Sara he could possibly share the future with.

Montgomery Barry arrived back at his office to find the back door open. "Well now isn't this interesting." He pulled the gun from his pocket open and checked the chambers snapping it shut. He adjusted the lighting just enough for him to see and went about in search of the intruder.

Jack sat there he could feel his heart start to race. He bit the inside of his cheek tasting blood. He went to spit when he saw a flash of light. He turned quickly to see that the light didn't fade and it was coming from the funeral home. He jumped to his feet swung the shovel over his shoulder.

Sara flew up the driveway with full barrels blazing. She leaned into the horn with enough effort to wake the dead. The backpackers stumbled out of their tents in a daze. Sara jumped from the truck running up the steps of the church screaming for Ken.

Ken met her at the top of the steps.

"Little lady I swear you're going to give this old coot a heart attack. What's all the noise about?"

Sara couldn't catch her breath and her throat was dry. When she tried to speak a mumbling of word came out.

Ken patted her on her back. "Calm down little lady take a deep breath." He pointed to the steps. "Have a seat." He handed her a bottle of water and she took a sip.

Sara slumped to the steps wheezing. Ken caught her in his arms. Suddenly the whole yard and woods illuminated with human fire fly's glowing briefly in and out of existence. Ken looked out and guessed at what had to be more than a hundred people glowing there in the woods.

"TRUCK, TRUCK BACK OF TRUCK." Sara yelled out.

Ken and four backpackers rushed to the back of the pickup finding Mike Shannon spread out on the bed clinging to life.

Everyone eyes widened in disbelief. One of the backpackers spoke up.

"I'm an outback emergency EMT. Let me look at him."

Everyone stepped back to give him room. He yelled out for another backpacker to fetch his med kit from their tent. He checked Mike's pulse.

"He's alive but in bad shape."

He took the pillows and put them under Mike's feet.

"The best we can do is to keep him stable until he can be transported to a hospital."

He checked Mike's face. How the hell did this happen to him? Who did this to him?"

"Pure evil." Ken replied, walking off to console Sara.

"What happened?" He asked. "Where's Jack?"

"It was horrible we found him like this in a body locker at the Barry Funeral home." Sara said through tears.

Ken shook his head. "I knew it." He said to himself.

Sara felt her head spinning and had difficulty keeping her balance. She couldn't hold it any longer and threw up from the pressure in her head. All the dead suddenly surrounding her was too much.

Ken, along with a backpacker picked her up and brought her inside and laid her on a door he had spread between too chairs. He then went to phone Roy.

When Roy picked up the phone Ken laid out a scenario of all hell breaking loose. "Roy we have an EMT here who says we better have a state E-VAC sent in."

"I'm on it. I'll be there in twenty minutes with the full Sheriff's department."

When Montgomery got to the body prep area he found two lockers open. Lou Mancini was still there stiff as a board. The other locker once holding Mike Shannon was empty. He knew that it would have had to have been a miracle for Mike Shannon to have gotten up and walked away. He hated miracles he had and never experienced anything close to a miracle and they certainly don't happen to Montgomery Barry. He returned Lou Mancini to the empty darkness and locked the door. Turning off the lights he walked back to his office.

The walls called to him he could hear the whispers.

378

"WHERE IS OUR FRIEND? HE'S MISSING. HE'S LOST. HE NEEDS HELP."

"Don't worry my dear friends I'm here. No one is going to hurt you. I'll find him." He brushed the face of Jenny Harrows. "Now, now don't cry." He said.

Montgomery turned out the lights and walked out into the dark holding the gun out in front him. He smiled loving the darkness. He was right at home there and could navigate through it like a bat having become accustom to it with years of experience.

Sara got up and went to the doorway to get some fresh air. She could see the emergency light flashing and herd the sirens wailing as Roy came up the drive followed by two other Sheriff Deputies. Ken came down escorting Roy to the back of the pickup truck. Five minutes later she heard the thumping of rotor blades and watched the helicopter hand on the front lawn.

Two paramedics attended to Mike setting up a saline drip into his arm and strapping him to a stretcher. They place him into the waiting helicopter and immediately took off for Bangor Hospital a twenty minute flight.

Roy came up the steps. "Who's your little lady friend?" He asked, but he already knew the answer.

"I'll explain everything." Ken said. "But first we got to get Jack. He's in serious danger out there."

Roy came up to Sara taking hold her hand. "Come on little lady tell me where Jack is."

"Funeral home." She managed.

Roy quickly walked outside. He waved a finger in the air and moved off quickly to his patrol car. "Let's go." He yelled out.

When Roy got to his car he was surprised to find Sara trying to get in the passenger side door. Roy waved her off. "Hold on their little lady you stay here."

"Not on your life." She answered opening the door and seating herself. "I need to be there can't you see what's been happening around here?" Sara pointed to the woods. Roy saw flashes of light everywhere he looked.

"Do you think it's natural to have all these people walking around popping in and out of existence like fire fly's on a hot July night? That bastard at the funeral home got something to do with it and I need to be there to help protect Jack."

Roy looked towards the woods and back to Ken. The woods were becoming alive with the dead.

Ken shook his head up and down. "I'm staying here. I would only be in the way."

Roy spoke into his two-way radio while firing up his car. "No sirens we go in silent." The patrol car spit up stones as he sped off the driveway.

Five minutes later the three patrol cars were in the driveway of the Barry funeral home. Two deputies were already out of their cars and approaching the front entrance. Roy pointed a finger in Sara's face. "Stay here." He warned. He took off running around the back of the building gun drawn.

Jack saw a tall shadow move through the doorway and out onto the porch just as the lights went out.

Montgomery didn't see the flashing in the woods at first as he walked up to the monument. He was standing in the center of his father's ossuary contemplating urinating on it again.

Jack saw movement in the middle of a large crypt when a flash went off in the woods. He quickly ducked behind a large headstone lying flat. He brought his head up just enough to take a peak around the stone. But the darkness returned and he saw nothing.

The two deputies found the dead body of Lou Mancini right where Montgomery and put him. Roy took the call over his walkie-talkie.

Sara saw her opportunity when Roy became distracted. He tried to grab Sara's arm but she slipped through his fingers and took off into the darkness. She removed the protection necklace from around her neck and hung it on the arm of a small cherub standing watch over a child's grave. She felt that the innocent needed protection from the darkness more.

Jack stood up in the protection of the darkness. A light flashed behind him. Montgomery caught the momentary flash in the corner of his eye. He turned toward the flash. In the darkness he made out Jack clear as day. Quickly pointing the nozzle of the gun in the direction of the movement he pulled the trigger and fired.

Jack saw the flash of the gun and hit the dirt hard banging his kneed on a tombstone as he went down. The pain instantly radiated throughout his leg. The sound of the gunfire echoed off the tombs sending up an alarm. Jack heard the bullet wiz above his head hitting the angel statue. He split the image in his mind. He saw Sara in one eye and the Lady of the Woods in the other.

Sara saw a flash off to her right side. She outstretched her arms and called out to the Lady of the Woods. "Come." She said. "The evil walks among you. I plead to all of you to send it back into the abyss from where it was born."

Jack turned his focus to the funeral home. He tried to get up when seeing three light coming fast from the area of the funeral home. His leg gave out from underneath him and he fell slumped over a grave marker.

A flash from behind in the woods gave Jack's position away and Montgomery seized the opportunity laughing as the shot hit Jack in the stomach. Jack fell doubled over in pain.

From her hiding place behind a large statue of a woman caressing a small child Sara saw Jack fall. She couldn't call out for fear of giving away her position. She stood still focusing all her attention on calling out to all the entities. She could see a flash of light materialize in front on Montgomery as he stood at the top steps of the tomb. Montgomery fired the gun again at the light source but he hit nothing.

Roy and the two Deputy Sheriffs came up alongside of Sara. Roy went to grab Sara trying to pull her to the ground. She pushed him off slipped away and knelt alongside Jack. Montgomery saw her movement and fired at her missing wildly.

Roy could see the shadow of Montgomery moving about at the top of the steps. He raised his revolver taking aim when suddenly he was blinded by a light that made it impossible for him to see.

Sara held Jack in her arms. From her vantage point she could see Montgomery surrounded by a dozen glowing entities with more rapidly approaching from all directions. They were surrounding him and walking in a tight diminishing circle. A shot rang out and Sara felt time come to a crawl.

She saw Roy come running up to her in slow motion. She saw the light from the tomb grow in intensity until it was white hot. She saw the two deputy sheriff's move in slow motion towards Montgomery. When they finally reached the top of the steps the light was too bright to look any more.

Ten seconds later darkness returned to reclaim its proper place in the universe. Roy was on his walkie-talkie calling in an ambulance. He knelt alongside of Jack and tore a sleeve off his shirt placing it on Jack's wound instructing Sara to keep pressure on it and hold it in place. "He's going to make it." He said smiling up to Sara.

Roy got up and walked up to the two deputies standing over Montgomery. "He's dead." One of the men said. Roy bent down to check the body. There was no pulse. He was certain that he had heard a gunshot but there was no evidence of it when he checked the body and there was no blood anywhere.

When Roy came back to check on Jack and Sara two EMT's had Jack bandaged, strapped to a stretcher and ready for transport to a hospital. "No need to check the other one, he's dead." He said to one of the EMT's. "What hospital you taking him to?"

"We are going to run him to Bangor." One of the men answered.

Roy called to one of the deputies to go with the EMT's and bring back a body bag for Montgomery.

He then asked Sara to accompany him back to where Montgomery lay. "Now little lady as I take it you're the authority here. So, tell me what we just witnessed here. Sure as hell I couldn't see a dam thing it was so bright. I know I heard a gunshot but I'll be dammed if I can find a hole in him anywhere."

Roy shone his flash light up and down the body of Montgomery.

He then held the light above Sara so he could clearly see her face and looked her straight in the eyes. "So, I want to know what you think."

Sara wanted to cut this questioning as short as she could. She knew that if she got into talking about her special abilities that the officer would have a hard time believing it and it would only lead to more questions.

"Deputy" She said. "It's late I'm sure we are all exhausted. What I can tell you is we are all safe nothing here will harm us. And as for him..." She pointed to Montgomery. "Let's say karma took hold of the situation and corrected the flow of the universe. He got what he deserved."

Roy nodded. "Okay little lady I'll take you back to Ken's place. You get some rest." Roy knew there was more to her story but he wasn't going to get any more info out of her this evening. He knew when to cut his losses. He walked her to his patrol car. The ride back was silent.

Sara sat there thinking about Jack and the possibility of his dying. Did life need to be this unfair to strip him from anything that had any meaning to him? It had already taken his grandmother away before he had the chance to make things right between them. Was the emptiness of death happily going to deny him fulfilling her final wish for him?

Roy pulled his patrol car up to the front steps of Ken's place and went around the passenger side to help Sara out. Ken saw them coming up the drive and was waiting for Sara at the top of the steps. Her demeanor was quiet and Ken immediately knew something was wrong.

"Jack?" Ken questioned.

"He'll be fine." Roy answered. "He's being taken to Bangor Hospital with a gunshot wound."

Sara walked pass them saying nothing and went straight to her room.

Ken followed Roy to his car. "What the hell happened out there?"

Roy got in his car and rolled down the window. "I'm still trying to process what I've seen. Damnedest thing but what I can tell you are, Montgomery Barry is dead and the investigation has taken a new turn. I'll see you in a few days." Roy stared his car and drove out onto the main road.

Ken went back inside and sat in the kitchen. He had many questions rolling around in his head. He thought about asking Sara but decided it was best to leave her alone for the rest of the night. Maybe over a hearty breakfast he wound let her come to him to tell what happened. He decided now was not the time to press her for information.

CHAPTER 31

LONG JOURNEY HOME

It was midmorning when Jack awoke with a splitting headache He felt groggy, but he felt alert enough to know his surroundings.

"Good morning Mr. Kahill I'm glad to see you awake. You had us worried there for a while. You lost a lot of blood. Do you understand what I'm saying?"

Jack saw a small man with oversized thick glasses in a white jacket standing at the side of his bed. He shook his head up and down. He watched as the man went to the end of the bed and pulled back the bed covers exposing his feet.

"I want you to wiggle your toes."

Jack did as the man asked.

"Good." The doctor said. "That bullet was close to your spine and we were afraid it might have affected your ability to walk. You're going to be fine and in a day or two we'll have you up and about."

Jack watched as the doctor checked his vital signs and looked over his charts. "A nurse will be in shortly to change your bandages." He said walking out of the room leaving Jack alone.

Awake and alive was a good thing but he suddenly felt terrible. Lying there in the bed all he could think about was seeing his grandmother and not being able to talk to her when he tried to visit. He felt ashamed that he didn't have the opportunity to rectify his odd disappearance some three years ago. He wanted to tell her how much he had loved her for all the things she was able to do for him even though she could never give him the proper home he so desperately had wished for as a child. He always hated being homeless and having to rely on someone else for his existence. Just once in his life he wanted to be in control and hold the cards. But the more he thought about it the more he realized he would have to play the hand dealt to him no matter where it took him as long as he knew deep in his heart that he was truly living with what old Mr. Sampson called it, *HONOR AND DUTY*.

Ken was standing on the church steps watching a few backpackers break down camp. They were getting ready for the hundred mile wilderness when Sara came out joining him.

"I couldn't sleep what with everything going on around here.
"How are you feeling?"

"Shaken and worried about Jack. I'm still trying to process what happened."

"Well you take your time, go to the kitchen and get some breakfast and when you're ready we can take a ride and see Jack."

"I'm ready now." She said. She wished she had her car even with the blown out windows. It still had to be better than climbing back into Ken's truck but she made no mention of it to Ken.

"You got to have something. I'll pack us a little breakfast snack some coffee for the ride." Ken disappeared into the kitchen. Sara went to the truck to fix the seat.

Ken came getting into the truck handing Sara a large heavy brown paper bag, thermos and two ceramic coffee cups. It seemed, she thought, he packed way more than they would need for an hour road trip. His genuine caring showed, and she was thankful for it.

Jack had his bandages changed and the young nurse informed him that tomorrow morning they were planning on having him walk some and depending on how that went he could be going home soon. When the nurse said the word home it hit him like a ton of bricks. He didn't have a home he was homeless since the time he left Elizabeth. He did have the cabin and it would have to do and he would try to make a go of it. Summer was coming and it would be easy until the coming of fall and the colder weather. The cabin was no place to stay in the harsh Maine winters.

He decided he would concentrate on finding what his grandmother and told him in the letter. He felt he had lost everything trying to gain his independence and find himself. The homeless problem he would cross that bridge when he got to it.

Closing his eyes he fell deep asleep seeing his grandmother sitting on a rocker on the cabin porch. But this time it was more. He saw the lady of the Woods standing next to his grandmother. His grandmother was singing to him as she often did.

"HUSH LITTLE BOY DON'T SAY A WORD. GRANDMOTHER BOUGHT YOU A MOCKING BIRD. THERE'S ONE GOOD SECRET THAT BIRD TOLD. SHE BURRIED IT UNDER THE MARAGOLD."

Jack heard heavy footsteps. Rubbing his eyes he opened them to find Sara and Ken standing at his bed. He reached out grabbing Sara's arm pulling her close and whispered in her ear. "I know where it is. It's buried under the marigold. It's in the garden."

Sara leaned in and kissed him on the cheek and as she came up she winked at him nodding.

Jack mouths the words to her. "GO GET IT."

Ken came up and putting one arm around Sara and the other he reached out to Jack shaking his hand.

"I want you kids to know that if there is anything I can do for you just let me know. As a matter of fact if you want to stay at the church you are more than welcome."

Jack squeezed Ken's hand and looked over to Sara. "No, I don't think that's necessary. We are going to make a go at it for a while at the cabin."

Sara took up Ken's offer. She asked to stay another night until she could make arrangements to get her car back.

Ken was glad to have Sara stay another night. He knew that he couldn't push them and that they wanted to make their own way. "Well okay." He said. "When you're better Jack you're going to need some work you come and see me. There is always plenty of work for a handy man around the church. No pressure it just a job if you want it."

"Thank you." Jack said. "I'll consider it. When I get out of here I want to visit an old friend first. Do you know old MR. Sampson at the orphanage?"

Ken tugged at his beard thinking for a moment. "I haven't heard that name mentioned in a long time. That orphanage has been close for a long time now. I wonder if he's still there."

CHAPTER 32

OUT OF THE DARKNESS

Twenty seven minutes past midnight exactly, he checked his watch. The air was warm and the evening still, with hardly a breeze. There was no moon even the stars were missing. He sat on the porch in a rocker enjoying the cigar Mike Shannon had left for him. He blew rings of smoke into the air watching them float away with delight.

The woods came alive with glowing entities popping into existence everywhere he looked. It was nothing new to him he had seen it many times before but this time something was different. They were all moving swiftly in one direction away from the orphanage.

Gabriel Sampson took a long puff on his cigar breathing new life into it. He took off his glasses placing them on a small table next to him. He wiped at his tired eyes with a clean white handkerchief and folded it into a perfect triangle. He watched as the forest again became black and the sounds from the darkness returned to normal. He smiled when he heard the crickets and saw only fireflies. Even the smell of the dampness of the forest had returned.

She called, and he listened cupping his hand over his ear. He could see one pinkish white light now appear in the woods. He knew who it was. The Lady of the Woods always came looking the same.

She spoke to him.

"Cast evil to the wind. You must bless the land clean once more, cherish all who came before and pass the knowledge to those going forth."

Sara awoke startled from a dream in the middle of the night she got up to go to the bathroom to splash some water on her face. She never liked when the night came calling. It had been many times when she was called upon in the middle of sleep by those seeking her help to cross over. She remembered the dream flooding in of seeing the Lady of the Woods and the Lady speaking to her.

"Cast evil to the wind. You must bless the land clean once more, cherish all who came before and pass the knowledge to those going forth."

Sara knew now what she had to do and in the morning, she would talk to Ken about having the land blessed in the hopes of putting all the spirits at rest. She would invite all faiths and the elders of the local Native American tribes to come and bless the land.

Sara tried getting back to sleep but it was hopeless. She kept thinking about having to answer questions when the deputy sheriff shows up. She desperately want to have her freedom back again by having her car. Lying there she wanted to go and dig where Jack had told her to dig, but she really wanted to wait for Jack to be better so that he could be there to be a part of it. It had been a long journey they shared together and he deserved that much. In an odd way if it hadn't been for him she would never know about any of her family's past or the possible future ahead.

In the morning she would contact Millie and tell her of the story she had to write. She had gone seeking the truth and found the unthinkable. For now, she would spirit the sleepless night documenting it all down in her journal.

The next morning Jack arrived in a patrol car driven by Deputy Sheriff Roy Halperin. He opened the passenger door. Jack came out leaning on a crutch.

Sara ran out throwing her arms around his neck.

Jack didn't hesitate. "What have you found?" He whispered in Sara's ear.

Sara didn't answer grabbing his hand and walking him into the kitchen of the church.

Ken and Roy followed taking a seat around the table.

As soon as everyone was seated Roy started. "I've got a lot of thing to say. But I'm going to cut to the chase here and tell you Jack, that all the charges have been dropped against you."

Ken shook Jack's hand and Sara started crying.

"Two things." Roy continued. "First your parole officer Mike Shannon is alive and well in the hospital recovering and he wants to see you when the time is right. Second, he is dropping all the charges. And I agree with him. You saved his life Jack. Oh the best news is that through our contacts in New York we come to the conclusion that the accident was not your fault and that the old man ran the traffic light. Sara your car will be returned to you today. Although your running didn't make matters any better but...Roy paused...in the measure of life you're free to move on and enjoy what comes next."

Roy got up from the table walking out to his car. He turned to Sara taking her hand in his. "Maybe someday, little lady, we can have that conversation about just what it was I'd seen out there."

Sara smiled. "They say God works in mysterious ways."

Roy said nothing nodding his head getting into his car leaving.

Jack turned to Ken. "What happened to our grandmother's remains?"

"I have the urn in the church tabernacle. It's safe and you can see it any time you're ready. It arrived too late for the backpackers to take it up the mountain. Maybe you and Sara would like to do that."

Jack asked Ken if he would take him to see old MR. Sampson in the morning. Jack got up and holding onto the cane. He walked out of the kitchen and into the great hall stopping in front of the tabernacle staring at the urn hold the remains of his grandmother. Tears filled his eyes.

Sara came up alongside of him putting an arm around his waist.

Jack thought about what he and Sara were about to do. Could there be something buried there in his grandmother's garden? Of all the things in his life, there was only one thing he was sure of, his grandmother never lied to him about anything. He thought about old MR. Sampson and how he could use the money to help children who like him needed a home. Most of all he thought about what Roy had said about the measure of life.

"You know." He said loudly, his voice echoing around the church walls.

"Maybe the measure of life is helping other people. Maybe it was doing the right thing when all of hell's fury is against you. Maybe it's the love of family there for you even when you didn't know it."

He held his arm around Sara holding her tight, tears rolling down his face. It had been a question he had sought an answer for since his going to prison the first time, and it was something he would forever seek an answer to.

FRANK BRINDLEY lives with his wife in New Jersey. He is a photographer, artist, poet and writer of two books: Bless Me Father and Tread'N Water.

*Special thanks to: SOCRATIC & LEVY AND THE OAKS for the use of their songs; DAYS I DID NOT BELONG, FLOWERS IN THE GARDEN.

64247437R00239

Made in the USA
Middletown, DE
28 August 2019